IN DARK WATER

A RARITY COVE NOVEL

LESLIE TENTLER

This book is a work of fiction. Names, characters, places, and incidents are either products of the author's imagination or are used fictitiously. Any resemblance to actual persons, living or dead, business establishments, events or locales is entirely coincidental.

In Dark Water

Published by Left Field Press

978-1-7335726-2-0 (paperback)

978-1-7335726-0-6 (mobi)

978-1-7335726-1-3 (epub)

All the art of living lies in a fine
mingling of letting go and holding on.
– Havelock Ellis

CHAPTER ONE

HE HAD BEEN GONE a year to the day.

Mercer Leighton stood at the shoreline, the sun setting in front of her, dappling the water with orange and gold. The mild fall breeze whipped her shoulder-length, honey-blond hair. Twelve months had passed, but she could still hear Jonathan's voice, his laugh. Briefly, she closed her eyes, picturing him as he had once been. Not the thin, fragile shell of a man he had become.

He had been nearly two decades older than her. Still, she had thought they would have more time.

She held the silver urn against her chest, her throat tight. They'd had only five years together, the last one marred by illness. The prostate cancer had returned, more aggressive this time, spreading to Jonathan's bones and leaving Mercer a widow at just thirty-three.

Drawing strength from the family who stood on the beach behind her, she removed the urn's lid and laid it on the sand among brown streamers of seaweed. Mercer stepped forward. The tide's cool, white foam licked her bare feet, the water lapping at her ankles and wetting the hem of her dress as she walked knee-deep into the breaking waves. Her eyes misted, but it was time.

"Goodbye, my love," she whispered and poured Jonathan's ashes out. What didn't disappear into the water lifted in the breeze, swirling in an iron-gray mist before vanishing, too. Head bowed, she said a silent prayer before turning back to the beach. Her eyes met those of her family—Mark and Samantha, Carter and Quinn, her mother and Anders. As she left the water, Mark and Carter came forward, both barefoot and in black pants and white dress shirts.

"It's done," she said.

Carter hugged her. He and Quinn and their little daughter, Lily, now almost three, had flown in from Hawaii where Carter was filming an action movie. Jonathan had wanted his ashes scattered on the water in Rarity Cove, a place he had grown to love as much as any St. Clair.

"Jonathan would be proud of you, Merce," Carter murmured as he held her. "You've been so strong."

As she stepped back from his embrace, Mark laid his hand on her shoulder. The family had gone to a more remote area of the beach to scatter the ashes, and he looked back to the hotel in the distance. "The room is ready for us. It's closed to guests tonight. We can go up whenever you want."

He was referring to the hotel's open-air loggia on its top floor. Another request of Jonathan's. One year from the day of his death, once they had given his ashes to the sea, they were to all have dinner together. They were to toast his memory a final time. After that, Jonathan had decreed that there would be no more sadness. He had told Mercer he would allow her to mourn him for just one year. And then he wanted her to dispose of his ashes—*you can't get on with your life with me sitting on the fireplace mantel*—he'd said, still trying to keep some sense of humor despite his failing health and terminal diagnosis.

"I know you still miss him. Every day, every week, gets a little easier," Mark promised. Both he and their mother knew what it was like to lose a spouse. But unlike their unexpected losses, she'd had time to try to prepare for Jonathan's death. She had been with him through the surgery, the chemo and radiation treatments, and their grueling side effects. Helpless, she had watched as he wasted away. Her guilt flared as she recalled the temporary relief that had at first mingled with her grief at his death. There had been some comfort in the knowledge that Jonathan was no longer in pain. He was free. But then the choking loss and loneliness settled over her. There had been a memorial service in Atlanta with the St. Clair family, Jonathon's son, friends, and members of the university faculty where he had taught in attendance.

You're young, Mercer. You can still have a life with someone else.

She hadn't taken kindly to Jonathan's words.

Mercer pulled herself from her thoughts as the others came down to the shoreline. Her mother smiled softly at her, sadness in her eyes. Both Samantha and Quinn stepped forward in turn to hug her. The small mound of Quinn's belly pressed against Mercer. She was pregnant again, four months along.

"Are you okay?" Samantha asked, concern on her pretty features.

Mercer nodded and tucked several strands of wind-whipped hair behind her ear. "I'm fine. But I've been dreading this," she admitted with a sigh.

Samantha touched her arm. A short time later, Mercer glanced back to the ocean. The sun had dropped lower, appearing half sunken in the plane of jewel-like sea, and the sky was streaked with purple and mauve. Seagulls screeched high in the air overhead. She reclaimed the urn's lid from the sand. Her heart filled as she looked at her family.

"I appreciate all of you being here. You mean the world to me. I couldn't have gotten through the last year without you." Doing her best to push aside her melancholy, she thought of Lily, Ethan, and Emily, who were waiting at the hotel with one of the on-staff au pairs. Ethan was now six, Emily eleven. Time moved so fast. "The kids are probably hungry. We should get back."

"YOU'RE FLYING BACK to Hawaii tomorrow?" Mercer asked, still seated at the long, rectangular table with Quinn. The dinner over, Mark and Carter had moved to the far end of the open-air space, their heads bent together in quiet conversation. Olivia and Anders had already departed for their residence in Charleston. On their way, they had dropped off Samantha, Emily, and Ethan at the Big House, the white-columned estate home on the edge of the St. Clair property where Mark had moved with his family a few years earlier. Ethan hadn't been feeling well, so Samantha had taken the children home.

"We're leaving for the airport after we have lunch with everyone at Anders and Olivia's." Quinn held Lily on her lap. She was a beautiful child, with Quinn's russet curls and Carter's midnight-blue eyes. "There're still another few weeks of filming, and it starts up again on Monday. Once Lily's old enough for kindergarten, we won't be traveling with Carter as often, so we're taking advantage now."

"Do you like flying on planes, Lily?" Mercer leaned closer and ran her finger over her niece's soft cheek. Lily nodded with enthusiasm, her dimples deepening, then gave a wide yawn.

"It's late. You guys should get going." Mercer thought of the

CHAPTER TWO

COMPARED TO THE PREVIOUS EVENING, the lunch at Olivia and Anders's had been a much less solemn affair. They had dined, picnic-style, in the verdant courtyard of the stately antebellum mansion on Charleston's East Battery Street, taking advantage of the family being together and the beautiful, early October day. Once Carter, Quinn, and Lily had departed for the airport, Mercer had left, as well. Although he had offered, she hadn't ridden with Mark and his family to Charleston, instead taking her own car since she planned to while away the remainder of the Sunday afternoon in the French Quarter. Mercer had strolled the district's quiet, narrow streets, past the historic churches and the old Dock Street Theatre. She'd even had a glass of chardonnay at a cafe that she and Jonathan had frequented on their visits to the city. A pair of young Citadel cadets had tried to flirt with her, but she politely deflected their attempts.

"May I help you?" A well-dressed, African-American woman inquired as Mercer entered The Bluth Studio, one of the

Quarter's many fine art galleries. Mercer knew her to be Alexa Rice, the gallery's owner.

"I'd like to just browse, if that's all right?"

"Of course. We close in a half-hour. I'm the only one here and I have a private appointment scheduled, but you're welcome to look around." The woman peered at her. "I'm sorry. Do I know you?"

Mercer hesitated. "I'm Mercer Leighton. My husband and I purchased a painting from you a few years ago. *Lowcountry Repose* by Eric Bledsoe?"

Her face lit in acknowledgment. "Of course. A lovely piece. I hope you're both enjoying it."

At the comment, Mercer felt a familiar void. Jonathan had bought the painting for her as a gift for their third anniversary, since it reminded her of home. "We are," she managed, not wanting to say more.

The woman smiled. "Maybe you'll find something else here today."

A phone rang at an antique desk, and she excused herself to answer it. Mercer went farther inside the large main gallery, which had polished hardwood floors and high ceilings. Paintings and sculptures were illuminated by the natural lighting that flowed in through a skylight overhead. Outside the centuries-old building, she heard the clopping of hooves against pavement, the sound of one of the many horse-drawn carriages that took tourists around the city. She was aware that the afternoon had been a nostalgic excursion to the places she and Jonathan had gone. Not the best activity for someone who was supposed to be *getting on with her life*. The owner remained on the phone, so after several minutes in the main gallery, Mercer wandered down the long hall that led to several smaller rooms where more art was displayed. It was in the first room, in fact, where they had found the Bledsoe watercolor. Entering the space, she noticed there were several more paintings by the artist among the ones displayed there. As she studied them, she heard the gallery's front door open. Mercer glanced back into the main area through a large glass window encased in an exposed-brick wall. A distinguished looking, older male with silver hair at his temples, wearing a tweed sport coat, entered. The owner was now off the phone, and although her words were muffled through the glass pane, Mercer heard her welcoming tone as she greeted him. He was apparently the private appointment she had mentioned. Not wanting to intrude, Mercer started to return to the main gallery so she could exit, but through the glass she saw the front door open again. Another man wearing a leather jacket stepped inside, closing the door behind him.

He raised a handgun with a long barrel and fired.

Thwap.

Mercer's muscles went weak, shock making her ears ring as the gentleman crumpled to the floor. The gallery owner started to scream, but the man fired again, shooting her in the face. *Thwap.* Stumbling backward, Mercer clapped a hand over her mouth to restrain her cry. The shooter stepped to where the man lay. Standing over him, he fired two more rounds. As he began to turn, Mercer dropped to her knees underneath the window, her pulse racing. *Oh, God.* He hadn't seen her, had he?

Her lungs cramped at the ominous echo of footsteps. She could tell by the sound that he was still in the main gallery. Probably looking for others. He would check the back rooms, too. Terror made her lightheaded. There was no way out without being seen.

Find somewhere to hide! Go!

Her panicked gaze swung around the space. A hulking, antique armoire sat diagonally in one corner of the room. She moved to it on rubbery legs. Her heart sank when she realized there wasn't enough room between it and the wall for her to squeeze behind. She hesitated, then opened the armoire's front with a soft snick. It was the kind that had been used for clothing storage a century or more ago. Drawers and shelves were in the top half of its interior but the bottom half was open, with hooks on the back panel for hanging garments. She had no choice. Mercer got inside it and, crouching, she closed its doors, her hands cold and perspiration beginning to bead on her upper lip.

Please, God. Please don't let him find me!

Moments later, footsteps came to a halt outside the room. Her flesh pebbled, fear sluicing through her as she huddled in the dark. If he opened the armoire, she was dead. Blood rushed in her ears. It was all she could do to keep her breathing shallow, to not gulp air. Through the keyhole, she could see him. Early forties, receding brown hairline and a coldly impassive face. He had been wearing sunglasses, but he had since removed them and clipped them onto his jacket pocket. His eyes swept the room as he entered, the gun gripped in his hand. As he began moving closer to where she hid, Mercer prayed.

Oh, God! I'll do anything. Please just let him go away!

He stopped a few feet from the armoire and looked directly at it, making her blood chill in her veins. She held her breath until her lungs threatened to burst. Mercer nearly went limp with relief when finally, he turned, exited the room, and traveled farther down the hall, based on the sound of his footsteps. What seemed like an eternity later, she heard him walk past the room again. Then the gallery's front door opened and closed.

She remained in the stifling, cramped space for several minutes, afraid to leave the dark confines of the armoire.

He's gone. I have to get out. I have to see if I can help those people.

I have to call for help!

Her legs had gone numb from the crouching position. She inched open the armoire's doors and slowly emerged. Carefully, she peered into the main gallery through the window. Seeing the two sprawled bodies, a hard tremor went through her. But the shooter was gone. Taking her cell phone from the small cross-body bag she wore, Mercer moved unsteadily down the hall. As she entered the main gallery, she placed a hand on the wall for support. Seeing the carnage at close distance, horror rose like bile in her throat. Still, she inched carefully closer, nearly panting in terror. *Dear God.* Nausea swept through her. The gallery owner didn't have a face anymore, just blood and tissue where her features had been. Blood covered the man's chest. Part of his skull had been blown off, and chunks of bone and gore lay on the floor. Crimson spattered the white wall and the paintings behind where they had stood. The coppery odor of blood hung in the air, mixed with an acrid odor that some part of Mercer's brain recalled. Gunpowder. Her father had taken her skeet shooting as a teenager.

Despite the grisly scene, she forced herself to bend down to shakily touch the side of the man's neck. She did the same to the gallery owner. But as she had already known in her heart, neither had pulses.

Standing upright again, she fought another wave of nausea. Mercer closed her eyes, trying to regain her equilibrium, trying to block out the slaughter. She had to get her too-fast breathing under control. Her shaking fingers somehow managed to dial 911 on her phone. When an operator answered, it took several tries for Mercer to find her voice. It finally emerged, sounding too high and unnatural, like it wasn't hers at all.

"I-I need help. Please! At The Bluth Studio on Queen...two people...they've been shot!"

"They've been shot?" the operator repeated. "Is the shooter still in the area?"

Her eyes darted to the closed door. "No. I mean, he left. He went out. I-I don't know where he is now."

"Are the victims breathing? Are they conscious?"

Mercer looked at the bodies again. She tried to swallow, but couldn't. Nothing seemed real. Her voice broke. "They're...gone. Please, just send help!"

CHAPTER THREE

CHARLESTON HOMICIDE DETECTIVE NOAH FORD studied the crime scene, a bitter taste in the back of his throat. The coroner's initial exam was over, and through the gallery's windows he could see the hearse waiting to transport the bodies once detectives had their look and Forensics processed the scene. Clad in jeans and a T-shirt, he wore latex gloves and paper booties over his sneakers, having been called away from an afternoon at his sister's house where he had been repairing his nephew's bike.

"Real shame about this. The Bluth Studio is practically an institution around here," the uniformed officer who stood beside Noah said. Since the officer's beat included the French Quarter, he had been among the first responders and Noah had brought him back inside to get a rundown on what he had found upon entering.

"And you were right," the officer added. "I talked to the coroner outside. The driver's license in the male vic's wallet is Sterling Deveau's."

Deveau was a U.S. district court judge. Noah had recognized

him. He had testified in his share of cases in his more than a decade of being a cop, and he'd been in Deveau's courtroom on numerous occasions. Noah peered down at the bodies. No matter how many crime scenes he had worked, the violence still hardened his stomach. Blood had begun to congeal where Deveau's right temple had been. It appeared that he had taken one to the head and two to the chest. They would know for certain following the autopsy.

The uniform spoke again. "So, what do you think, Detective? A robbery? The Quarter's usually a safe area, especially in daytime."

"I'm not thinking anything yet." He still had an eyewitness to talk to, hopefully some security footage to review. Noah's attention shifted to the doorway. Tyson Beaufain stood just outside the gallery's high-ceilinged foyer, where he was donning the latex gloves and foot coverings required to enter the scene. An African American with close-cropped hair, he was in his late thirties and was a few years older than Noah. They had been partners for the past six years.

"Thanks for holding down the fort, man," Tyson said as he reached Noah, his gold shield on his hip along with his holstered gun. "I was halfway back when my phone starts blowing up."

"Fish biting?"

"Reeled in a largemouth bass this morning the size of my arm. It fought like a real badass, but I won. Got him in my cooler in the trunk along with some other beauties."

Noah knew that Tyson had been at the remote fishing cabin on the upper end of Lake Marion. Tyson's wife and twin daughters were away for the weekend to visit family and, as soon as he'd gotten off duty on Friday, he had headed up to the place that he had recently inherited from his grandfather. Noah had been invited, but had declined. He'd had a date—a recent divorcée his sister had been pushing him to ask out—but there had been no real spark. Probably his fault, he conceded.

"You can go back out," he told the uniform, who exited.

Tyson gave a low whistle. "The male vic. That who I think it is?" He frowned as he peered down at the bodies. Around them, crime scene techs were doing their jobs—dusting the gallery's interior for prints, swabbing for touch DNA and marking shell casings on the floor with small yellow cones. A tech with a camera was photographing the high-velocity impact spatter that looked like a fine, rusty mist on the expensive oil paintings.

"Sterling Deveau," Noah confirmed. "We're also pretty sure the female vic is Alexa Rice, the gallery's owner."

"There's not much left to ID."

"It's her gallery and her purse with her driver's license is in a desk drawer."

Extracting a ballpoint pen from his shirt pocket, Tyson dropped down onto his haunches and used the pen to lift up the edge of Deveau's sport coat, revealing a holstered handgun. Noah had looked for it himself earlier, since it was widely known that the judge carried a concealed weapon due to threats that he had received over the years.

"That piece didn't do him much good." Tyson let the coat drop again as he stood. "He didn't even get a chance to draw."

Noah filled Tyson in on what he knew so far. Several other pairs of detectives were also milling about, but Noah had already been informed by the cap—Captain Walter Bell, head of Charleston's Police Investigations Bureau—that he and Tyson were being assigned as lead detectives on the case. They had recently closed a major investigation, which meant they had more bandwidth, at least more than some of the other detectives in the busy unit.

"I hear we have a witness. Where is she?" Tyson wanted to know.

"At the Fleur-De-Lis, for discretion. A uniform's watching over her."

Tyson looked down again at the two bodies. "How'd she not end up like them?"

"My understanding is that she hid. She got a good look at our guy, though."

"You talked to her yet?"

"Not yet," Noah said. "I'm about to go over there. Do you want to come?"

"You go ahead. I'll take over chain of command here."

Removing his gloves and shoe coverings at the door, Noah left the gallery. Outside, controlled chaos prevailed. Luminescent yellow tape cordoned off the sidewalk and a portion of Queen Street as uniforms worked to keep onlookers outside of the crime scene's perimeter. A crowd had gathered once police had ascertained that there was no active shooter in the area and partially reopened the street. Tony Garber and Bobby Durand, another pair of detectives, were talking to some of the bystanders, and a team of uniforms was conducting a grid search around the gallery's perimeter, looking for evidence. As Noah began walking toward the Fleur-De-Lis Hotel, the blue lights of patrol cars flashing into the fading, late afternoon sky above him, Bruce Tan, who worked in IT for them, called out, halting him.

"You're not going to like this, Noah," Bruce said as he approached. "I just got off the phone with the security company. Those cameras mounted inside the gallery are dead—they were scheduled to come out to repair them tomorrow morning."

Frustrated, Noah ran a hand through his dark hair. This made their witness even more important. He preferred digital proof over eyewitness testimony, which was notoriously fallible. "How long have they been out?"

"The company noticed the outage midday, right after the gallery opened, and contacted the owner. They're short-staffed on the weekend and tomorrow was the earliest they could get someone out."

Noah pressed his lips together. He didn't believe in coincidence.

He thanked Bruce for the information before walking the three blocks to the old hotel, which had a cocktail hour going on in its lush courtyard despite the disorder just down the street. Waiting for a horse-drawn carriage to pass, he then jogged across the asphalt and strode up several steps to the hotel's front.

"She's in the manager's office, Detective." A uniformed officer who had been leaning against the back of a Victorian sofa straightened as Noah entered the lobby. Giving a nod, Noah walked to the closed door. He knocked before entering.

"Ms. Leighton?" he said to the attractive blonde who rose from the couch as he came inside. "I'm Detective Noah Ford."

They shook hands. Her slender fingers were cold, he noted, her face pale and soft-blue eyes reddened. Noah felt a tug of sympathy. He had arrived at the scene after the first responders had already whisked her off-site, before the media had gotten word of the shooting. Based on what he'd been told, Mercer Leighton had been able to view the shooter through the keyhole of the antique armoire where she had taken refuge.

Nervously, she glanced down at her hands. "They tested me for gunpowder residue."

"It's routine. It's to eliminate you as the shooter." He indicated the couch where she had been seated, and she sat down again. "Can I get you a glass of water?" he asked.

"The officer outside brought me a bottled water earlier, but thank you." She absently rubbed at her upper arms, her anxiety palpable.

The only other seat in the office was behind the desk, so Noah sat on the other end of the couch and turned toward her. "I know you've already gone through it for the officers, but could you recount to me exactly what happened? What you saw and heard?"

Taking a tremulous breath, she relayed what she had seen from a back room in the gallery. How she had hidden when she realized that the shooter was looking for others. She struggled to speak, her eyes misting as she described returning to where the bodies were. Noah reached for a box of tissue on an end table and, moving closer, he handed it to her.

"You're doing good," he assured her in a low voice. He waited a moment before probing further. "And you had a clear view of the shooter?"

She nodded, wiping at a tear on her cheek. "He...came into the room and stood just a few feet from where I was hiding. I could see him through the keyhole."

Noah imagined the terror she must have felt. "Ms. Leighton, I'm going to ask you to close your eyes and focus. Tell me everything you remember about him. His face, his height, what he was wearing."

Tightly clutching the crumpled tissue, she closed her eyes and described the man she had seen.

"...He also wore a ring on his right hand, the one that held the gun," she added after she had given a physical description. "I was crouched inside the armoire, so I was at eye level with it. It was yellow gold and had some kind of design, maybe Celtic? I couldn't see it all that well, but it looked like a cross inside a circle."

She paused reflectively, biting at her full bottom lip. "The gun had a long barrel. He pulled it out from underneath his jacket after he came into the gallery."

The barrel she described was most likely an attached silencer, something Noah had suspected. The shooter had used it to mute the sound to some extent. It had worked further in his favor that it was late on Sunday afternoon, which meant many galleries in the Quarter were already closed, including the ones on either side of The Bluth Studio.

He asked a few more questions about the man's appearance before telling her that she could open her eyes again. Her long, silky lashes fluttered open and her bleary gaze met his. She appeared somewhere in her early thirties. Despite her casual clothing, there was something decidedly high-end about her.

"Why were you at The Bluth Studio today, Ms. Leighton? I understand that you're a tourist. Were you sightseeing?"

"I'm not a tourist," she corrected, rubbing faintly at her brow. "I live in Rarity Cove. I just moved back there a month ago."

The first responder that Noah had talked to must have confused that information.

"We...I...bought a painting from Alexa Rice a few years ago." She shrugged weakly. "I just wanted to go back and browse, I guess."

It hadn't escaped him that although her hands were bare, she wore two rings—white-gold or platinum, one with a diamond and the other a simple band—on a delicate chain around her neck. Noah guessed that she was widowed, probably fairly recently, the latter based on the fact that she had initially said *we* before changing it to *I*.

"What happened today, Detective Ford?" she asked, her face tense. "Was it a robbery? Some kind of domestic violence situation?"

"We don't know at this point. I'm sorry."

"Who was the man who was killed?"

"We're still trying to identify him," he lied, unable to give out such information until Deveau's next of kin had been notified.

She bowed her head and lightly pressed her fingers to her eyes. "Those poor people," she whispered.

Unsure of what else to do, Noah placed a comforting hand on her shoulder. "We're done for now, Ms. Leighton. Thank you.

But we may have other questions. I'd also like to get you with a forensic artist as soon as—"

The room's door opened and a man entered with the uniformed officer on his heels. It had been years, but recognition as well as surprise flickered through Noah. The woman stood and went into Mark St. Clair's arms, pressing her face into his chest.

"I got here as soon as I could," he said as he held her.

"I know Mom's closer." Her voice was muffled against his shirtfront. "But I-I just couldn't call her."

Noah had risen from the couch, as well. The officer who had ushered in St. Clair spoke to him, sounding apologetic. "I checked his ID, Detective. He says that he's her brother. Your witness called him."

CHAPTER FOUR

"I CAN'T STOP THINKING about Carter's call for help." Sitting in the passenger side of Mark's Volvo, Mercer stared absently out at the passing scenery that was shrouded in darkness. It was unsettling that just a few years after the attack that had nearly taken Carter's life, she had made a similar 911 call, caught in her own nightmare. Her hands twisted together in her lap. "I'm starting to think we're not the luckiest family."

Mark glanced at her from the driver's seat. "You managed to leave that gallery alive, Mercer. That seems like a lot of luck to me."

She released a soft breath and changed the subject. "I could've driven myself home," she argued for not the first time. She had traveled on foot into the Quarter that afternoon, leaving her car in the cobblestone alley behind Olivia and Anders's home. Mark had insisted on leaving it there for now and driving her back to Rarity Cove, since she didn't want to go to their mother's.

"You're trying to hide it, but I know you and you're too rattled to be driving. We'll get your car picked up tomorrow." He turned the car onto the peninsula road that led to the St. Clair. Mercer hardly remembered the drive from Charleston, her thoughts too fractured. Gruesome images from the gallery replayed in her head.

"I think we should consult an attorney," Mark said. "One who specializes in criminal law."

Mercer looked at him. "Why?"

"Because I want to understand what your rights are as a *witness*." Even in the car's shadowed interior, she could see the hard set of his jaw. "I just want to get in front of this. If they find the guy who did this, they'll want you to testify."

"If I can identify him in court, I will." She tamped down her unease. "He killed two people, Mark. I have to do whatever I can."

Mark fell silent. Despite her words, Mercer understood his concern. She was the link that could put a killer in prison. But that was if the police were able to find him and she had no idea if they even had any leads. She thought of the detective who had interviewed her. Noah Ford had an air of authority about him, as well as a physical intensity that was magnified by his gold detective's shield and firearm. He looked to be in his mid-thirties, tall and solidly built with thick, dark hair, a strong jaw, and intelligent hazel eyes that seemed to shift from amber to moss-green.

"So, you know Detective Ford," she said, aware of the silvered moon that was intermittently visible between the gnarled limbs of the ancient, moss-draped live oaks lining the road.

"Not that well. It was a long time ago. I didn't recognize him until he introduced himself. He used to work at the St. Clair back when he was in high school—lifeguarding during the summer, valeting or busing tables at night. I was already in college but I remember him because I worked for Dad, too, on summer breaks." Despite the situation, Mark smiled softly in recollection.

"Dad used to call it my *internship*. He was training me to take over the business one day, although at the time I mostly saw it as a nuisance. Something to keep me from hanging around the beach or heading off to Europe with my friends."

"What do you know about him? Detective Ford?"

"I remember that he didn't talk much. He was a good athlete —baseball. His high school team won a state championship."

"Did he go on to play in college?"

"I'm not sure," Mark answered. The St. Clair's gated, wrought-iron entrance was just up ahead. Bronze sconces illuminated the hotel name, and a tiered, granite fountain cascaded water. "He stopped working here after he graduated high school."

Mercer sat up straighter as Mark made a right instead of heading through the resort's gates. "What're you doing?"

"You're staying with us tonight. You shouldn't be alone."

"Mark, I'd rather not." She heard the tension in her voice, but she was in no mood to be around anyone, or to keep pretending that she was all right. All she wanted to do was have a drink and crawl into a corner somewhere. "Just take me to my bungalow? I'm fine, really."

"This isn't up for argument." A short time later, he pulled into the circular drive in front of the Big House. Shutting off the car's engine, Mark turned to her. "What you saw today...what you've been through...you need to be with family, Mercer. Samantha has one of the guest rooms ready. You can borrow something from her to sleep in. We can talk about this again tomorrow."

As he exited the car and went around to open her door, Mercer stared at her childhood home. It appeared stately with its brick front, white columns and hurricane-shuttered windows. Lacy ferns spilled from planters on the porch, not yet brought in for the fall season. Warm, golden light emanated from the home's interior. Mercer's throat ached. In that moment, she yearned to be a child again, to go back to a time when she felt safe and carefree.

A time when she hadn't lost her husband and witnessed a double murder.

As she entered the home's elegant foyer with Mark, Samantha greeted them, her expression concerned. Brock, the family's Lab mix, and Doug, Carter and Quinn's dog who was staying here while they were away, padded over, their tails wagging.

"Mercer, thank God you're okay." Samantha hugged her. "Mark said you haven't eaten dinner. I've put out food in the kitchen."

"Thanks, but I don't think I can eat anything."

Mark touched her shoulder. "Just have a few bites. You'll feel better."

The three of them walked into the gourmet, black-and-white tiled kitchen in the home's rear. The space had been updated to accommodate Samantha's culinary prowess, with new, high-end appliances as well as airy windows that overlooked the old carriage house and landscaped terrace with its kidney-shaped swimming pool. Farther back, a children's swing set, barely visible in the dark, sat nestled under the outstretched branches of a live oak. Samantha had laid out a veritable feast on the wide granite island. It included several artisan cheeses, olive tapenade and other spreads, grilled bread and crackers, assorted cold cuts, and Café Bella's signature brownies.

Emily called down to her mother from the upstairs.

"I'll be right back," Samantha told Mercer. "Ethan's already in bed, but Emily's still up watching television in her room. She doesn't know yet that you're here. I figured you don't need her bothering you right now."

Mercer tried to smile, but wasn't certain that she had pulled it off. "Emily could never be a bother to me, Sam."

"Just the same, I think I'll keep her in the dark for a while about you being here." Once Samantha had gone upstairs, Mark withdrew his cell phone from his pocket.

"Go ahead and make yourself a plate. I'm going to my study to call Mom and then I'll have a bite with you. If she and Anders discover your car still in the alley, they're going to be worried."

Mercer was grateful that Mark had offered to contact them for her. The news about what had happened today would upset them. "What're you going to tell them?"

He released a breath. "I'm not sure yet. Mom won't take this well. That's why I agreed to not take you over there tonight. I'm going to leave a message for Carter, too. He's probably still in flight unless they're on a layover. I'll be back soon."

He departed to the paneled study that had previously belonged to their father. Mercer stared at the food Samantha had prepared. As she fed the two canines small bits of turkey and roast beef from the counter, her eyes fell on the open bottle of wine that sat under a wine rack built into the overhead cabinetry. Taking a crystal goblet from one of the cabinets, she poured a generous portion of merlot and gulped half of it before she put the glass back down. The wine churned in her empty stomach.

You're doing good.

She recalled Detective Ford's praise, the pleasant drawl of his voice. But despite his words, she felt weak and vulnerable. Her eyes burned.

Get it together, Merce.

She had another fortifying gulp of wine, then stood there in silence until Brock and Doug finally gave up on getting more food and padded off down the hall. The grandfather clock chimed from the foyer, indicating it was nine p.m., still too early for the late-night news. Mercer's cell phone was nearly dead, but Mark's laptop from his office at the hotel sat nearby on the counter. She hesitated before taking her glass and moving to it. Tentatively, she rubbed her finger over its trackpad to wake up its darkened screen. Entering Mark's password, she then opened the browser and did a web search, looking for news from Charleston. Her muscles tensed as she saw the headline about the double homicide at the top of the search results. Still, she clicked the link which led to the website of a Charleston television station. Taking a tight breath, she played the video.

The Bluth Studio appeared in front of her, cordoned off by fluorescent crime scene tape. The flashing lights of police cars stained its brick front and reflected off its windows. Plainclothes detectives and uniformed officers wandered about on the sidewalk. Pinpricks of unease traveled over her skin as her mind flashed on the slaughter inside the gallery. The voiceover on the video relayed the latest news on the shooting. Mercer's breath bottled up in her lungs. They had identified the male victim now, too.

The man who had been missing part of his skull, whose white dress shirt had been soaked with blood, was Sterling Deveau, a U.S. district court judge.

IT HADN'T TAKEN LONG for the media to learn the identities of both victims. The local television stations had broken the news, in fact, less than a half-hour after Noah and Tyson had gone to see Deveau's wife. Noah swallowed heavily. He hated notification of death visits, but he hadn't wanted to pawn it off to someone else. They had left Carol Deveau, alone and weeping, in the living room of her home in an upscale, gated community in Mount Pleasant.

There hadn't been a need to notify anyone of Alexa Rice. She had been a longtime resident of the French Quarter and her partner of more than twenty years had caught wind of the gallery shooting. Darlene Rollins had arrived at the scene as Rice's body, covered by a sheet, was being rolled out. Eyes squeezed closed, Noah pressed the cool glass of the beer bottle against his forehead, Rollins's wails still echoing in his ears.

He wandered into the small kitchen in the second-floor, single-bedroom apartment that he rented in an old building a few blocks off King Street. He had considered moving to one of the new loft apartments going up around the Charleston metro area, but he liked the place's character, there was a nice balcony perfect for reading the paper and drinking coffee on his mornings off, and it was just minutes from the downtown precinct. He opened the fridge and scanned its sparse contents, reflective of his bachelor status. There was a takeout carton that contained leftover Thai, and Noah took it out, dumped the food onto a plate, and placed it in the microwave to heat. While he waited, he rinsed the container, then placed it in the garbage can under the sink. The kitchen was spotless, without even a coffee mug or cereal bowl left from breakfast on the counter or in the basin. Tidiness had been part of his U.S. Marine Corps training and it was a habit he kept even years after an honorable, medical discharge from ANGLICO Special Ops.

Thinking of that time in his life, a familiar darkness fell over him. He had lost a lot to the military. A fiancée, and for a time, his health and very nearly his sanity.

As the microwave continued running, his cell phone rang in the living room. Noah went to retrieve it, noting the time on his wristwatch. It was getting late.

"I talked to Jill tonight," his sister, Corinne, said when he answered. Jill was the recent divorcée from Corinne's church that she had roped Noah into going out with. "She said you were polite—a bona fide gentleman—but that you gave off a distinct *not interested* vibe."

At the judgment in her tone, Noah drew in a slow breath. "Sorry to disappoint you."

"What's wrong with her, Noah? She's nice and attractive, and from what I can see, she's got a great rack."

The microwave beeped in the kitchen, the scent of spicy noodles wafting in the air. "If it's all right with you, I'd just as soon not hear my sister describing another woman as having a *great rack*."

She laughed softly. "Chalk it up to Keith's trucker talk rubbing off on me." Keith was her husband, a veteran of the U.S. Coast Guard who now drove an eighteen-wheeler for a transportation company. He was away from home regularly, which was why Noah had gone to help his nine-year-old nephew, Finn, with his bike that afternoon.

"I just think you need to settle down. You spend too much time alone, and I worry about you."

"I'm capable of finding my own dates, Corinne. And I promise you I *do* go out on occasion."

"Well, I tried. What's the saying? You can lead a horse to water but you can't make it drink. Pardon me for putting a pretty, available woman in your path." She must have decided to let him off the hook, because she added, "Thanks for coming up to help Finn with his bike today. I'm sorry you had to leave before dinner."

"Me, too." Phone tucked between his chin and shoulder, he pulled the plate with the mound of Thai food from the microwave, placing it next to his gun holster with his Glock still inside it on the counter. He reached for a fork in the drawer.

"Was it that double homicide in Gallery Row? It's been all over the news tonight."

"Yeah," he said, spearing several noodles. "Ty and I caught it. It looks like it's our case."

He moved the conversation to another topic. A short time later, they said good night. The food gone, Noah washed and dried the plate and put it back inside the cabinet. Corinne was eight years older than him. She could be nosy as hell about his personal life, but she was also an angel, in many ways more of a mother to him than a sister. Their father—an abusive drunk—had run out on them as kids, and their mother had died when Noah was just thirteen. Corinne had only been twenty-one herself, but she had obtained legal guardianship over him. They had no extended family—it was either that or him being placed in foster care. They hadn't had much growing up, but things had gotten tougher on their own. Corinne barely kept them afloat with minimum-wage jobs and Noah had pitched in as soon as he was legally old enough to work. They had lived in the county halfway between Charleston and Rarity Cove. Corinne, in fact, still lived there in the same house, only now with her husband and son. The home's relatively close proximity to Rarity Cove was how Noah had come to work at the St. Clair. He had spent three years there, full-time during the summer and part-time when school was in session. Harrison St. Clair had admired Noah's athleticism and had been willing to let him work his schedule around the baseball that he had hoped would get him a college scholarship. When it didn't, Noah had gone into the military with an ideal of serving his country while sending checks to help his sister and, ultimately, using the GI Bill to pay for a college education.

I checked his ID, Detective. He says that he's her brother.

The officer who had been stationed in the lobby of the Fleur-De-Lis had appeared apologetic about letting Mark St. Clair inside. The uniform wasn't a rookie, he knew better, but the St. Clair name carried weight, even here in Charleston. And it wasn't enough that the family owned one of the top independent hotels in the Southeast—one of them was an A-list movie star. Carter St. Clair *had* done good work, Noah conceded, thinking about the Charleston fitness complex that was specially equipped for disabled veterans that the actor had been largely responsible for. His nonprofit foundation had two other centers and three more in the works in other parts of the country.

Noah had been fighting it for most of the night, but Mercer Leighton's soft-blue eyes appeared in his mind. Her first name was unusual and he should've picked up on it, but the last name *Leighton* had thrown him off. Noah loosely recalled seeing her around the resort all those years ago. She had been a few years younger than him, in his eyes at that age, still just a kid. He remembered her trying to appear grown up as she lounged by the pool. His memory of her was vague, but there was no forgetting her now.

A St. Clair. The family was like royalty in these parts. Noah drained the last of his beer, tension in his stomach. Mercer Leighton was a definite complication.

Beautiful, richer than God, and she's my freaking eyewitness.

CHAPTER FIVE

"THANKS FOR CALLING to check on me," Mercer said to Carter as she sat behind her desk in her office at the St. Clair. She had put him on her cell phone's speaker while she leafed through a contract for an acoustical guitar player she was hiring for a *Bonfire on the Beach* event. Since arriving at work mid-morning, her mission had been to keep occupied. "I'm sorry I didn't call you and Quinn back last night. I wasn't really up to talking, and I knew Mark had already called you."

"That's okay. But what I don't understand is why you're at work."

"Did you and Mark compare bullet points? Because I've already had this conversation."

"Merce..." Carter's voice lowered nearly to a whisper. It was still early in Hawaii, and he had mentioned that he was in Makeup, waiting for shooting to start. "You can't just pretend like it's business as usual. Not after what—"

"I'm not." She released a soft breath, the fragile composure she had been holding on to temporarily slipping. "But I have to focus on something *else*. I just got off the phone with Mom and she's so worried that she's practically taken to her bed with all this."

The wine that Mercer had drunk last night had put her to sleep for a while, but she'd awakened in the dead of night, the reality of what she had witnessed, what she had gotten herself into, making her heart race. She stared unseeingly at the contract in front of her, then pushed it aside. The murders had been the lead story on the news again that morning.

"Come to Hawaii," Carter pleaded.

"I can't. I should stay here in case the police need me."

"I wish I were there."

"You will be in a few weeks." Redirecting the conversation, she asked how filming was going. They talked for a bit longer, until he was interrupted by a member of the production crew. Disconnecting the phone, Mercer passed a hand over her eyes. When she looked up again, Mark was standing on the room's threshold.

"If you came to jump me again about being at work, Carter already beat you to it."

Mark studied her, but didn't respond. Instead, he shoved his hands into his pockets and came into her office. "How was your run with Samantha this morning?"

Between the children and her business, Samantha was busy, but she had turned the cafe's management over to someone else and now focused primarily on the Bella Café products that were being sold in upscale grocery stores and gift shops. Upon Mercer's return home, she and Samantha had resumed their regular runs on the beach. Quinn often joined them when she was in town.

"It was a good distraction. Sam picked my brain about some marketing ideas. I'm going to help her get ready for that trade show in New York."

Mark picked up a mock-up of an ad for the hotel from Mercer's desk.

"I'm placing that in *Southern Living*'s February issue," she said. "It'll run when people are getting sick of cold weather and are starting to make spring break plans."

He laid the ad back down. "You okay?"

"Yeah." Aware that she was fidgeting, Mercer stood and walked to the nearby window that was framed by coral, raw-silk drapes. It provided a view of the landscaped terrace with its Olympic-size swimming pool and, beyond it, the gray-green ocean. The midday sky was a vibrant blue. Arms crossed over her chest, she looked out at the picturesque scene, wishing that she could concentrate on something else.

"You don't have to be here," Mark reminded gently. "There's nothing you're doing that can't wait."

"I'm still trying to get everything prepared for that sandcastle-building workshop this weekend," she argued, turning back to him. Since resuming her position at the hotel, Mercer had been coordinating activities that would attract guests during the slower fall and winter seasons. "There's also the sea turtle recovery project with the South Carolina Aquarium. I have a meeting for it the day after tomorrow and I need to—"

Her words halted as her cell phone that lay on her desk sprang to life. Anxiety traced over her skin. *Charleston Police Department.* Mark's tense expression told her that he had seen the caller's identity, too. Her chest tightening, she picked up the phone and answered, hearing Noah Ford's voice.

"It's Detective Ford. How're you this afternoon, Ms. Leighton? I hope you were able to sleep last night?"

"I...did," she fibbed.

"That's good. I'd like to get you with our forensic sketch artist today. Maybe around four?"

"All right," she managed, glancing at her wristwatch. Mark

had sent two of the hotel employees for her car that morning, so she had transportation. She smoothed her hair, trying to tamp down her nervousness. "I'll be there."

"I'd prefer it if we came to you, actually. We're trying to keep your involvement off the radar."

"Oh. Four o'clock is fine, then."

"I'll see you then, Ms. Leighton."

Her throat dry, she said goodbye, disconnected and met Mark's searching gaze. "Detective Ford's coming here in a few hours. He's bringing a sketch artist with him."

Mark frowned. "Call him back and tell him today's not good."

"No." Mercer shook her head, then absently chewed on her fingernail as Mark began to pace the room.

"I have a meeting scheduled tomorrow with an attorney. I want him to advise you before you talk to the police again."

"Mark. It's not like the attorney's going to tell me not to cooperate with the sketch artist." She swallowed with difficulty, her voice sounding a bit breathless. "If they find this man, they can and will serve me with a subpoena to testify. We both know that's the case. I love you...but you can't protect me from this."

GRAY-HAIRED, barrel-chested, and nearing retirement age, Captain Walter Bell had requested an update on the case and now stood inside the debriefing room with Noah and Tyson.

"If this does turn out to be a hit on a federal judge, expect more hands on it," Bell said as he brushed at a piece of lint on his uniform shirt.

Noah capped a marker that he had been using on a dry erase board to list the facts of the investigation, at least what they knew so far. "That's what it's shaping up to look like, Cap. The gallery's inventory is valued at nearly a million dollars according to insurance assessments, but nothing was taken. Both victims still had their cash, credit cards, and cell phones, so robbery doesn't appear to be a motive."

"Unless it was a robbery gone wrong. Maybe the gallery owner or the judge resisted?"

"That doesn't match the eyewitness account, or the fact that Deveau had a concealed gun that he never got a chance to pull." Noah replaced the marker on the board's tray. "Ms. Leighton said that the perp walked in and just started shooting. No hesitation, no demand for money—"

"Then this cat puts two more bullets into Deveau for good measure before taking a stroll through the gallery, looking for others," Tyson chimed in from where he sat on the edge of the conference table, his long legs stretched out in front of him. He and Noah had already discussed, in theory, the possible reasons why Deveau had been targeted inside the gallery rather than the courthouse or his home. It was most likely to avoid the high security at both places. When they had visited the gated community where the judge lived, they'd seen firsthand the guards patrolling the neighborhood on golf carts, as well as myriad security cameras. The gallery had only required taking out two cameras—one in the foyer and the other in the main room.

"It takes some stones to plug two people in Gallery Row in broad daylight." Tyson crossed his arms over his chest. "The smooth way he slid in and out points to a real pro."

"What about the security company?" Bell shifted his stance. "Did they have an explanation for the cameras going down?"

"They were alerted by the system when they went out, but they haven't been able to identify a reason for it," Noah said. "We think the perp knew that Deveau was carrying, so instead of wearing something to conceal his face that would be a tip-off, he took the cameras out instead."

Bell appeared to consider this. "Maybe someone at the security company was in on it."

"We're looking into that," Noah assured him. "Although the company said that they do background checks, we're running employee names through the database to see if anyone has a record." His cell phone beeped, indicating that he had a text. He looked at the screen and, seeing that it wasn't urgent, decided to respond to it later. "Bruce said it's also possible for someone to hack in and take out the wireless transmission remotely. Either way, we're still looking at all the angles and possible other motives, although considering who the male vic was, retribution is high on the list. We need to get access to Deveau's docket. We also want to look at recent judgments as well as past cases, see if anyone sticks out."

Bell gave a nod. "Keep me in the loop, detectives."

Once the captain left, Tyson spoke. "What doesn't make sense with this *payback is hell* theory is how the shooter would've known in advance that Deveau was coming into that gallery. Taking out those cameras required planning. You think someone in Deveau's office with access to his calendar told the shooter where he would be and when?"

"It's a possibility, but a remote one," Noah said. "The people around Deveau have worked with him for years. They're devoted to him. But we should still interview them."

Tyson paused thoughtfully. "So, let's say it wasn't someone in the judge's office. Maybe some kind of spyware was used to access Deveau's computer or cell phone? His wife said that he had a scheduled appointment at The Bluth Studio—he was commissioning a painting of his hunting dogs. I bet that appointment was on his personal calendar."

"You'd still need access to the devices to install spyware,"

Noah reminded. "And it can be removed remotely once it's done its job."

Tyson pushed off from the table. "Worth a look, though, right? Deveau's cell is in the evidence room. I'll check it out and take it to Bruce. I'll try to get access to the judge's laptop, too."

"As far as courthouse employees go, I'm sure Deveau had a secretary—most judges do. She probably kept up with his schedule."

"I'll pay her a visit while you're having high tea in the St. Clair ballroom." Tyson smirked as he departed. "Keep it classy, Noah. Make sure you stick your pinky finger out while you're holding that china cup."

Noah tried not to smile. "Kiss my ass, Ty."

His partner's chuckle echoed down the precinct's hall. They had already decided that Noah would go with the forensic sketch artist to the St. Clair while Tyson would remain here to handle other aspects of the investigation. There was no point in both of them traveling to Rarity Cove and Noah had already established a relationship with Mercer Leighton. He could have had her come here, which was the usual protocol, but he didn't want to risk anyone seeing her walk in and put two and two together. Maybe he was being overly cautious, but reporters hung around here in hopes of getting a sound bite from a detective, or seeing something that would make them first to report breaking news. And the Gallery Row double homicide was the story *du jour*. If she showed up here, and especially if she had her prominent civic-leader brother with her, as Noah suspected she would, it would be too easy for a reporter to recognize him in particular and start wondering why the St. Clair family had business with the Charleston Police.

CHAPTER SIX

"IS THAT HIM?"

At Noah's question, Mercer looked up from the drawing that the forensic sketch artist—a bespectacled, middle-aged man named Jim—had created based on her description. She sat with him in the twin upholstered wing chairs in her office while Noah alternately stood or paced in front of the window. While his attire had been casual last night, he now looked more official in dark trousers, blue dress shirt, and tie. He waited for her answer, his hands planted on his lean hips just above his badge and holstered gun. Mercer looked again at the sketch, a knot in her stomach.

"Not exactly, but it's closer." They had been working on the drawing for well over an hour. She had asked for repeated adjustments—to the receding hairline, the eyes, eyebrows, nose, and jaw.

"What happens now, Detective Ford?" she asked once they had taken the sketch as far as they could. Mercer rose to her feet as the artist began gathering his materials.

"I'll meet you in the lobby, Noah." Tucking the drawing pad under his arm, the artist slipped from the room.

"That's it, for now," Noah said once they were alone. "You have my card, so if you remember anything else that you think might be helpful, don't hesitate to contact me."

"But what exactly happens if you find him? I'm not a fan of the unknown. I want to be prepared."

He appeared to measure her for a moment. "If we identify a suspect, we'll come back to you. Probably with a photo array to see if you can pick him out from a group."

"There won't be a line-up with me behind a two-way window?"

His faint smile, a surprise to her, caused attractive crinkles to form at the corners of his eyes. "You see that a lot on television, but it doesn't happen as often as you think. It can be hard to get that many people together with similar physical characteristics. A photo array is easier." He paused, his trademark seriousness back into place. "We do appreciate your cooperation, Ms. Leighton. You're no doubt still trying to deal with what happened yesterday. I know a little about post-traumatic stress disorder and I encourage you to seek out counseling if you're having a hard time."

"Thank you for the advice." Mercer moved restlessly, still unable to stop thinking about the *what next* of her situation. "If you *do* find this man, I'll be expected to testify against him. I know that. He'll be there in the courtroom when I do."

"That's a long way off," he said gently, apparently sensing her trepidation. "But yes, you'll be asked to point him out in front of a jury. In addition to telling the court what you witnessed, you'll be cross-examined by the defense. Eyewitness testimonies can be tricky. The DA's office will put you with the prosecuting attorney beforehand to help you prepare."

She nodded her understanding, although she felt disquieted at the prospect. Trying to ease her nerves by lessening the formality between them, she changed the subject. "I can't believe you used to work here. I guess it's true about it being a small world."

"Your father was a good man."

Mercer's heart pinched. She had been away at college in Atlanta when Harrison St. Clair—whom she adored—had passed away unexpectedly from a heart attack.

"He was. I still miss him," she said softly, then hesitated before speaking again. "Considering things, I'd really prefer it if you'd call me Mercer. Chances are that we met here years ago."

She felt the beat of her pulse inside her throat as that intense, amber gaze held hers for several seconds. He didn't take her up on her request, however.

"It was nice to see you again, Ms. Leighton, although I'm sorry for the circumstance."

His dark lashes flickered downward, and she realized that she had been absently fiddling with the rings she wore on a chain around her neck.

"I'm also sorry for your more recent loss," he rasped. He bid her a polite goodbye and departed her office.

"DETECTIVE FORD."

As Noah walked out through the luxurious, marble-floored lobby, he turned to see Mark St. Clair headed toward him.

"Go ahead, Jim. I'll catch up to you outside." As the sketch artist continued on, Noah repressed a sigh. He was good at reading faces, and tension was etched onto the approaching man's features.

"Could we have a word in private?" Mark inquired when he reached him. When Noah agreed, he was led from the lobby back to a corner office that he knew had once belonged to Harrison St. Clair. It had been redecorated, the paneled walls now painted in neutral tones that complemented the rich, Oriental carpet covering the hardwood floor. There was also leather-upholstered seating and a barrister's bookcase, although the large, antique mahogany desk was the same one that Noah recalled. The space was as masculine as Mercer Leighton's office had been cheerful and feminine.

"Did you get what you wanted?" Mark asked, his tone somber, once he had closed the door behind them.

Noah gave a faint nod. "We have a sketch to work from now."

"Do you have any leads?"

"Not at this time, but we're hoping that will change soon."

Mark paused for several moments before speaking again. "I'm concerned about my sister's role in your investigation, Detective."

Noah had a sister, too, and he empathized. "I understand."

"This man committed a double homicide without qualm. Based on the news reports, it's starting to sound like it was an assassination on a federal judge. What're the chances this man will come after Mercer if he finds out there's a witness?"

Noah had expected the question. "Mr. St. Clair, I want you to know that we're doing everything we can to keep your sister's identity confidential. We had her escorted from the crime scene last night before reporters arrived and a crowd gathered. It's why I had you leave the Fleur-De-Lis with her through the back entrance, and it's why I came here today to see her instead of having her come to the precinct."

The assurance seemed to calm him somewhat. He tiredly rubbed at his brow. "You need to understand...Mercer's been through a lot. She lost her husband to cancer just a year ago. She moved back here from Atlanta to try to pull her life together, and now this." His shoulders slumped under his white dress shirt. "My sister's a good person. She took care of my daughter and me during a rough patch several years ago, and she single-handedly cared for her husband during his illness, which wasn't easy on her. If I could change places with her on this, I would." His voice roughened, but his gaze remained direct. "I need your word that you'll protect her."

"You have it," Noah promised.

A short time later, he walked back through the lobby, his thoughts occupied with what Mark St. Clair had told him about his sister. But as he pushed through the revolving doors that led outside, Noah's cell phone rang. Walking past a uniformed valet who was packing luggage onto a brass pushcart for arriving guests, he fished the device from his pocket. He could see Jim awaiting him in the distance, leaned against the side of Noah's black Ford Explorer in the parking lot. Noah put the phone to his ear and answered.

"How'd it go?" Tyson asked. "Do we have a likeness of our shooter?"

"Let's hope so." Human memory was malleable. As a detective, Noah had had training in reconstructed memories. The brain had a way of filling in missing gaps with false information, which was why he had wanted to get Mercer with a sketch artist as quickly as possible.

"You were on the money, Noah. Deveau had a secretary. Her name's Anne Sheridan. I paid her a visit at her home. She's pretty broken up—she and the judge were tight. They worked together for over twenty years. Ms. Sheridan was responsible for keeping up with Deveau's schedule and kept his calendars, both business and personal, on her cell phone and laptop. I asked if we could get a look at them to check for spyware."

Noah had already learned from an earlier conversation with Bruce that no spyware had turned up on the judge's cell phone. Nor had the phones in his home or office been tapped. Nearing the SUV, he used his key fob to remotely unlock the doors. Although Jim went around and got in on the passenger side, Noah remained standing outside the vehicle. The pleasant, briny sea air that carried inland on the breeze ruffled his hair and made his tie flap against his shirtfront.

"Find anything?" he asked.

"Both her laptop and cell phone were clean." There was a loaded pause over the airwaves, however. "But you should know that she's only had the phone for a couple of weeks."

"What happened to her old one?"

"Weekend before last, Ms. Sheridan took her seven-year-old grandson to the Mount Pleasant Towne Centre to buy him some new clothes. They had lunch in the food court, and she placed her cell phone on the table—said she's positive of it. When she turned her back to look through her shopping bags, the phone disappeared. Looks like someone lifted it right off the table."

Noah's chest tingled. It could have been just some teenager engaging in theft, but again, he didn't believe in coincidence.

His gut told him that whoever had taken that phone had gotten access to Sterling Deveau's calendar.

CHAPTER SEVEN

MERCER WATCHED from the bungalow's front door as Olivia and Anders's Bentley pulled away, its headlights sweeping over the sand dunes as it left the driveway. She'd had dinner with them in the hotel dining room, although her mother had spent most of the meal fretting over her, something Mercer understood but still didn't need. She had also declined Mark's offer to spend another night with his family, but the quiet here was more unnerving than she had expected.

She went to the bedroom to change into something more comfortable—a well-worn T-shirt of Jonathan's and pajama pants—then returned to the living area with the intent of watching television. But as she walked past the end table where she had placed her purse, she hesitated before withdrawing Noah Ford's business card. Printed on plain white card stock with raised black letters and the logo of the Charleston Police Department, it was as no-nonsense and businesslike as he was.

Her curiosity about him won out. Getting out her laptop, she sat cross-legged on the sofa with the device in her lap and powered it up. She was savvy enough to know that a police officer's personal data, such as a street address, was unlikely to be located online out of security precautions. The only thing she knew about him was his occupation and that he wore no wedding band, which didn't mean that he wasn't in a relationship. Mercer did a search using his name and keywords that she thought might pull something up. She did find a group photo of the Charleston Police Department's softball team, which had played in a charity league that past summer. Noah stood in the back row, the brim of a baseball cap pulled low over his eyes. She went back to scan the rest of the search results. A moment later, her fingers paused on the trackpad, her stomach fluttering at one of the headlines her search had found.

Marines Rescue Four POWs from the Taliban.

The online article was from 2009.

Marines today rescued four troops from a compound eleven miles outside of Kabul, Afghanistan, in a covert operation that took place fourteen days after the soldiers' Apache helicopter gunship went down over mountainous terrain. Also recovered during the mission were the remains of two U.S. troops who had been executed...

A chill fell over her as she read the article's description of the torture that the soldiers had endured. Her throat dry, her heart beating hard, Mercer scanned the rest of the article until she came to the names of the freed soldiers.

First Sergeant Noah Christopher Ford, ANGLICO Special Operations, from Charleston, South Carolina, was among those listed.

THEY HAD BECOME LESS frequent over the years, but occasionally the nightmares still came for him. Noah awoke from a black abyss, bathed in sweat, his pulse racing. What had happened to him nearly a decade ago would always be with him, lurking somewhere in the back of his mind. But he was one of the fortunate ones.

He had come home while others, his brothers, had not.

Blowing out a breath, he scrubbed his hands over his face, trying to push away the images that cut at him like a knife.

Aware that sleep wouldn't be returning to him easily, he reached for his cell phone on the nightstand and squinted at its lit screen. Five-fifteen a.m. He would have to be up in another hour or so, anyway, especially if he planned to hit the gym before work. Pushing back the covers, he rose and pulled on the sweatpants that he had folded and left at the foot of the bed the night before, then walked barefoot and bare-chested into the kitchen to start the coffeemaker. He turned on the small television set on the counter to keep him company while he ground beans and cracked a couple of eggs into a skillet.

The television was turned to a twenty-four-hour cable news station. He was about to switch it over to ESPN, but he put down the remote when the station moved to a different story, catching his attention. A female field reporter stood in front of a gracious row house in Savannah, Georgia, according to the caption at the screen's bottom.

U.S. Attorney Found Dead Inside Savannah Home.

A microphone gripped in one hand, the reporter spoke.

"U.S. Attorney Richard Townsend was found dead from an apparent gunshot wound in his home here in Savannah's Historic District late yesterday. According to investigators, Townsend lived alone and appeared to have been deceased for several days —possibly as long as a week—prior to the body's discovery by a housecleaner. Investigators do not believe it to be a suicide. Townsend had a successful thirty-year legal career that included time prosecuting federal cases in Charleston, South Carolina, and more recently, here in Savannah..."

The coffeemaker gurgled behind him. Noah resisted the impulse to call Tyson—not only would he be rousing him early, he would also be risking awakening his wife and little girls. Noah decided to can the gym and go directly to the precinct as soon as he showered and dressed.

A judge and a prosecutor, both working in Charleston, both shot dead within a week of one another. There was at least a fair chance the murders were related.

They were poring over Deveau's current docket but still needed to look at past trials, which numbered in the hundreds. If they could find a defendant who Townsend had prosecuted in Deveau's courtroom, things might be about to break their way.

SUNLIGHT SLANTED through the barred windows in the visitation room as Lex Draper peered at the approaching, white-haired male in the orange jumpsuit. Flanked by two muscle-bound guards, he rolled a mobile canister of oxygen behind him, a nasal cannula clipped under his nose. As the old man stiffly eased down at the table across from Lex, the guards receded, their attention turning to the handful of other prisoners who sat at tables with visitors of their own. The guards gave the old man a wide berth, just like they gave him the table in the far corner that allowed the most privacy for business—as they should, since they were on his payroll.

"You've got a problem, Lex. A big one." The old man leaned forward, his features stern in his creased face. His voice, roughened by a lifetime of tobacco use, dropped to a gravelly whisper. "You left a witness behind at the gallery."

Lex's heart skipped a beat, but he kept his face impassive. The others at the compound called him *Iceman* for a reason. His chin raised fractionally. "That's impossible."

"You think my sources lie?" He narrowed his jaundiced, pale blue eyes, a flash of the imposing man who had led them all these years reappearing despite the frailness of his body. "I'm letting you know out of courtesy, son, so you can do something about it. If I were you, I'd find out who she is—"

"I will," Lex stressed, lifting his palms from the table. "I'll take care of it."

"You damn well better, unless you want to end up in here with me." Their conversation moved to other business until the old man began to cough, a phlegmy, wheezing sound. He pulled a handkerchief from his pocket and spat into it before stuffing it away again. Scraping back the plastic chair, he stood slowly, then tottered out with one of the guards in his wake.

There were a few whispers that this need for retribution was the product of a failing mind. But the old man was their leader and was still widely revered. He still called the shots, even from behind bars.

Lex frowned as he stood, his hands balling involuntarily into fists at his sides. He wanted to be named the new leader when the old man finally bit the dust. Having his blessing was imperative. The old man had chosen *him* to do his bidding and Lex had accepted the task to seal the deal. But if he went down as the trigger man, it was over.

A goddamn eyewitness.

Biting the inside of his cheek to control his outrage, Lex waited impatiently for a guard to open the door. Then he strode from the visitation room, the laminated guest pass flapping against his shirt pocket as the heavy thud of his boots echoed along the empty corridor. He understood now why the old man had sent for him. The phone lines here were monitored.

His mind worked to think of some room in that gallery, some closet or cubbyhole that he had missed. He had planned too carefully for this. They had known all along that the police would eventually figure out the connection between the shootings. But the plan had been for there to be no evidence. The old man *wanted* them to know that he had gotten his revenge and they couldn't do a damn thing about it.

So, the situation had changed some, Lex conceded tensely as he walked through the metal detectors, then waited for another guard to allow him to exit the building. When the last set of electronic bars finally clanged open, he stalked through the lobby and outside, leaving the bleach-over-piss odor of the penitentiary behind. He scowled to himself despite the warm afternoon sun on his shoulders, aware of the guards with rifles patrolling from the widow's walk above him as he reached his pickup truck in the high-walled parking lot.

Briefly, he regretted having stuck his neck out again for the old man. But there was no way in hell that he was spending the rest of his life rotting in some jail cell, awaiting execution.

Relax, Lex. You can fix this.

He took a deep breath. This was a hiccup, was all.

One that could still be easily handled.

CHAPTER EIGHT

AN EMPTY FEELING in her stomach, Mercer looked up from the photos that Noah had laid on the desk in her office. There were a dozen images of balding, Caucasian males who appeared to be in their early forties in front of her, all of them with sullen expressions and a hardness in their eyes. But she had recognized the man from the art gallery immediately, his image turning her blood to ice.

"Who is he?" she wanted to know, unable to keep the breathy tremor from her voice. When Noah seemed reluctant to answer, Mercer rose from behind the desk. Arms wrapped around her midriff, she went to stand in front of him. "I have a right to know, don't I?"

"His name is Lex Draper," he said finally. "He's a member of an extremist organization called The Brotherhood. It's classified as a sovereign militia group."

"Sovereign militia?" She had heard the term before but wasn't exactly certain of its meaning.

"Groups like these espouse an anti-government, conspiracy-oriented ideology. They're obsessed with weaponry and defending themselves against what they believe to be attacks on their freedom. As groups like these go, The Brotherhood's particularly *out there.*" As he spoke, Noah rubbed tiredly at the back of his neck. It was late Wednesday afternoon and he was casually dressed in sneakers, jeans, and an untucked, button-down shirt that partially concealed the gun at his waist. Mercer herself wore athletic clothes, her hair in a ponytail since she had already left work for the day but had returned when she had received his call to let her know that he was coming to the hotel with photos. The news had rattled her.

"How'd you zero in on him?" she asked. "Did you get some kind of tip?"

"There was a U.S. attorney named Richard Townsend who was murdered in Savannah last week. He previously worked in Charleston. My partner—Detective Beaufain—and I went through Sterling Deveau's trial history, looking for cases that Townsend had prosecuted in Deveau's courtroom. It was a process of elimination, but we found a case from seven years ago that got our attention. From there, we went through mugshots of The Brotherhood's known members until we came across one that fit your description."

"This man, Lex Draper—he was the one on trial?"

Noah shook his dark head. "The leader of The Brotherhood was. His name's Orion Scott. He was convicted and is serving out a twenty-five-year sentence in federal prison."

"For what?" Mercer asked in a quiet voice.

"For ordering the murder of his son's ex-wife's fiancé. He was African American, and Scott didn't want his grandchildren being raised in a mixed-race household. The Brotherhood also has white supremacist leanings. The murder attempt was unsuccessful—the victim survived but will spend the rest of his life in a wheelchair. Scott was convicted for conspiracy to commit."

Sickened by what she had been told, Mercer absently laid a hand against her stomach.

"Scott's also seventy-nine. We found out this morning he's in late-stage heart failure. Even with a terminal illness, he was turned down for parole again last month and won't get another hearing for two years. He'll most likely be dead before then. Richard Townsend spoke at the parole hearing and stated his belief to the board that Scott should remain incarcerated." Noah shifted his stance. "We think that the murders were retribution against Townsend and the judge who sentenced him—a final act, since he has nothing to lose at this point. Draper was the hit man. Draper's been a person of interest in other investigations over the years but nothing's stuck."

Mercer swallowed past the dryness in her throat. "So, you're just going to go arrest him now?"

"Your identification should be enough to get a judge to sign-off on an arrest warrant, as well as a search warrant for the compound," Noah said. "Draper lives there, as do some of the other members. We'll serve the warrants hopefully overnight. The compound's in a rural area about an hour north of here."

"You and Detective Beaufain aren't going out there alone, are you?"

"We're taking a SWAT team and several other detectives. There's always a chance with this group that things could get ugly."

Things were moving much faster than she had expected. Mercer looked away, suddenly feeling ill-equipped to handle all this.

"Are you all right, Ms. Leighton?"

"I'm...fine," she lied. Mercer thought of what she had learned about him. "You should know that I'm guilty of Googling you." At the impulsive admission, she felt heat rise on her skin. "I didn't know that you were a military hero, Detective Ford. Mark didn't, either. I'm sure it was on the news back then, but we somehow missed it or didn't make the connection."

A shadow seemed to pass over his face. "That was a long time ago. And I don't consider myself a hero."

Looking up at him, she shook her head. "What you went through...I can't imagine."

He slid the photos back into their envelope. "I need to get going. Thank you again, Ms. Leighton. I'll keep you updated."

He made an abrupt exit from her office. Left in his wake, Mercer took a tight breath. Noah Ford remained a mystery. Thinking about what he planned to do tonight—arrest the man who had filled her nightmares as of late—she felt a strong sense of unease. Through the window, she was aware of the approaching evening. Samantha couldn't go with her tonight, but she needed a run to try to burn off her anxiety.

HE SHOULD HAVE ALREADY LEFT, but Noah sat inside his SUV in the St. Clair parking lot, one elbow propped against the window as he stared blindly out. Mercer Leighton's mention of his past had thrown him. He had talked a little to Corinne and Tyson about it over the years but if anyone else asked, Noah typically would just shut down on them.

Many soldiers who had seen active duty suffered from some form of PTSD. Noah had a better reason than most to succumb to it, but he hadn't, at least not to the extent that ruined so many veterans' lives. After returning home, he had seen the mandated military shrinks while hospitalized for his injuries. Then, after his medical discharge from service, there had been the twice weekly counseling sessions for nearly a year, something the police department had mandated as a condition of his returning to work. Noah had been able to go on with his life. He had learned to compartmentalize the trauma, but that didn't mean that what had happened didn't still grab him by the throat sometimes.

Still, he regretted the curt way that he had left Mercer Leighton's office. Despite her apprehension, she was cooperating fully with the investigation. She had tried to reach out to him and he'd put up a wall between them.

Noah straightened as he saw her emerge from the hotel's front. It was impossible not to notice her shapely figure, especially in the tight spandex running pants that stopped at mid-calf and equally fitted shirt that clung to her breasts and revealed a glimpse of the hot pink straps of a jog bra. He watched as she spoke to one of the valets, then headed toward the boardwalk, her honey-blond ponytail swaying with her movement. Noah frowned. Based on her attire, he had hoped that she was on her way to the hotel's fitness studio and not the beach. This was a high-end resort and Rarity Cove was generally a safe place, but it was nearing dusk and he didn't like the idea of her running alone so close to dark. Once he had gotten a positive ID on the shooter, he had called Tyson to get him started on the paperwork for the warrant. Considering what faced them tonight, he should be headed back himself. But instead, Noah got out of his vehicle and traveled in the direction that Mercer had taken. He was uncertain whether he could catch her before she ran off, but as he reached the boardwalk he saw her, stretching her legs on a sun-bleached wood railing on a ramp that led down to the beach. Between the lighter tourist season and the fact that it was dinnertime, there were only a few hotel guests out strolling on the boardwalk. Still, he was glad for the untucked shirt he wore that pretty much concealed his gun so that he didn't attract attention.

She appeared surprised, the heavy lashes that shadowed her cheeks flying upward as he descended the ramp and reached the railing beside her.

"Detective Ford."

"I...want to apologize for earlier. The brusque way I left your office. I didn't mean to be impolite. You just caught me off guard."

A long strand of her hair had escaped her ponytail in the ocean breeze, and she tucked it behind her ear in what seemed like an almost nervous gesture. "I get that you don't like to talk about it. I shouldn't have brought it up. I shouldn't have Googled you, either, but..." Her slender shoulders rose in a shrug. "I guess that I was curious about you."

He sighed softly as seagulls cawed in the air above them. "It's all right."

She seemed to consider that a tentative invitation, because she asked carefully, "How long were you in the Marines?"

Noah breathed in the scent of brine and looked off across the water before speaking. "I enlisted right after high school. I served four years overseas, then came back here and became a cop. I got my degree in criminal justice at night, and I'd just made my way up to detective when I got called back as a reservist. I was redeployed to Afghanistan." He paused, uncomfortable, but felt an inexplicable need to reveal some part of himself to her.

"I was nearly at the end of a six-month tour when my team was sent out on a reconnaissance mission for another Special Ops force. The helicopter we were in was shot down by the Taliban." He stared down for a time at his hands. "The pilot was able to crash-land, but we were captured."

She touched his arm, and Noah felt his chest tighten. "Anyway, I'm sorry if I seemed rude earlier. You shouldn't be running alone so late, by the way."

"It's okay. I'm staying in one of the guest bungalows. It's only about a half-mile down. I'm going to run about a mile past it and then come back. I'll be home before dark." She hesitated before adding, "I already went for a run with my sister-in-law this morning, but with everything going on, I'm a little wired."

He indicated the earbuds that hung around her neck by a

cord, companions to the ever-present wedding rings. "Just don't use the earbuds, all right? You should always stay aware of your surroundings, even here."

The sun's hue had dimmed to a deep gold as it sank lower in the sky. Their gazes held in the waning light.

"Be careful tonight?" she asked.

He felt some bond form between them, tenuous and fragile. "Absolutely."

"And I know that you probably consider it unprofessional, but I really *would* prefer it if you called me Mercer. At least when it's just the two of us. And I'd really like to call you Noah."

He gave a faint nod of acceptance. "Good-night, Mercer." He took a few steps back up the ramp, then turned to her again. "For what it's worth, I Googled you, too."

Her smile, the first time he had seen it, lightened his heart. He headed up the ramp toward the parking lot, but halfway up, Noah's head jerked at the muted *thwap* and splintering of wood. He spun, flinching at another round as it whizzed past his ear. Mercer cried out as the railing exploded beside her. He charged back down.

"Get down!"

He tackled her hard, falling on top of her. The handful of others who had been on the boardwalk above them began to scream. Heart hammering against his ribs, Noah rolled Mercer closer to the protective jut of the ramp as more wood exploded, this time just over their heads. Still on top of her, he reached for his gun, peering carefully upward to scan the area. The hair on his nape prickled as he spotted a man in a Halloween mask, his hoodie pulled up, looking over the railing at them. The long barrel of a silencer was visible.

"Are you hit?" he asked Mercer, his voice strained.

Her face was ashen and she gasped for air, the wind knocked out of her, but she shook her head.

"Stay down!" Noah leapt up and began to run, his gun poised in both hands in front of him. The man had been striding down the ramp to close in on them, but upon seeing Noah's weapon, he turned and sprinted back up, disappearing from view.

"Police! Stop!" Noah reached the boardwalk in time to see the masked shooter jumping into the back seat of a waiting car at the edge of the parking lot. He ran after it as it screeched away. Chest heaving, perspiring, he dug into his jeans pocket for his cell phone and called the local police, giving his badge number, stating what had happened, and relaying the car's description and the partial number he had gotten from its tag. Noah cursed inwardly. He hadn't been able to get off a shot at the gunman or the car since he had feared hitting bystanders who had scattered across the parking lot in an attempt to distance themselves from the fray. Holding his badge in the air to let them know that he wasn't a threat, Noah then raced back down the ramp to Mercer. She was standing now, appearing dazed, her chest rising and falling rapidly with her breathing. Blood trickled down her left leg. It was scraped from where he had knocked her to the ramp's rough wood planks, but she didn't appear to be otherwise injured.

"They're gone. You're okay," he murmured as she went to him and hid her face against his chest. Her body shook like a cold, soaked kitten. Still gripping his gun, his arms closed protectively around her. Noah swallowed, in disbelief that they had come after her right here on her family's resort.

If I hadn't been here...

Had the shooter been Draper, or someone else from The Brotherhood? Either way, they knew about her now. Anger radiated inside him.

Somehow, they had a leak.

CHAPTER NINE

NIGHT HAD DRAPED a blanket of darkness over the boardwalk and ocean.

"How do you think they found out about her?" Tyson asked as he and Noah waited for techs to process the scene. Noah had called them over from Charleston since the Rarity Cove Police Department was too small to have its own forensics unit. Mobile lights had been set up around the boardwalk for visibility and hotel guests watched police activity from behind yellow crime scene tape.

"It could've been someone at the Fleur-De-Lis, or even one of our officers working the scene." Noah's jaw clenched at the latter possibility. "Regardless, they made a bold move here. They'll try again if they get the chance."

Tyson grunted in agreement. He had driven up from Charleston after hearing about the shooting. The rubberized mask the shooter wore—a macabre, grinning werewolf—had imprinted itself onto Noah's brain. Despite the lulling sound of waves sweeping ashore below them, he released a tense breath. "She's only been living here for about a month in one of the bungalows. In the eyes of the hotel, that makes her also a guest and they won't give out patrons' room numbers or addresses. They probably had no choice but to surveil the hotel and wait for an opportunity."

"You said that she was going for a run. They must've gotten impatient. If they'd followed her onto the beach to a more remote location..." Tyson made a popping sound with his mouth. "Game over."

Noah felt a dullness inside him. But it would be difficult for a shooter to make an escape in the soft sand if he were spotted. Taking shots at her from the boardwalk while she was on the ramp below had nearly the same advantage as a hunter in a deer stand. Not to mention, the parking lot's close proximity made for a fast getaway. Noah stared at a patrol car, its lightbar flashing strobe-like into the night. He recalled how Mercer's body had trembled against his as he held her. It had been clear the shooter hadn't known that Noah was a cop. He had come down the ramp after her and had retreated only upon seeing Noah's gun.

"You've been holding out on me." Tyson's lowered voice pulled Noah from his thoughts. "You never mentioned that Mercer Leighton was so *fine*. Now I know why you weren't bitching about being point of contact."

Tyson was only trying to lighten his mood—his partner was one of the happiest married men that he knew—but Noah wasn't biting. He had introduced Tyson to Mercer in the third-floor hotel room where he had left her with her sister-in-law and a Rarity Cove police officer stationed outside the door. Mark St. Clair was with her now, too. He had been at a South Carolina tourism meeting in Myrtle Beach some two hours away when the shooting occurred, but Noah had seen his Volvo drive up and park under the hotel's black awning about fifteen minutes ago.

"You know I'm just riding you, man." Tyson peered at a uniformed officer who stood nearby, scribbling on a notepad as he talked with a witness. Noah had also talked to bystanders prior to Tyson's arrival, although technically, it was the Rarity Cove Police's crime scene, not theirs.

Tyson scratched at his cheek. "So, you're telling me the local boys saw *nothing* on the drive out here? That peninsula road is the only way in and out. Should've run straight into them."

"There's dense brush behind the trees lining the road," Noah recalled. "They probably drove in and hid until the units went past."

"Looks like they got the entire force out for this." Tyson indicated the four police cars that were on-scene. It was a jab at the department's small size.

"What's the status on the warrants?" Noah asked.

"Garber and Durand should be at the judge's house right now. They offered to do it since I thought I should get up here to check on you. I let them know about the attempt on Ms. Leighton's life. It's another big checkbox for probable cause, although most of the judges in Charleston County are worked up about the homicides already, considering that Deveau and Townsend were two of their own." Tyson studied him, his expression serious. "You know you're damn lucky that the shooter didn't blow your head off trying to get to her. I'm not in the mood to break in a new partner, Noah."

He didn't respond. Instead, he looked up to the hotel's third floor, counting the windows to find the room where Mercer was located. The curtains were closed as he had instructed. Noah had done the right thing in not risking bystanders' lives, he knew that. But if he had shot the gunman and it was Draper, as he suspected it was, all this would be over. There would no longer be a target on Mercer's back.

"You've had one bitch of a day already," Tyson pointed out. "You sure you still want to go with us to serve that warrant?"

Noah burned with the need to take Draper in, as well as

anyone else who had been involved in what had happened here. "We're the leads on this. I should be there."

He repressed a sigh as Mark St. Clair appeared at the edge of the boardwalk's cordoned-off area, his features hard. A uniform stopped him from going farther.

"That must be the brother," Tyson said. "You ask me, he looks loaded for bear."

"He has good reason." Steeling himself, Noah called to the officer. "Let him through."

I need your word that you'll protect her.

He had done that, but he figured the approaching man wouldn't see it that way.

"I'll let you field this one." Tyson made his escape, walking off in the direction of the forensics techs, who were wrapping up.

"What happened?" Mark demanded, eyebrows drawn down as he reached Noah. "You *said* her involvement was being kept confidential."

"I said we were trying—"

"You could've gotten her killed tonight, you know that?"

Noah's muscles tightened, but he didn't argue. Instead, he waited until Mark took a calming breath.

"I'm sorry. That wasn't fair. Mercer told me that you shielded her when the shooting started."

"How's she holding up?"

"She's scared. We all are." His mouth slackening in obvious disbelief, he looked around the boardwalk at the police activity.

"Mr. St. Clair, I want to do everything I can to make sure something like this doesn't happen again. But the stakes are raised and I need your family's cooperation."

Mark looked at him. Noah continued carefully. "I have a call in to my captain. I want to take your sister into temporary protective custody."

"No." He shook his head vehemently. "My family stays

together. I have hotel security. We'll keep her confined to a room."

"Your guards aren't even armed. They aren't trained for something like this, not even close," Noah argued. Although he didn't say it, the two hotel security guards were the equivalent of mall cops. Indicating the Rarity Cove officers who were working the scene, he lowered his voice. "To be honest with you, neither are they. They have zero experience handling a major crime. I'm not even happy about the uniform who's inside watching her, but that's all I've got right now. I need your sister back in my jurisdiction. I might be able to convince my department to let us watch over her here on the property, but I don't recommend it. The man she witnessed at the gallery knows where to find her now. She needs to be somewhere else."

When Mark still appeared uncertain, Noah added, "If she stays here, at the least, our presence will be a disruption to your business. At worst, it could put others—your guests and staff, even your wife and children—in danger. It's a miracle that no one was killed or hurt today. I know you don't want to take that risk again."

Mark dragged a hand through his hair. "My brother's in Hawaii, filming a movie. I could send her there."

"You could. But your brother's fame doesn't make for an ideal situation for someone trying to hide. He has photographers trailing his every move."

Mark stared off in the direction of the beach, clearly struggling with what to do.

"You'll be the one watching over her?" he asked finally.

"As much as I can. I'm working the investigation, but my partner and I will take an active role in her protection." He pointed out Tyson, who was now in conversation with one of the local officers on the far side of the parking lot. Noah was committing to a lot, but some part of him needed to keep Mercer close. He had taken responsibility for her safety, had given his word.

"Tell me about this man," Mark said heavily. "This killer."

"He's part of a militia group known as The Brotherhood. They've been on the news over the years—stand-offs with police, tax evasion, gun running to fund themselves. They're also on several watch lists for domestic terrorism."

"Mercer said his name is Lex Draper."

Noah nodded. "We believe the murders at the gallery and another one in Savannah were ordered by the group's leader. Draper was the gunman. We're going to attempt to serve an arrest warrant for him tonight. But even if we take him into custody, your sister could still be in danger. Draper has help. Someone was driving his getaway car today. Our understanding is that he has a small group of loyalists within The Brotherhood who want him to be named the next leader. Even if Draper's arrested, arraigned, and denied bail, it doesn't mean one of them won't take up the charge to make sure this never goes to trial."

Mark looked briefly up into the dark night, clearly overwhelmed. "I don't like this."

"I don't, either," Noah said somberly. "But if I hadn't been here tonight, your sister would be dead. I gave you my word that I'd keep her safe, but I need you to let me do that."

"I-I DON'T WANT TO LEAVE."

Noah's throat ached as Mercer looked pleadingly between him, Tyson, and her brother, panic in her eyes. Samantha St. Clair, who Noah had met earlier, was no longer in the room and, based on the rumpled duvet on the large, four-poster bed, it appeared that Mercer had been lying down until the men knocked on the door. A flat-screen television housed inside a mahogany armoire was on, but the sound had been muted.

"I believe it's for the best, Mercer," Mark said gently. "Detective Ford and Detective Beaufain want to take you somewhere that Draper and anyone who's helping him won't be able to find you."

Mercer pressed her fingers against her closed eyelids.

Tyson spoke, filling the strained silence. "It'll be safer for you, Ms. Leighton, and for your family and the hotel guests."

He seemed to strike a nerve because she opened her eyes again. "You're right. I'm sorry. I-I haven't been thinking clearly. Anyone could've been hurt or killed today. I can't stay here and put anyone at risk again." She looked at Mark. "I can't even go to Carter. I could put him and his family in danger."

She turned her eyes to Noah. "For how long? Please don't tell me until there's a trial. That could take months."

"I don't know for how long." He wanted to be honest with her. "We need to take this one day at a time. My goal for right now is just to get you somewhere besides here."

"But you said that you're going to arrest Draper *tonight*."

"We're going to *try*," Tyson interjected. "But Detective Ford and I are concerned that even if he's arrested, he may have others in his group who could take up the charge—"

"To make sure that I never get to testify against him," Mercer said thickly.

Mark softly clasped her upper arms. "You need to go with them, sweetheart. I can't let anything happen to you. I wish there was another way, but..."

They turned at the knock on the door and Noah put a hand on the gun at his hip, then relaxed it when he heard the officer who was stationed outside, letting them know that Samantha St. Clair had returned. Noah unlocked the door and opened it, and she entered with a blond girl and a younger, dark-haired boy in tow. Both of them ran to Mercer.

"I went down to get the kids from the au pair," Samantha explained. "They overheard the staff talking about what happened and they were worried about Mercer. I thought it'd be okay to bring them up so they could see that she's all right."

Her expression was apologetic, having apparently sensed that they had walked in on something.

"I'm glad you did." Despite everything, Mercer managed to put on a smile and talk with the children. Once she had hugged both and reassured them that she was fine, the girl wandered over to the bed and reached for the television remote, although the little boy remained leaned against Mercer's thigh. As she ran a hand through his hair, he shyly stared up at Noah.

"May I turn up the TV, Aunt Mercer?" the girl asked.

"Of course, sweetie."

The sound of a television show blared into the room.

"I'm sorry. I can tell we shouldn't be here." Samantha's tone was hushed as Noah overheard her speak to her husband. "I didn't know the detectives were here, and I thought with the police in the lobby and the officer right outside the room it'd be safe to bring them up."

"Ethan, why don't you go watch TV with Emily?" Mercer gave him a gentle nudge and he skipped over to join his sibling, climbing onto the bed beside her. Touching Samantha's arm, Mercer said, "I have to go. Mark will explain what's happening."

Her voice faltered as she spoke, causing another spark of guilt inside Noah. He stared at the fire exit plan posted on the back of the door, feeling as though he were intruding on a private family moment. Mark embraced his sister.

"It's going to be okay," he told her. "They'll take you to your bungalow so you can pack a bag. I promise that I'll see you soon."

Appearing defeated, she gave a small nod.

MERCER WATCHED from inside Noah's Ford Explorer as he entered the bungalow from the covered front porch, his gun poised in front of him. Detective Beaufain, who had trailed them from the hotel in his own sedan, now stood guard outside the SUV. Her mind wrestled with anxiety as she imagined hearing a gunshot and seeing a flash of light through the bungalow's windows, but it remained dark inside. Relief filtered through her when, a minute later, Noah reappeared. Detective Beaufain opened her door.

"Detective Ford will wait inside with you while you pack," he said as he helped her from the SUV. "We weren't followed, but just the same, I'll stay out here to make sure we don't get any unwanted company."

Noah had gone back inside the bungalow. As Mercer entered, she saw him walking through the darkened rooms and closing the plantation shutters.

"You can go ahead and turn on a few lights, but stay away from the French doors," he told her when he returned. She reached to the pull chain on a Tiffany lamp and turned it on, bringing him into focus.

"You should change into something a little warmer while you're packing," he advised. "There's a cold front coming through. It's unusual for this time of year, but it's supposed to drop into the low fifties overnight."

Mercer pushed up the sleeves of the too-large, navy Charleston PD windbreaker she wore over her running clothes. It belonged to Noah, who had insisted that she put it on before they'd escorted her from the hotel through a rear service door and into the SUV.

"How's your leg?" he asked.

"It's just a scrape." She glanced down at the bandage on her shin. The town's lone ambulance had arrived at the hotel along with police, and although she hadn't thought it necessary, a paramedic had cleaned and treated the minor injury.

"I'm sorry that I had to take you down like that."

She stirred uneasily at the memory of his hard, male body on top of hers. "Don't be. I'm alive because of it."

Their gazes held in the lamplight, until she looked away, seeing her computer on the kitchen island. "Am I allowed to take my laptop? I have a hotspot device in case there's no wireless access where I'm going."

"I'd prefer that you don't." His dark eyebrows slanted downward in seriousness. "But if you do, I want to be absolutely clear on this—no posting on social sites and no sending emails. And I don't want you using your cell phone at all. It stays turned off."

Despite her nod of acceptance of his rules, another wave of anxiety washed over her. Mercer wondered for how long she might be away. She had drawn so much strength from her family since Jonathan's death, but it seemed that now even that support system was being stripped from her. Her emotions were running high and a lump formed in her throat at the unfairness of it all. Turning away, she walked to the fireplace, not wanting Noah to see the mist in her eyes. She stared up at the silver urn on the mantel, an ache inside her, until she became aware of Noah's presence close behind her.

"You can take that, if it'll help," he said, his voice low.

She shook her head, her heart heavy. "There's nothing inside it anymore. I scattered his ashes last weekend."

She wiped at her eyes, embarrassed, before turning to face him. His expression held sympathy. "Your brother told me that your husband died a year ago."

She felt the lump in her throat grow larger. "I...guess I've had a hard time letting go."

"He was quite a bit older than you."

Defensive, her chin lifted faintly. "Did Mark tell you that, as well?"

"I Googled you, too, remember? There was a photo of you with him in the *Atlanta-Journal Constitution* from a few years back. It was taken at an awards ceremony at the university where he taught."

Mercer felt a pang at the memory. Jonathan had received the Dalmouth Award, a high honor for professors of English.

"We were married five years," she said quietly. "The last nine months of our marriage were...difficult. Jonathan was very ill prior to his death."

As his somber gaze held hers, Mercer was again made aware of the vitality he exuded. She imagined that women found his alpha-male *take-chargeness* and dark, brooding good looks deeply appealing. Unsettled by the observation, she glanced down at her hands.

"You should go pack," he said.

A short time later, she had changed into a sweater and jeans and was zipping up her large travel bag in the bedroom when Noah knocked on the door.

"You can come in," she told him. Once he entered, she handed him his jacket. "You'll probably be needing this tonight."

He accepted it and shrugged into it. "Let's go. If you've forgotten anything, we can buy it or send someone back for it."

Mercer picked up her own jacket from the bed and put it on as Noah placed the bag's strap over his shoulder to carry it outside. She followed him into the living area. With their pending departure, however, her anxiety spiked again. "Where're we going? To some kind of safe house?"

"This is a fast-moving situation and we're still working on that," he said as he turned to face her. "But I have a place where

I'm leaving you while Detective Beaufain and I meet up with the SWAT team."

"I need to know where I'm going, Noah."

"You'll be with my sister, Corinne, and her husband. They live in the same general direction we're headed, so we're dropping you off before traveling to the compound. Two of my friends—both former military—will stay outside to watch over the place. They're more than likely already there. My brother-in-law will sit guard inside. He's a civilian now, but he served in the Coast Guard for five years, working in its Drug Interdiction unit."

"Your sister and her husband agreed to this?"

He frowned slightly at her questioning. "Yeah, they did. They've sent their son to stay at a friend's house, so it'll be just the three of you inside. As long as we're not followed there, and we won't be—Detective Beaufain and I know how to spot a tail—there's not a chance they'll find you. If I thought there was, I wouldn't endanger my family."

Her chest tightened. She didn't want to be left alone with someone she didn't know. And for all she knew, Noah had strong-armed their cooperation. Nor did Mercer understand why he was having friends watch over her instead of police.

"I don't want to be an imposition on anyone. Can't I just stay at the hotel for the night? We can ask the Rarity Cove Police to keep guard. You can come back and get me once—"

"We need to do this my way and we need to go *now*, Mercer," he said with forced patience. "I want you off this property as soon as possible. Don't fight me on this, all right?"

At his tone, she bit down hard on her lower lip. Noah released a soft breath of resignation. Putting down her bag, he came to stand in front of her. "I'm sorry. What happened has me on edge, too. I trust the men who'll be watching over you completely. Until I know who leaked the information about you, until I can rule out that it came from somewhere inside my own department, I'm not leaving you with just anyone. I need time to figure out who I can trust. You'll only be at my sister's place for a few hours. At the most, until morning."

She nodded mutely, unwilling to tell him the truth: that the prospect of being without him frightened her. Her hands trembled faintly as she closed her laptop on the kitchen island, put it in its carry case and picked it up along with her purse.

Hoisting the large bag over his shoulder again, Noah moved forward, then halted at the door with Mercer behind him, waiting until Detective Beaufain gave them the go-ahead to proceed.

"I want you to slink down in the seat like you did when we left the hotel. The local police have checked the peninsula road to make sure there's no one waiting to ambush us, but I still want you to keep down until we get outside the property and off that road," Noah instructed once they were both inside his SUV. Snapping his seatbelt, he started the engine. The twin headlights of Detective Beaufain's sedan flared to life behind them.

A few minutes later, sitting huddled low in the seat, Mercer's heart constricted as they left the St. Clair behind.

CHAPTER TEN

"SO, this is where Noah grew up." Mercer made nervous small talk as she accepted the mug of decaffeinated coffee that Corinne Salling handed her. They stood in the tidy kitchen with its patterned, linoleum flooring and white appliances. Her husband, Keith, a big bear of a man, sat in the adjacent living room in front of the television, a shotgun across his lap, which he had calmly told Mercer was just a backup to the men who were stationed outside.

"The very place." Corinne was dark-haired like her brother, although she appeared older than him, her locks streaked faintly with gray and fine lines on her face that suggested she'd had a hard life. She indicated one of the wooden chairs tucked around a well-used dining table, and Mercer sat. Corinne sat across from her, her intelligent brown eyes assessing.

"I'm sure this house doesn't look like much," she remarked, although the comment seemed to be made without malice. "But as our Mama always said, it keeps us dry and warm in the winter and cool in the summer—at least as cool as one gets in South Carolina."

Mercer figured that Noah had told Corinne that she was a St. Clair and his sister had made assumptions about her.

"I like your house," she assured her. "You can tell there's a lot of love here."

When she had entered with Noah a half-hour earlier, Mercer had noticed the multiple groupings of family photos and the shelves that held cheerful knickknacks, including several homemade items that looked like a child's school art projects. There were also photos of Noah in uniform, both police and military. The home was modest—an aging ranch with a low-slung roof—but it was well cared for and appeared to be on several acres of property. As she had been ushered inside, Mercer had also noticed the shadowed structure of a large greenhouse behind the home.

"I saw the greenhouse," she mentioned, still trying to keep conversation flowing. "What do you grow?"

Corinne took a sip of coffee. "Oh, this and that. I supply nurseries with shrubs and plants. *Local sourcing* is a thing now, so I also sell seasonal organic vegetables to a few restaurants in Charleston."

"Is that what you've always done? Horticulture?"

She smiled wearily. "I've had more jobs than you've had birthdays, honey. But I always liked gardening. It wasn't until I met Keith and we had our Finn that I started taking it seriously, though. The money Keith makes driving made it possible for me to start a business so I could be at home when Finn was little. It's grown from there," she said, a note of pride in her voice. "I'm not getting rich by a long-shot, but doing something you love and making some money along the way isn't too bad."

Mercer nodded in agreement. "I'm sorry about being left here. I know this is an inconvenience. Noah told me that your husband's away from home a lot. I must be ruining one of your few nights together."

"Keith does most of his driving at night, so he's okay with staying up. And he's no slouch with a gun, I promise you." Corinne pressed her lips together before speaking again. "I heard you call my brother *Noah*, not Detective Ford. I heard him call you by your first name, too. That's unusual."

"Oh..." Self-conscious, Mercer cupped her hands around the warmth of her mug. "It looks like he might be stuck with me for a while, so I convinced him to dispense with the formality."

Corinne arched an eyebrow. "But Ty's still Detective Beaufain?"

"Well, I just met Detective Beaufain today," she tried to explain, aware of the implication. She attempted to make light of things. "You're as observant as Noah. Are you sure that you don't want to change your line of work to law enforcement, too?" Her eyes moved to the small handgun that lay on the table between them. "You also seem pretty comfortable around *that*."

"Noah says we're safe with his friends outside, and I believe him. But like Keith said, a little extra precaution never hurts." Corinne toyed pensively with one of the whimsical, ceramic salt and pepper shakers on the table. It was in the shape of a rooster, the other a hen. "It was just Noah and me for a long time. Things have grown up some around here, but back in the day this house was truly out in the middle of nowhere. We learned to protect ourselves, including knowing how to use a gun."

"Just you and Noah? What about your parents?"

"Our father walked out on us when Noah was eight. Good riddance—he was a drunk who couldn't hold down a job and liked to knock us around. Noah especially, since he'd try to defend Mama and me. Our mother died when Noah was thirteen. I took over after that."

A swell of sympathy inside her, Mercer shook her head. "My goodness. You couldn't have been much more than a child yourself."

Corinne got up to reach for the carafe that sat on the coffeemaker's burner. She brought it to the table to top off Mercer's mug. As Corinne returned it, Mercer paused thoughtfully before speaking. "Your brother seems like a good man. He's definitely a brave one. He saved my life tonight." She fidgeted with the spoon that she had used to stir milk into her coffee. "I...know about his military history. About his time as a prisoner of war."

"He told you?" Corinne turned back around to her.

"I brought it up," she admitted. "I'd read an article online. Noah told me a little, but he seemed reluctant to say much."

Corinne sank back down at the table. "If he didn't walk out on the conversation, you're ahead of most everyone else. He's told me a little, but I only know the details because the Marines offered counseling to family members to help them deal with the trauma the men brought back." For a time, she stared down at her hands that were folded on the table in front of her. "He came home with three broken ribs, a fractured jaw, and scars on his chest and back. He'd lost twenty-two pounds. For several years, he had recurring tinnitus in one ear because of how badly he was beaten. But I think the mental strain was worse. The Taliban was using their captors to try to get some of their own men released from our prisons. When the U.S. wouldn't budge, they started executing their prisoners, one by one, to show that they meant business. Noah never knew if he'd be next."

Mercer's heart beat almost painfully at what she had been told.

Corinne shook her head. "He stayed here for a while after his medical discharge from the military. He'd have some pretty bad dreams." She lifted her chin faintly. "Noah's tough, though. He managed to move on from what happened, but it pretty much finished off Allie and him."

"Allie?"

"His fiancée," she supplied. "Although truth be told, I don't think they were ever really right for one another. When Noah got called up again, Allie couldn't handle it. I think that she might've even slept around on him, but I don't know for sure. Once Noah got back home, he just became more and more distant, and they called things off. She married someone else less than a year later and moved to Missouri. Noah's stayed single ever since."

She rose from the table and poured the remainder of her coffee into the basin before turning around again, her expression pained. "I've said too much. Noah wouldn't approve of my big mouth. It's just that I worry about him, and...you seem like you might care."

They stared at one another in silence, until Corinne glanced at the wall clock. "You very well might be here for the night, Mercer. You can sleep in Finn's bedroom, if you like. It's the second one on the right. I changed the sheets. I'm going to go get ready for bed myself. Do you need anything?"

"No, but thank you for your hospitality."

Corinne smiled softly. Taking the gun with her, she headed down the hall.

Mercer remained in the kitchen.

You seem like you might care.

And Mercer *did* care. Of course, she did. Just as she had told Corinne, Noah seemed like a good man. But any spark of attraction she felt to him was purely physical, she assured herself.

Still, guilt flickered inside her.

"HE'S NOT UP THERE," the point man on the SWAT entry team announced as he jogged back down the wooden flight of steps in the main building inside the gated compound. Like the others on his team, he was outfitted for war, his AR-15 rifle pointed downward at his side.

Frustration gnawed at Noah's gut. Draper's bedroom was believed to be the last one on the second floor.

"It's been cleared, Detective. You're free to go up."

Noah holstered his firearm. Around him, SWAT team members had a dozen people—men as well as women—prone on their stomachs, fingers laced behind their heads on the floor. Many of them shouted slurs at the law enforcement officers standing over them, but there had been no exchange of gunfire, at least not yet. Leaving the chaos, Noah took the stairs two at a time, aware of the yelling, the cries of frightened children, and the splintering of wood coming from the outside, indicative of the other buildings that were simultaneously being breached. Although The Brotherhood's compound was some eighty miles outside the city, the warrants gave the Charleston Police Department authority for the raid outside its jurisdiction. Still, they had given the local county sheriff's office notification of their plans.

At the top of the rough-hewn landing, Noah traveled down a hall and entered the last bedroom on the right. It appeared almost military in nature, with unadorned walls, a plain, twin-sized bed covered by tightly tucked sheets, and an army-green, wool blanket. A footlocker sat in front of the bed. Noah opened it and rooted through its contents. But there was no weaponry—a .22-caliber handgun, specifically—that might be a match to the striations on the bullets used in the murders or the ones recovered at the St. Clair. Nor was there a Halloween mask or anything else that could be considered evidence. Noah went through the sparsely filled closet and desk next, then tipped the mattress from the bedframe, looking for anything that might be hidden underneath it.

Minutes passed before he gave up his search. Scowling, he turned at the sound of footsteps.

"Draper's not here," Tyson said as he entered. "Neither is the band of men he runs with. We've gone through all the buildings. You think they knew we were coming?"

Placing his hands on his hips above his badge and gun, Noah drew in a slow breath. It was nearly two a.m. and he'd had hope that Draper would be present. "If he figured that we'd already connected Deveau and Townsend's murders, he probably knew our eyewitness either already had or was on the verge of making an ID."

He brushed past Tyson.

"Where're you going?"

"Back down." Detectives were combing through the other upstairs rooms as Noah went down the hall with Tyson in his wake. "Someone here has to know where he is," Noah said tightly.

Upon reaching the main floor again, he spotted Tony Garber, one of their detectives, emerging from the building's rear.

"Came across materials for making explosives, as well as an impressive gun and ammunitions stash, but no .22-cal handguns," he said. "There's a false panel in the wall back there that leads to a staircase down to some kind of bunker-style storage room."

Noah called out to two burly SWAT team members, then gave one of the males lying on the floor a hard nudge with his shoe. "Take him in there." Noah nodded to a back room. "He and I are going to have a talk."

"I don't know anything!" the man snarled as he was hauled upward. He wore boxers and a white underwear shirt, apparently having been pulled from bed. A Nazi swastika adorned his right biceps. He glowered at Noah through greasy hair that hung into his face. "And even if I did, I wouldn't tell you jack-shit. Iceman and his pals aren't here—we got nothing to do with this!"

Noah's cell phone rang. Seeing on the screen that it was a patch-through from the county sheriff's office, he caught Tyson's gaze.

"Go ahead. I got this," Tyson said, trailing the two SWAT officers as they propelled the struggling man into the room. Noah went outside so he could hear the caller over the din. Standing on packed-down dirt, the black night above him, he answered the phone.

"This is the sheriff's dispatch, Detective Ford," a female operator said over the airwaves. "I thought you'd want to know that a car matching your description was located. The partial's also a match."

Based on the partial license plate number that Noah had gotten at the hotel, they had already learned that the car had been reported stolen earlier that day. "Where?"

"Just over the county line, near rural highway seventeen. It's been burned. It's still too hot to get near, but the deputy who called it in said there's not much left."

Noah pressed his lips into a hard line. That meant that fingerprints, hair, or DNA from something like the inside of a Halloween mask would likely be gone, too. The location of the burned-out vehicle was about six miles west of here, he estimated. He thanked the operator and asked her to have the deputy stay with the car until he could get there. After disconnecting, Noah stared briefly at the wild grass and weeds growing along the inside of the property's high wall. The cry of a predator bird somewhere in the woods mingled with the noises coming from the buildings behind him.

It was entirely possible that the guns that had been found here were registered and legal. But even if that was the case, they could still make arrests for possession of explosive materials. If he were lucky, one of the group might give up Draper's whereabouts, if he or she knew it, in exchange for a promise of leniency from the DA.

Thinking again of what had happened at the hotel, Noah's chest tightened under his Kevlar vest. They had failed tonight. Draper was still out there. And with the continued lack of other evidence against him, Mercer's eyewitness account was still all they had.

Which meant that she also remained the lone threat to Draper.

CHAPTER ELEVEN

IT WAS Mercer who let Noah in at the door.

"Did you find him?" She wore plaid pajama bottoms and a long-sleeved sleep tee, her blond hair mussed and tumbling loosely around her shoulders. Her state of attire was Noah's fault for giving them only a minute's advance notice of his arrival, but he had been on the phone until he had reached the gravel drive that led to the house. He checked his wristwatch, noting that it was just after six a.m.

"No." Shoulders slumped under his navy CPD windbreaker, Noah closed and locked the door behind him. "We located yesterday's getaway car, though."

She took a step closer. "At the compound?"

"About six miles from there. It was stolen in Rarity Cove yesterday. It was torched, so I doubt we'll be able to gather much evidence. You should go ahead and get dressed—"

"Because we need to go." She finished his statement on a tense sigh, then went down the hall and disappeared into Finn's bedroom.

"How'd it go?" Corinne stood on the kitchen's threshold. She wore a bathrobe over her pajamas.

"It didn't. Our perp wasn't there." Noah's eyes burned from lack of sleep. "Other than confiscating enough ammonium nitrate and aluminum powder to blow up half the Battery, it was a waste of time. Hazmat and the ATF's taken over. At least the situation didn't turn into another Waco and it damn well could've."

Corinne frowned at him. "You look like death warmed over, Noah."

"You try an all-nighter. Keith can tell you what it's like." As he walked past her and into the kitchen, Keith was seated at the table, and Noah clasped his shoulder in appreciation. "Thanks for staying up."

"Hey, I live vicariously through you these days, Noah. What you do is a hell of a lot more exciting than driving a rig." Chuckling, Keith shook his head. "Not that anyone was getting past those two hosses you stationed outside, anyway."

"Have you made coffee yet?" Noah asked Corinne.

"I was about to, along with some egg sandwiches to take out to your friends. Let me feed you before you leave, at least."

"Can I get it to-go? And I already sent Tom and Remy on their way," Noah said, referring to the men—both Special Ops, both career military and retired—that he had stationed outside overnight. He turned on the faucet at the sink. Cupping his hands under the stream, he splashed cold water onto his face, then reached for a paper towel. When he opened his eyes, Corinne was beside him at the counter, taking the coffee canister down from a shelf.

"You might as well have a seat while I'm cooking," she said.

As Noah sat at the table across from Keith, Corinne began measuring grounds for the coffeemaker. "I've got to admit—being a St. Clair, I expected Mercer to be stuck-up, but she's the farthest thing from it. She's real sweet and down-to-earth." She glanced at Noah over her shoulder. "She's a pretty thing, too. Judging by the rings she wears around her neck, I'm guessing she's a widow."

"Yeah," Noah replied quietly. He tried not to think of how Mercer had looked when she greeted him at the door. It wasn't as if she had been in some silky piece of lingerie, but the intimacy of seeing her in what she had slept in, her porcelain skin devoid of makeup, was a pleasant image that he couldn't shake. He tried instead to focus on Corinne's compact Kimber handgun that sat on the counter beside the toaster.

As the coffeemaker began to gurgle and hiss, a knock sounded on the front door and Tyson loudly announced himself. Wiping her hands on a dishtowel, Corinne went to let him in. Noah heard her greet him as she opened the door.

"Good morning, Ty."

"You know something good about it, let me know," Tyson replied in his usual dry manner as he followed Corinne back to the kitchen, then greeted Keith. "I see Corinne's still feeding you well."

Keith smiled and raised his glass of orange juice in a mock toast. "Body by biscuit and gravy in the veins. I'll leave all that CrossFit stuff to you and Noah."

Tyson had remained at the compound while Noah went to get a look at the burned-out vehicle, and they had planned to meet up here. Noah had made arrangements to have what was left of the stolen car towed to the Forensics department in Charleston.

"I'm making breakfast," Corinne said to Tyson as she returned to the stove. "I'll throw on a couple more eggs and another sausage patty for you."

"You're a goddess, Corinne."

She smiled and went back to cooking.

"We need it to-go," Noah reminded.

A short time later, the enticing aroma of the breakfast sandwiches that Corinne had made and wrapped in aluminum foil mingled with the scent of coffee as Mercer appeared in the kitchen. She had changed into jeans, a blouse, and a soft-looking cardigan. As Noah and Tyson rose from their seats at the table in preparation to go, Corinne walked over to her, touching her shoulder. "Take care of yourself, Mercer. I'll say a prayer that all of this is over soon."

"It was good to meet you, Corinne. You, too, Keith. Thank you for everything."

Corinne handed the sandwiches out. Noah put his in his jacket pocket.

"Thanks, Sis." He kissed her cheek. "I'll get the mugs back to you."

"You better." Corinne handed one of the large, earthenware cups to Mercer. "Fill up, honey. It's the real stuff, not like last night. Noah's on a schedule, as usual, so you'll have to drink it on the run."

Noah wasn't deterred by his sister's tone. He *did* have a lot to do, including a mountain of paperwork related to the raid on the compound. He also hoped to talk privately with a few more of the arrestees before they were either bailed out or a lawyer shut them up. Most of all, he needed to get Mercer to the safe house that had been secured overnight. It was why he had been on the phone on his drive here, and it was also why he had sent Tom and Remy on, in fact. They would meet them at the house in an hour or so. One of them would take the first shift while the other slept. Noah would hopefully catch a few hours of shut-eye himself before he went to relieve them overnight, and Tyson would take the shift the next morning. He had discussed the situation with Captain Bell, who had agreed that until they were sure that the leak hadn't come from inside, he would look the other way and let Noah handle security in whatever manner he chose, at least for the time-being. He studied Mercer as she splashed milk from a carton into her coffee.

"I've had enough caffeine. I'll leave my cup here. Thanks, Corinne," Tyson said. His gaze shifted to Noah. "I'll head out first and make sure it's all clear." Stuffing his sandwich into his jacket pocket so that he could have his gun at the ready, he also bid goodbye to Keith and headed out.

As Noah watched him depart, he noticed that Mercer had placed her jacket and luggage in the living room. When he turned back to her, she was looking at him over the rim of her coffee mug as she took a sip, her eyes worried in her perfectly oval face. Noah wondered whether she had gotten any sleep last night or if she was as dog-tired as he was. "Let's go."

THE HISTORIC EASTSIDE neighborhood was located on the peninsula over which the old Cooper River bridges once ran. Through the SUV's windshield, Mercer stared out at their destination—a narrow, shotgun-style house that sat at the end of a street and was shaded by a massive live oak hung with Spanish moss. Noah pulled into the single-car driveway that ran alongside the home, although Detective Beaufain's sedan didn't follow, instead making a U-turn on the street and heading back out.

Hands folded tensely in her lap, Mercer tried to calm her nerves. Her mother lived not too far from here, but like most old cities, Charleston could go from upscale mansions to increasingly more derelict homes in the matter of a dozen blocks. This particular street was still undergoing revitalization, with shabbier residences interspersed with renovated ones that reflected the area's resurgence. Mercer estimated that the house was about a century old. It needed a paint job and there were several windows boarded over, she noticed as the SUV entered the backyard that was enclosed by a high, weathered-wood fence.

She wondered again how long she would be here.

Noah parked the SUV on a slab of asphalt. Cutting the engine, he moved the domed, blue strobe light that he kept in his vehicle farther under the dashboard so it couldn't be seen. "This place is owned by a friend of mine. It's completely off the radar. The house next door is vacant."

"The police don't have a safe house they use for situations like this?"

"We do, but it's currently occupied. And considering yesterday, I prefer keeping the number of people who know about your location to a minimum."

She yearned to see his eyes, but couldn't through the dark tint of his sunglasses. As Noah exited the vehicle, Mercer looked out at the small backyard, which consisted of a flagstone patio, cracked with age, and a small patch of untended lawn. A cement statue—a timeworn angel missing one of its wings—stood watch over what looked to have once been a flower garden, although it now held mostly dried stalks and weeds. A yellow Jeep was also parked in back. Mercer recognized it as the same vehicle that had sat in front of Corinne and Keith's house overnight. Although she hadn't met them yet, hadn't so much as laid eyes on them, Noah had told her that the same men that he had called upon for security last night would be staying with her today. Noah himself would take the overnight shift so that Detective Beaufain could be at home with his family.

"Your friend lives here?" Mercer asked.

Noah shook his head. "Steve renovates and flips houses. I help him with some of the work—refinishing floors and overhauling kitchens and bathrooms, that kind of thing. I've even invested in a number of fixer-uppers along with him."

Mercer glanced down at his lean, masculine hands, imagining

him working with them. Carpentry wasn't a skill she expected in a homicide detective.

"This place was foreclosed on six months ago and Steve bought it at auction." Noah looked up at the house. "He hasn't had time to get started on it yet. He had to call in a few favors, but he got the power and water turned on for us this morning."

"Steve's former military, too?" Mercer had begun to suspect that most men that Noah called his friends were.

"He is." He indicated the mostly uneaten sandwich that she'd rewrapped in its foil. It sat in the SUV's center console between them, along with the two empty coffee mugs. "You should take that with you. I asked Tom and Remy to try to pick up some things on their way here, but I don't know what they were able to get in the amount of time they had."

As it had earlier that morning, her stomach rioted at the thought of food. Still, Mercer obediently took the sandwich and placed it in her purse as Noah exited the SUV. Hand on the holstered gun at his hip, he scanned the property's perimeter before he went around to open her door.

"I'll come back for your things. Let's get you inside first."

The step down from the SUV's passenger side was considerable, and Mercer misjudged the distance. She stumbled slightly but Noah caught her.

"Easy..." His hands were at her waist, steadying her, and her breasts pressed against his hard chest. Her entire body, in fact, was in contact with every inch of him, making her stomach flutter.

"Sorry," she murmured, heat rising on her skin despite the cool morning air. She patted his chest to let him know that she had her feet under her now, although she couldn't bring herself to look at him, her traitorous senses brought to life by his hands on her. The reaction felt like a betrayal to Jonathan and she felt another stab of guilt. Noah cleared his throat and released her. A moment later, she felt his right hand again, though, this time at the small of her back as he guided her up the rather rickety wooden stairs that led to the home's rear stoop. At the entrance, he rapped on the door three times, waited several seconds, then rapped again once more. A moment later, the door opened and they were greeted by a tall, broad-shouldered male who, despite being well into his fifties, had the rock-hard frame of a gym rat. He, too, wore a holstered gun at his side. He took a step back to allow them entrance.

"Mercer, this is Remy McAllister," Noah said, introducing them as he closed the door behind them and locked it. "Remy was my CO for my first tour in Afghanistan."

"Noah was the best forward air controller on my team," he told Mercer. His silver hair cut military-short, he smiled and shook her hand, engulfing it in his own. "Pleasure to meet you, Miss. I'm sorry for the trouble you've gotten yourself into."

"Thank you for watching over me last night."

"Where's Tom?" Noah removed his sunglasses as they followed Remy down a hall and farther into the home's interior. The hardwood flooring underneath them creaked with age.

"He's already taking a siesta in the front room. We're going to do three hours on, three off. I drew the short straw so he's getting his beauty sleep first," Remy answered as they entered a main parlor with more bare flooring and minimal, worn furniture that looked as though it might've been left behind by the home's former occupants. The place was austere but dirt-free, and she figured that the bank had had it cleaned prior to putting it up for auction.

Remy indicated the staircase. "There're a couple of bedrooms upstairs—one even has a bed. There's also a bathroom up there, so you can have your privacy, Miss."

"Please, call me Mercer."

He bobbed his head. "As long as you call me Remy."

She trailed the men into a kitchen with faded Formica countertops and ancient appliances. A card table and folding chairs sat in the room's center where a dining table should have been. A cardboard box with an image of an automated coffeemaker had been placed beside the sink and there were also some basic grocery items—paper towels and toilet paper, a case of bottled water, a loaf of bread, jars of peanut butter and grape jelly, bananas, and a coffee tin.

"We stopped for a few essentials, but it's slim pickings," Remy warned.

Noah nodded. "I'll make sure you're reimbursed for anything you've spent. Make a list of whatever else you think that we need here and I'll bring it with me tonight."

Mercer placed her purse on the counter and put the remains of her sandwich inside the fridge that she noticed was only slightly cool inside due to the electricity just having been turned on. As the men talked protocol, she wandered back into the home's front room, her arms crossed over her chest as she looked around. As empty and unadorned as the structure was, she could see what Noah's friend, Steve, did. The interior had high ceilings, a wide, white-bricked hearth and recessed, built-in bookcases. Shutters covered the windows and a brass-and-glass chandelier, its pendants clouded with age, hung in the room's center. Old-fashioned panel doors closed off what she guessed was a second parlor. The room was apparently where the other man, Tom, was sleeping. Curious, she took the stairs to the second floor.

As Remy had indicated, there was a small bathroom, its one luxury a vintage, claw-footed tub that would most likely go for a high price tag in an antique shop. Passing by the unfurnished bedroom, Mercer went into the other one, but all it contained was a slowly moving ceiling fan and a bedframe with a bare, blue-tick mattress—no pillows, sheets, or blankets. Her chest tightened again at the prospect of how long she might be here, and she tried to shove away a growing sense of panic.

A window with an accordion-style radiator below it was on the other side of the room, facing the property's rear. Fighting claustrophobia, she moved to the window and opened the shutters, discovering to her surprise that she had a partial view of the Cooper River, including the newer, often-photographed cable-stayed bridge with its diamond towers that led over to Mount Pleasant. Due to the high fence surrounding the property's rear, she hadn't realized how close they were to water. From this angle facing outward, there were no other houses behind it and she felt certain that no one would be able to have a view into this room, short of flying a camera-equipped drone. Placing her fingers against the cool, paned glass, she swallowed hard, feeling imprisoned already. She wanted to be back at the St. Clair with her family, not alone here, without Noah and with these men she didn't know.

"Are you going to make me keep this closed?" she asked, still standing at the window as Noah entered a few minutes later with her travel bag and computer case. She was unable to keep the strain from her voice. "Because I just might lose my mind if you do."

He sighed as he placed her things on the mattress. "I'll bring some bedding back with me tonight. Some towels, too."

She turned back to the window, morose. "Maybe I should just figure out how to pry this window open and throw myself out." She stared onto the broken flagstone patio twenty or so feet below. "I could do Draper's work for him. Just get it over with."

"Mercer."

She was aware that he had moved to stand behind her, but she remained stock-still.

"Turn around and look at me," he ordered softly.

Releasing a breath, she turned and looked up into his face.

She couldn't help it; Mercer felt a carnal pull low inside her. Noah's strong jaw was masked by stubble so dark it appeared nearly blue-black against his skin. Faint lines fanned out from the corners of his eyes that were the color of a fine bourbon and hooded by thick, sensual brows.

"It's going to be okay," he said in a low voice. "Things seem a little bleak right now and this place leaves a lot to be desired, I know. But you'll be okay."

She could only nod in response. Unable to help herself, she briefly touched his shirtfront. Noah swallowed, but didn't step away.

"When will you be back?" she asked, an ache in her throat.

"Around ten tonight. Is there something I can bring you? Any special food you'd like? Maybe a book or some magazines?"

She shook her head. She wanted to beg him not to leave her here but she understood that he had serious responsibilities, and that she was just one of them. "You need to sleep."

"Yeah." He cupped the back of his neck. "I'm going to get a few hours before I head back here. At least, that's the plan."

NOAH DROVE past the bustling Eastside stores and old homes in various states of repair and decay, but his mind remained on Mercer. He couldn't shake the despair that he had seen in her eyes. She felt abandoned, he knew, separated from her family and left to fend for herself in a house with two male strangers. But he hadn't had a choice. He had to get to the precinct, had to figure out who else he could trust to help keep watch over her, then he had to get a few hours of sleep if he planned to stay up all night again. Noah trusted Remy and Tom—he would trust them with his own life. It had to be enough for him right now just to know that Mercer was safe even if she wasn't happy.

Braking for a red light, he removed his sunglasses to rub his fingers over his closed eyelids.

You're getting too personally involved. You need to take a step back.

It was getting harder to deny to himself the attraction he felt to her. When Mercer had stumbled getting out of his vehicle, his hands had nearly encircled her small waist. Noah tried not to think of how her blouse clung to her round, heavy breasts, or how her nipples had instantly pebbled against his chest, sending fire through him. Since Allie, he had dated a handful of women but he always kept them at a distance, and he would cut bait as soon as he got the impression they wanted something from him that he was unable or unwilling to give.

Frustrated with himself, he fisted his right hand and absently tapped it against the padded steering-wheel column. Mercer Leighton wasn't just his eyewitness, which made her off-limits. She was a widow and she was also a St. Clair. Still, Noah sensed that she felt some draw to *him*, too.

A car horn blared and he realized that the light had changed to green. He shot a glare at the driver behind him in the rear-view mirror, then accelerated and went through the intersection.

He had faced a hard truth, at least.

His feelings for Mercer were beginning to go beyond protectiveness, and that was dangerous for them both.

CHAPTER TWELVE

"WHAT THE HELL, Mark? What do you mean, you don't know where she is?"

Sitting behind the desk in his office with Carter on the phone's speaker, Mark released a tense breath. He had put off getting in touch with his brother last night since there wasn't much that could be done at this point, anyway.

"Someone tried to kill her and then you just let these men take her away—"

"Not men, *police*," Mark interjected. "And I didn't have a choice. You weren't here, Carter. This man came after her right here on our boardwalk. Anyone could've been caught in the gunfire. If Detective Ford hadn't been here last night..."

Unwilling to voice his thought, his words trailed off.

"God," Carter murmured. "Does Mom know?"

"I went to see her early this morning. I wanted to tell her what happened before she caught word of it." Mark's heart pinched at the recollection. Olivia had cried, fearful for her daughter. "She's scared."

"I'll call her."

"That'd be a good idea." Mark knew that Carter had always had a way with their mother, who practically floated in his presence. If anyone could console Olivia, it was him.

"Carter...we need to present a united front on this, even if you disagree with what I've done. If Mom thinks that I made a mistake in letting the police take Mercer, it's only going to upset her more."

"You trust this Detective Ford?"

"I have to. I just got a call from him, letting me know that they have her at a safe house."

"For how long? Until there's a trial?"

"I don't know and I'm not sure they do, either," Mark admitted. "It's a fluid situation and they're still trying to figure things out. All they know is that she can't be here anymore."

"Send her to me—"

"I thought of that, but it isn't a good idea. You've got Quinn, Lily, and a baby on the way. We can't put them at risk. At least with the way things are now, she has police watching over her."

Carter cursed softly. "I'll be home in two weeks, hopefully. I'm going to meet this detective and I'm going to see Mercer, even if I have to tear through the entire Charleston Police Department to do it."

Mark looked at the framed family photos on his desk as he let Carter continue to rail. He understood his upset, since he had been dealing with the same roller-coaster emotions himself, going from disbelief to anger to self-doubt by turns. They talked a while longer, until Carter seemed to have run out of steam.

"I'm not angry with you, Mark," he said finally. "I know you tried to do what was best. You had to make a fast decision. But I still can't believe this. I just talked to Mercer yesterday."

"She's going to be okay," Mark said, praying that he was right. He promised to keep Carter posted on any detail he learned, no matter how small. Once he disconnected the call, Mark picked up a sterling silver letter opener and absently turned it around in his hands a few times before returning it to his desk and standing. He walked to the window and stared out onto the ocean.

He wished that Mercer had never gone into that art gallery.

"LET us know once you've worked out a schedule, Noah." Rising from the sagging couch, Remy picked up his backpack and hauled it over one muscled shoulder, preparing to head out.

"Will do." It was nearly eleven p.m., and Noah had arrived back at the house only a few minutes earlier. He had brought in several bags of items that he had purchased, which he had left on the floor near the bookcases. "I appreciate it. Truly. I'll send you a text."

"I'm bringing a television next go-round," Tom announced as he appeared from the parlor. A powerfully built African American with a shaved head and salt-and-pepper goatee, he was somewhere in his fifties like Remy and also wore a gun at his hip.

"Good luck with that, Washington. There's no cable," Remy pointed out.

"Then I'll just have to siphon some by running a line off one of the other houses. Use some of the skills I acquired in my youth before the USMC straightened me out."

Remy shook his head at him. "How about just getting in this century, brother? You know you can watch Netflix on your cell phone these days."

"Nah. I'm *old school*, man." Picking up his own backpack, Tom stifled a yawn. "Any luck with your perp?" he asked Noah.

"Draper's in the wind." Ballistics had determined that the bullets recovered from the St. Clair had indeed come from the same gun as the one used at the art gallery and at Townsend's home in Savannah—no real revelation, but at least it was evidence tying all three incidents together. Despite the several-hour nap that he had taken after finishing work, Noah tiredly dragged a hand through his hair. He and Tyson had spent most of the day chasing dead-end leads. He glanced to the staircase, figuring that Mercer was upstairs. "How is she?"

"Seems okay. She's kept to herself most of the time, though," Remy said. "She did come down and break bread with us. Good sport, too—no complaints about PBJ sandwiches."

"What's to complain about? Peanut butter and grape jelly are foods of the gods," Tom declared.

"That's another of your better qualities, Washington. Your discerning palate." Remy playfully shoved at Tom as the two headed down the hall to the home's rear. Noah followed them, thanked them once more, then locked the door behind them as they exited. When he returned, Mercer stood at the bottom of the stairs.

"It looks like you survived the Tom and Remy show," he said, searching for something to say as she came closer.

"I came down to make some fresh coffee."

"You'll be up all night."

"I was making it mostly for you. I heard your SUV pull up outside and I figured you could use the caffeine." Her gaze held concern. "Did you get to sleep at all?"

"I went by my place to shower and catch a long nap before coming here." Picking up the shopping bags that contained groceries and cookware, he followed her to the kitchen and placed them on the card table. "I also brought some towels and bedding, straight from *Tarjay,* as Oprah calls it. It's not the thousand-thread-count sheets and goose-down comforters from the St. Clair, but it'll have to do."

Mercer peered into one of the plastic bags. "Mac and cheese?"

"And frozen dinners and pizzas. The kitchen's limited, so I

went for simplicity." At her expression, he asked, "You don't like pizza?"

"I don't think I could like someone who doesn't. But I'm pretty careful about what I eat. You probably don't remember, but I was a little overweight when I was younger."

"I don't remember you being like that."

She shook her head in rueful self-recrimination. "Of course, I suppose now isn't the time for me to be worrying about being off my running schedule and staying in my skinny jeans."

She looked damn good in the jeans she was wearing right now, Noah thought, her shapely bottom in full view as she went onto her tiptoes and tried to reach the top shelf in the cabinet where one of the men had placed the coffee tin. Needing a distraction, he moved beside her and retrieved it. As she measured grounds into the coffeemaker with a plastic spoon, Noah put the frozen items he had brought into the freezer. He'd also bought a skillet and pizza pan, a dozen eggs, bacon, milk, and orange juice, and he placed the food items inside the refrigerator.

"Do you pay them?"

Closing the fridge's door, he turned to her. "Who?"

"Tom and Remy. For helping out."

"No. They, uh, owe me a favor."

When she lifted one delicately arched brow, Noah explained. "Tom's got a twenty-year-old daughter, Keisha. Pretty girl—she's done some local modeling, which also landed her a stalker who was getting bolder by the day. Tom wanted to kill the creep, but wasn't too keen on going to prison, so he asked for my help. I pulled the guy over on the pretense of a busted taillight. I let him know who I was and used my badge to put the fear of God into him. He's left Keisha alone ever since."

Mercer hooked her thumbs onto her jeans pockets. "I just bet that you're the one who busted the taillight, too."

Noah merely pressed his lips together.

"What about Remy?" she asked.

He grew more serious. "Remy lost his wife to a brain aneurism a few years back. He went through a pretty dark time." Noah figured that Mercer could relate. "We were worried about his state of mind, so Tom, me, and a couple of others took turns staying with him until he stabilized. To be honest, I think Remy's enjoying the assignment here. It gives him something to do besides ride Tom's ass. By the way, you should know that despite their constant bickering, they're the best of friends. They served together in Desert Storm."

The coffeemaker gurgled, for several seconds the only sound in the room. Mercer scraped a hand through her hair. "Since you haven't mentioned it, the answer is probably *no*, but is there anything new in the investigation?"

He filled her in on the little ground they had gained that day, which was practically nothing at all. Despite pressure, none of the arrestees from the compound had given up much on Draper that could be of use. Whether it was because they knew nothing, Noah wasn't certain. As of late that afternoon, those who hadn't been transferred to lockup to await arraignment on possession of explosive materials had been bailed out by a lawyer representing the group. They *had* learned that Draper had an elderly mother in a nursing home outside Beaufort, but the facility's records indicated that despite regular visits for years, he hadn't been there for the past two weeks. Nor was interviewing the mother a possibility, since she was in late-stage Alzheimer's.

Mercer took two foam cups from the stack beside the sink and poured coffee, then handed one to Noah.

"I thought you weren't having any."

"One cup won't hurt. I thought it might warm me up. When your friend gets around to renovating this place, it could use some better insulation." She went to the refrigerator for the milk and poured some into her coffee.

"This cold spell—if you can call it that—is supposed to stay with us for a while," Noah said. "It's nice out during the day, but a little chilly at night, at least by Lowcountry standards." Of course, she hadn't been allowed outside, so she wouldn't know that, Noah thought to himself. "Remy said that you spent most of the day upstairs."

"I put some of my clothes down to cover the mattress and took a nap, since I didn't get much sleep last night. I also have some books I've been meaning to read loaded onto my iPad, and I did some work on a springtime marketing plan for the hotel on my computer." She frowned slightly at him. "Although who knows how I'll get it to Mark when it's done, considering your *no emails* policy."

"We'll find a way."

Taking their coffee, they moved to the home's lone sofa, although with the sliding parlor doors now open, he could also see that a single cot—belonging to Tom or Remy—had been set up under a row of tall, shuttered windows. The old house *was* a bit drafty, and Noah went to retrieve the bedding he had purchased. Removing a blanket from a shopping bag, he broke it free from its packaging and took it over to Mercer. Appearing grateful, she placed it around her shoulders as they sat together on the couch. As she blew on the coffee's surface before taking a sip, Noah studied her fine features. Despite being in her early thirties, he was certain that she could still pass for a pretty coed at the nearby College of Charleston.

"What're you thinking about right now?" she asked, apparently aware of his gaze on her.

Noah hesitated, but something inside him made him speak the truth. "I'm just wondering about you and your late husband. How you came to marry someone so much older than you."

"Oh." Appearing self-conscious, she tucked her long hair behind one ear. "Jonathan was my English professor. I'd already graduated and he was single, by the way. It started out as just a fling, really, at least for me." She shrugged, an attractive blush appearing on her cheekbones. "I'd always been a good girl. I was raised to be a proper Southern lady and do all the right things. I was a debutante and an honors student. But I guess I needed to rebel. There was something exciting and taboo about being with an older man and my former professor, to boot."

He watched as her expression grew pensive.

"But then things started getting serious. It wasn't something that I expected or planned. When Jonathan told me that he was in love with me and wanted us to have a future together, I guess I did get scared by the age thing. It was about the same time that my brother Mark's first wife, Shelley, was killed in a car accident."

Noah recalled hearing about Mark St. Clair's first wife. Due to the family's prominence in the area, the car accident, caused by a drunk driver, had made the news in Charleston.

"I left Jonathan in Atlanta and moved back home to help out with my niece, Emily. She wasn't even three at the time." As she spoke, Mercer absently picked at a worn spot on the sofa. "Mark and Emily needed me, but I was also using them to avoid making a decision about Jonathan and me."

"But you eventually went back to him."

She nodded reflectively. "We lived together for a while before finally getting married. We were happy, but we also created quite a scandal. Our families got past the age difference eventually, but Jonathan's friends and colleagues never really accepted me. I know they talked behind my back. To the men, I was just some trophy that he'd managed to score. And their wives..."

Noah was aware of the shadows in her eyes as her voice dropped off.

"Still, Jonathan and I were happy," she said. "I always figured that I'd be without him one day, but just not this soon."

A short time later, Noah had gotten up from the sofa to peer between the slats of the shuttered windows when Mercer spoke.

"Now that I've made my confession, what about you? Corinne told me that you were engaged at one point."

"My sister talks too much," he rasped, still looking out although there was no activity outside, just deep, dark night. But it was his turn, he supposed, payback for having asked her such a personal question.

"Corinne thinks Allie cheated on me when I was overseas," Noah said quietly. "Maybe she did, but it didn't matter." He felt a familiar hollowness open up inside him. "When I came back home, I wasn't capable of having a relationship with anyone. I certainly wasn't capable of being a husband."

"I'm sorry."

Noah realized that Mercer had gotten up and now stood behind him. Closing the shutter slats again, he turned to her. She had left the blanket behind on the sofa, her coffee cup on the floor in front of it. Looking up at him, her gaze was as soft as a caress. Noah felt something in the air shift around them. Each time he saw her, it seemed that the attraction between them was stronger, and for the space of a few heartbeats, he imagined what it would be like to slide his hand around the back of her neck and pull her to him. To lower his mouth to hers and taste her. If he did, he wondered whether she would stop him. But Noah reminded himself of who he was, who she was, and that their situation was creating an intimacy that was out of place. Clearing his throat, he brought himself under control.

"I need a refill." He indicated the empty cup he held. "It's going to be a long night." He took a step back from her and went to the kitchen.

"Who'll be here tomorrow?" she asked, having followed him.

Noah filled his cup at the coffeemaker. He was reminded that Mercer didn't like surprises.

"Detective Beaufain has the day shift. Either Remy or Tom will most likely be with you again tomorrow night." He saw the disappointment on her features.

"I won't see you tomorrow at all?"

"I've got to take care of some things. For starters, I have a court appearance for another case. We're also planning to stake out Draper's mother's nursing home, and I need to get that coordinated. I'm going to have one of the staff call and say there's been an emergency with his mother to see if he shows." He sat his cup on the counter, his mood resigned. Even with Tom and Remy's help, they needed more resources here, especially since they didn't know how long this might go on. Now that they'd had time to catch their breaths and have a real discussion about exactly who they could trust, Tyson had finally convinced Noah to call in a couple of others on the force. "There're two other detectives we're going to have help out here. They're men that Detective Beaufain and I know well. They're good cops. You don't have to worry."

"It sounds like I won't be seeing you for a while." She dropped her lashes as she spoke, her soft mouth downturned. Repressing a sigh, Noah moved to where she stood, tamping down the urge to touch her. To explain to her that he had to put some space between them before he acted on his attraction to her. "I'm still part of the rotation, Mercer. I'm not abandoning you."

He sensed her doubt as she looked up at him again. Noah thought of what he had told her earlier, about why he had called his marriage off.

"After coming back from Afghanistan, I pulled it together enough to be a cop again. But outside of my job, I couldn't go back to the life I had before. I couldn't go back to *who* I was before and Allie was part of that." His voice lowered as he once again found himself opening up to her. "But I'm okay with the life I have now. I...hope the same for you, Mercer. I know the loss of your husband left a big hole. But things *will* get better for you. I'm sorry that you've been separated from everyone you care about just because you were in the wrong place at the wrong time." His jaw clenched in determination. "I'm going to find Draper and our judicial system is going to see that justice is done. And then you can finally get back to rebuilding your life."

His heart pinched at the hurt that remained in her eyes. She took a small step back from him.

"Thank you for the towels and bedding," she said. "I'm going to take them upstairs. Good night."

A thickness in his throat, Noah watched as she walked back to the sofa. Gathering the blanket and the shopping bags that contained what he had bought her, she went upstairs.

MERCER LAY IN BED, aware that the coffee wasn't the reason she was unable to sleep. She turned restlessly onto her side under the fleece blanket, embarrassed with herself for the disappointment that she had been unable to hide downstairs. Despite Noah's assurance, she did feel as though he was abandoning her. But here in the dark, she also asked herself a hard question.

What *did* she want from him?

The moon shone through the window, spilling silvered light across the bed. She sighed softly and thought of Jonathan, her chest squeezing with guilt. Had she become some kind of sex-starved widow? Noah had been nothing but a gentleman with her. They barely knew one another. So, why was she lying here imagining his mouth, his hands on her? She rolled onto her back again in frustration and tried to block out the mental picture, as well as the slow heat that the fantasy had caused to spread through her.

Staring up at the high ceiling, her fingers toying with the platinum rings that lay against her breastbone, Mercer swallowed down her remorse and confusion. What she was feeling was only a fleeting, physical attraction brought on after a long, lonely year, she rationalized once again. It was nothing more. At the most, it was just some sad case of hero worship. Noah *had* saved her life yesterday. It made sense. And he was watching over her right now, even if that wouldn't be the case come morning.

Still, as she finally drifted into a troubled sleep, she was thinking of him.

CHAPTER THIRTEEN

"DON'T LET those innocent blue eyes fool you," Detective Bobby Durand said as Noah followed him into the kitchen from the home's rear. He indicated Mercer as she sat at the table with playing cards fanned out in her hands. "She's a real card shark."

Noah felt a pain in his throat as Mercer looked up at him, her gaze cool. It had been several days since he had taken a shift, with Tyson handling Friday and Tom and Remy taking turns over the weekend. They had put Durand into the rotation today and he appeared to have made himself at home. A decade older than Noah, he was tall with a lanky build and light-brown hair. Another hand of cards lay face down on the table across from Mercer, apparently how he had left them when he had gone to let Noah in for the night.

"You didn't sneak a look at my cards while I was away, did you?" Durand gave Mercer a wink.

She smiled faintly. "I don't need to cheat to beat you, Detective."

"Ouch." Chuckling, he placed a hand over his heart and staggered backward a few steps as if he had been wounded before turning to Noah. "Based on that dour look on your face, I'm guessing Draper still hasn't shown up at the nursing home?"

"No." They'd had the facility staked out all weekend and there were still several plainclothes officers stationed there now. But Noah believed that if their scheme was going to work, Draper would have already shown himself. They'd had a nursing home staff member leave him an urgent voice-mail message about his mother. Draper's cell phone also appeared to be turned off, making it impossible to use its GPS function to track his location. Noah removed a lavender-colored envelope from the pocket of his CPD windbreaker.

"It's from your mother," he said to Mercer.

Her face paling a bit, she laid the cards on the table, stood and took the envelope that he held out. "You saw her?"

"I was summoned to Anders Bauer's home about an hour ago. He's a friend of the mayor's, apparently." Noah thought of the elegant Greek Revival mansion that he had been called to. He had expected Olivia St. Clair-Bauer to demand to see her daughter or complain about her treatment, but she had told Noah that she only wanted to meet him and to give him a letter for Mercer. Noah had assured her that her daughter was fine and that she was safe. He knew at least the latter to be true, but he had no idea what her mental outlook was. Admittedly, he was surprised to see her downstairs playing cards with Durand. But it was clear that the letter had shaken her.

"I'm going to go upstairs to read this," she said quietly and slipped from the kitchen.

"Everything okay here?" Noah asked as he shrugged out of his jacket and hung it over the back of one of the folding chairs.

"Quiet as a tomb," Durand said. "I've been doing a scan of the perimeter every ten minutes or so. Other than a cat with a dead mouse cutting through the backyard, there hasn't been a soul in sight." He lifted a foam cup filled with coffee from the table and took a sip. "Hey, did you know that Spanish moss isn't really moss? It's in the same family as pineapple and succulent houseplants."

"That's random."

"Funny what comes up in conversation when you have hours of nothing to do but kill time." Durand glanced stealthily to the staircase, apparently making sure that Mercer was out of earshot. "You might be on to something here, Noah. Can't say that I minded spending the day here while everyone else is out busting their asses on this case." Taking another sip of coffee, he smiled into his cup. "Not to mention, Ms. Leighton's definitely easy on the eyes. I've always had a thing for blondes. Rocking little body, too."

A muscle jumped along Noah's jaw at the comment. Durand was married, although it appeared that he had *misplaced* his wedding band. Noah moved to the shuttered window over the basin, adjusting the slats so that he could peer out onto the graying street. Garlands of the aforementioned moss that hung from the large tree out front had begun to sway, a harbinger of an approaching line of thunderstorms. He had been scheduled to relieve Durand at seven p.m., but had come early.

"Looks and money, too—can you imagine how much she's worth?" Durand was still talking behind him. "That hotel runs nearly four-hundred dollars a night in the off-season." He chuckled lewdly. "Let me tell you, I wouldn't mind spending some *quality* time with her in one of those swanky rooms, if you know what I mean, then swim like *Scrooge McDuck* in a pool of all that St. Clair money—"

"You can go, Bobby." Noah cut him off, barely keeping his ire on simmer. He turned as Durand rose from the table, seemingly oblivious to his irritation.

"Yeah, good idea. Maybe I can beat those storms that're on their way in. When do you think you'll need me here again?"

"I'm not sure. I'll let you know."

"Are we getting paid overtime for these babysitting gigs? I could use the cash."

A burning sensation in his chest, Noah didn't respond. He followed Durand down the hall to the home's rear, then locked the door behind him once he exited. Durand and his partner, Tony Garber, were good cops. Noah knew that. But even if it was just typical male shower-room talk, Durand's comments about Mercer had raised Noah's hackles.

Scowling to himself, he decided that Durand had served his first and last watch here.

YOU'RE *my only daughter and youngest child. I love you with every fiber of my being, Mercer. I'm so proud of the woman that you've become. But my heart breaks for what you've been through and what you're going through now...*

Sitting on the bed's edge, Mercer reread the letter and brushed at the tear on her face. She had choked up the moment she had glimpsed her mother's elegant script. The letter had been intended to be comforting, but instead it had drawn the emotion that she had been holding inside herself for days now to the surface, like a poultice applied to a wound. Mercer had always been independent, but she ached for her mother's presence now.

Stay strong, darling. You've always been my strong girl...

But Mercer didn't feel that way. The boredom and tension that she had been doing her best to keep at bay now assailed her full-force, just as the first heavy raindrops thudded on the roof. Convulsively, she pressed her hands over her eyes. She had been under lock and key for days now with nothing to do, the faces of the men watching over her a blur as one departed and the next one arrived.

Worst, for the past three days none of them had been Noah.

At least not until now.

Hastily, she wiped again at her face as she realized that he stood just outside the bedroom, his amber gaze sympathetic. She had been so lost in her own self-pity that she hadn't heard him ascend the stairs. Embarrassed, she put the letter aside and looked away, noticing the rain that now trailed down the window pane in jewel-like rivulets. The world had turned dark outside.

"I thought I should check on you since you didn't come back down." Somber, Noah entered the room and she felt the mattress dip as he sat beside her. "I won't ask if you're okay. You're obviously not."

"I've been feeling emotional and I guess the letter got to me." Mercer's face felt hot. "How's my mother?"

"She's okay. She's worried about you."

"She's sixty-eight. She shouldn't have to be dealing with this." Mercer frowned as thunder rumbled in the distance. "I'm sick of being here, Noah. I just want to go home."

"You know that's not possible—"

"I don't care." She rose from the bed, also not caring that she sounded like a petulant child. A dam of resentment about this situation and her helplessness in it had opened up inside her. "I've been here for five days. I miss my family. I'm sick of bad coffee and card games. My muscles are sore from no exercise. I'm tired of men with guns babysitting me..." She stared at him, an ache inside her. "...and none of them being you."

At her admission, a heaviness centered in her chest and she closed her eyes. A moment later, she became aware of him moving to where she stood.

"I'm here *now*, Mercer," he rasped, his voice low and patient.

She opened her eyes and looked at him. "You know as well as I do that this could go on for weeks, maybe even months. I'm going to lose my mind if I haven't already."

"Let's just focus on tonight, all right? What can I do to make things a little better for you?" When she didn't answer, he drew a thoughtful breath before speaking again. "It's dinnertime. Why don't we give you a break from frozen pizza and sandwiches? We'll order in. Whatever you want. It's not something I want to happen all the time since delivery cars parked out front could attract attention. But we should be fine for tonight if you stay out of sight when the food arrives."

She bit her lip, hopeful. "You'll eat with me?"

He gave a nod. "Go online and look at some menus. Decide what you want and I'll place the order from my cell."

She hung her head. "I'm sorry that I'm being such a baby."

"You're just understandably frustrated by having your life hijacked."

Touched by his attempt to soothe her, her fingers briefly grazed the side of his hand. In that bare space of time, neither spoke. Then, swallowing, Noah took a step back and moved to the doorway.

"Let me know when you're ready to order."

"IT'S NOT the chargrilled oysters—they're my favorite but they wouldn't have traveled well—but these are pretty great, too." Mercer pinched the tail from another of the barbecue shrimp before biting into it. Noah tried not to watch as she licked the sauce from her fingers in an almost sensual way.

"With all your talk about healthy eating, I expected you'd be getting a salad," he said after swallowing a bite of the crab cake sandwich with spicy rémoulade that he had ordered for himself.

"At Huey's? No way. How's yours?"

"Killer." The food had been delivered from a nearby seafood

dive that mostly only the locals were familiar with. "How do you know about Huey's?"

"Rarity Cove isn't that far away. The place is a favorite of Carter's. He's always had a knack for finding these fabulous hole-in-the-wall places. He first took me there years ago and I've been a fan ever since." Breaking open a hush puppy, she playfully rolled her eyes. "Now that he's a big-deal movie star, they give him a private room overlooking the marina whenever he comes in."

Noah dragged a fry through a puddle of ketchup. "Your brother's doing a great thing with the fitness centers, by the way. He's making a real difference in the lives of a lot of disabled vets."

Mercer smiled softly. "I'm proud of what he's doing. It's kind of become a family project, too. His wife, Quinn, is a physical therapist and sits on the board. And I've been donating some of my time to help direct marketing for the fundraising campaigns."

She poured a bit more of the chardonnay—a cheap brand, the only white wine that the seafood restaurant offered—from its bottle into her foam cup. Outside, rain slammed against the house as the storm intensified. Heavy drops thudded off the shuttered kitchen window, and an antiquated, plugged-in radio that Mercer had turned on played music from the living room, mingling with the sound of the deluge. Noah guessed that the radio belonged to one of the other men who had been here, probably Tom with his avoidance of anything modern. He watched as Mercer devoured another of the messy shrimp.

"Thanks for the wine. I wasn't sure if they'd deliver it," she said. The distraction the meal had provided had eased some of the tension from her face.

"How is it?"

"Pretty bad," she admitted with a laugh. "But as long as it gives me a buzz, I'm not complaining. Are you sure you don't want some?" She held the bottle out to him, but he shook his head.

"I'm on duty. Besides, I'm more of a beer man."

Lightning flashed around the shutter's edges as another clap of thunder boomed overhead, this time loud enough to rattle the window panes. Mercer startled with the explosion, then smiled and shook her head. "That was close. It's really coming down outside." Her honey-blond hair had fallen forward as she ate, and she pushed it back over her shoulder again, focused on her food. "That poor deliveryman."

"You didn't see him. He was just a kid. He was dripping wet and looked so miserable that I tipped him extra." Prior to the deliveryman's arrival, Noah had sent Mercer upstairs and temporarily removed his shield and gun holster. The less curiosity he drew, the better, although he had covertly tucked the weapon in the back waistband of his pants just to be on the safe side.

Tossing the last shrimp tail aside, Mercer reached for one of the moist towelettes that had come with the delivery and tore it from its package, using it to wipe her fingers. "Thank you for a wonderful meal and a great distraction." She closed the lid of the foam box that the food had come in. "I obviously enjoyed it—maybe a little too much. I feel like I'm covered in barbecue sauce."

"You wear it well." He indicated her tresses that had again fallen forward over her shoulder. "You've got some in your hair."

"Oh, God." Her laugh was musical as she tried to peer at the ends of her long hair to find the offending sauce. "I guess you could say I really got into my food."

Chuckling, Noah tore open another moist towelette package.

"Here." Leaning forward and reaching across the table, he gathered a thick lock in his hand and wiped the strands clean with the damp paper. Her hair was heavy and as silky as he imagined, his fingers tingling faintly where he had touched it. He lowered his hand and sat back again.

"Thanks." Her still somewhat bleary gaze held his, and Noah drank in her closeness. She took another sip from her cup and for a moment they sat without talking, listening to the rain and the music coming from a golden oldies station.

"All this seafood reminds me of the St. Clair's oyster roasts. We have one every year for guests, usually in late summer. But this year I talked Mark into moving it to fall. Jonathan and I always made a point to be here to attend them." At her words, sadness passed over her features. "I'll be missing this year's, most likely. It's just around the corner."

"I remember those. I worked a couple of them." Noah recalled the live music and dancing, the delicious aroma of roasted oysters. "I was too young to bartend but I set up and broke down the tables and dance floor. I dug the pit for the trestle, too." Not wanting to further pique her memories, he attempted to change topics but Mercer held up a hand and sat up straighter in her chair.

"Listen..."

Through the rainfall, Noah heard a familiar song—beach music—coming from the radio. Mercer stood as more thunder rumbled overhead. "You do shag, don't you?" she asked with a mischievous grin, holding her hand out to him.

Noah indicated the half-empty wine bottle on the table. "That's it. I'm cutting you off."

"C'mon, Noah, please?" When he remained stubbornly seated, she looked at him pleadingly, her slender fingers still held out to him. "You asked what you could do to make things better for me, remember? Time to put your money where your mouth is, Detective. I need to move."

He chuckled again and shook his head. "I'm not much of a dancer."

"You're a Lowcountry native. I don't believe for one second that you can't do a decent Carolina Shag. Now get up and dance with me before the song is over."

She looked so appealing with her wide blue eyes, her hair tumbling carelessly around her shoulders and her skin like peach-tinted cream. With a sigh of resignation, Noah stood. Laughing, her fingers laced with his, she tugged him from the kitchen to an open spot closer to the radio in front of the sofa. The music was louder here, melding with the shush of the steady downpour outside. To his surprise, the popular dance, a slower form of swing dancing, came back to him and he led her through the basic triple step, triple step, rock step of the dance in time to the music. Her smile was radiant as he executed an underarm turn, spinning her around.

"I've been accused of having two left feet," he admitted as they fell into a rhythm, keeping the steps and turns simple. "Don't expect me to pull off a *Funky Applejack* or anything else advanced."

"You're better than you give yourself credit for. Jonathan and I used to shag-dance all the time."

They continued dancing until the song faded and was replaced by a commercial jingle for a local restaurant. Laughing, still standing close, Mercer's cheeks were flushed. Noah's fingers still clasped hers, and her expression grew more serious. What had felt like fun now shifted into something different, charging the air around them once again. Lightning flashed, a powerful clap of thunder exploding overhead at the same second. The house's lights went out, plunging them into grainy darkness. Into silence save for the downpour outside. Unable to stop himself, Noah closed the scant few inches between them and lowered his mouth to Mercer's. Her lips parted for his, sending the pit of his stomach into a wild swirl. As their kiss slowly deepened, she moaned her pleasure into his mouth, the sound of it heating his skin. Her palms slid up his chest, her arms encircling his neck as she pressed her body purposefully into his. Noah's hands moved to her waist, masculine need spreading through him. He was vaguely aware of a tree branch scraping the house outside, his senses too overcome with the taste of her and the feel of her body molded to his. They clung together, kissing, touching, for how long he didn't know.

When finally, his mouth left hers, they were both breathing hard with desire. He walked her backward several steps, until her back met the wall beside the open parlor door. Pinning her there, his mouth seared a path down her slender throat, sucking at her skin as she arched her neck to give him greater access, undulating her hips against him and sending fire through him. He felt her hands thread into his hair as he lightly bit at her neck.

"Noah," she moaned softly. "Oh, God..."

Lost in need, his hands slid up her sides, cupping her breasts and massaging them gently through her blouse, his thumbs brushing back and forth, teasing the hard points of her nipples. She pressed her open mouth eagerly to his in response, begging for his tongue to explore her again. At the same time, her hands left his hair and began to work at the buttons on her blouse. She trembled against him, making his blood pound.

The lights flickering back to life was like a douse of cold water on Noah's senses. The short circuit in his brain corrected itself. *Christ.* Regretfully, his mouth left hers, his hands releasing her soft body. She stared up at him, confused, her pupils dilated and her lips appearing swollen from their kissing.

"We can't...this isn't..." His emotions whirled and skidded, his knees weak at what he had done.

"I don't understand." Her eyes were liquid and filled with need.

"Mercer...we can't do this," he managed, his voice hoarse. Taking a step back from her was one of the hardest things he had ever done. "I'm sorry. I'm way over the line here. That shouldn't have happened."

He saw her swallow. She was still panting slightly, her hair mussed. Several buttons on her blouse were undone, exposing her cleavage and the lace edges of a blue, satin bra.

"I'm attracted to you and...I let my feelings get the best of me," he tried to explain, swimming in a haze of self-recrimination. "You're my witness in a major investigation. I'm supposed to be watching over you, not taking advantage. I'd never want to do anything to—"

"What about what I want?" Longing in her expression, she touched his chest and he became aware of his own labored breathing. "You weren't taking advantage, Noah. What happened took both of us."

"That doesn't matter. I *know* better."

Her chin lifted faintly. "I know what I'm doing. I'm a grown woman."

"Who's under a great deal of stress right now. You're not able to make the best decisions," he pointed out gently. "There's a man out there who wants you dead. You've been uprooted from your entire life." His guilt flared, and he dragged a hand through his hair. "Not to mention, you just lost your husband."

"I've been alone for a *year*," she emphasized in a choked voice. "*Twelve months*. If you want, I can tell you how long right down to the days." She fisted her hand over her heart, emotion in her voice. "Do you know how long it's been since a man held me? Made love to me? My husband was ill for months before he..."

Her words died off, causing Noah's throat to tighten. He touched her shoulder. "It's not that I don't want you, Mercer. God, believe me, I do. But I can't let things go any further between us. If this were a different situation..."

Her soft-blue eyes had darkened with pain and possibly embarrassment.

"*It took two of us,*" she repeated softly, an ache in her voice. "I'm inviting you into my *bed*, Noah." The vulnerability on her face made his chest squeeze. "No one has to know except us. I... I'm going upstairs. You can follow me up there or you can stick to your rules and keep your white hat intact."

A branch again scraped the house's side as more thunder rolled overhead. A heaviness inside him, Noah watched as she headed up the staircase, her posture rigid. As she disappeared on the landing, he scrubbed a hand over his face, cursing softly under his breath. Every part of him wanted to go after her. More than anything, he wanted to pin her down on that bed and give her exactly what she wanted. But if he acted on his desires, he would be doing something far worse than Bobby Durand's shower-room talk. Noah *would* be taking advantage of her, whether she understood that or not. Her world was in shambles and she was looking for something, someone, to cling to.

But what scared him most was that if he gave in to his needs and followed her upstairs, he didn't think that Mercer was someone he could just use and then walk away from.

CHAPTER FOURTEEN

NOAH ENTERED the bullpen where the precinct accommodated its detectives. After being relieved by Remy at the safe house early that morning, he had gone by his apartment to shower and catch a few hours of sleep. His outlook was bleak. Mercer hadn't returned downstairs last night or that morning, either. His rejection of her—and he feared she saw it that way—had hurt her, he knew. He was angry with himself for letting his attraction to her overrule his better judgment. It wasn't like him.

"Noah."

He sighed inwardly as Bobby Durand called to him over the ringing phones and conversation of other detectives.

"So, how'd it go last night?" Durand followed as Noah made his way to his desk that was situated by the old building's bank of windows. Tyson's desk that was directly across from his was vacant, however.

"Fine." Noah's tone was distracted. He picked up a file from his inbox and shuffled through it.

"You're just now getting here? It's after eleven."

"I went by my place to get some sleep. Aren't you supposed to be at Shirley Draper's nursing home?"

"Not until three. Tony and I are headed to Beaufort after lunch." Durand lowered his voice. "I figured you'd know, so I'll ask—the scuttlebutt is that one of The Brotherhood is willing to give up some real information on Draper in exchange for leniency on the explosives charges, so long as he remains anonymous. Is that true?"

Tyson had sent Noah a text an hour ago, letting him know that an arrestee had changed his mind and was willing to talk, although what exactly he knew remained to be discovered. Worried about confidentiality, he had agreed to speak only to the two lead investigators and the district attorney who could offer a deal.

"We're interviewing him this afternoon," Noah confirmed.

"Any idea what he knows?"

"No." Noah watched as Durand studied the photographs of Draper and five other members of The Brotherhood that were pinned on a corkboard behind Tyson's desk. The other men were believed to be close allies of Draper's. They all had mugshots in the database due to previous arrests, and two had outstanding warrants. And, like Draper, they had all vanished into thin air. The corkboard also held grim photographs from all three crime scenes, including ones from Townsend's home in Savannah that the local police there had shared.

"Well, I know the mystery squealer isn't one of these guys. So, who is it?" Durand turned from the corkboard to face Noah again.

"I can't say. I'm under DA's orders."

Durand took a sip from the coffee mug he held before changing topics. "Since you were up all night with nothing to do, I thought you might've made out a schedule for the safe house for the rest of the week." He grinned and waggled his eyebrows suggestively. "It's a tough job, but somebody's got to do it."

Noah released a slow breath. He hadn't wanted to get into this today. "Yeah, about that. You're off the schedule, Bobby. Thanks for your help yesterday."

The other detective appeared surprised. "I thought you were short-handed—"

"Turns out we're not." Leaning over his desk, Noah turned on the computer and peered at its screen, waiting for it to power up. He had some notes from an earlier conversation with the arrestee that he wanted to review prior to the meeting at the DA's office.

"What about Tony? Is he off the schedule, too?"

Noah remained focused on the computer screen. "No, just you."

"Did I do something wrong? Hey, this isn't about what I said yesterday about Mercer Leighton?"

Noah looked at him. The answer must have been evident on his face, because Durand rolled his eyes. "Jesus, Noah. You know I'm just talking. Don't tell me that you haven't noticed that she's—"

"It was disrespectful." Noah straightened and faced him.

Durand gave an incredulous laugh, his face reddening. "Are you freaking kidding me? Since when did you become such a Boy Scout?"

He turned on his heel and stalked off. Noah knew that he was being a hypocrite considering what had happened between Mercer and him last night. Berating himself again, he scraped his hair back, then sat behind his desk. Whether he was being protective or territorial where she was concerned, he wasn't sure. Maybe it was a little of both.

"What's up with you, Noah?" Tyson appeared at Noah's

desk a short time later. He wore his shield on a chain around his neck. "Bobby just told me that you threw him off the watch. Said you had a bug up your ass about something he said about Ms. Leighton."

Noah looked up from the computer screen at him. "He's not the right fit. We'll find someone else to help out."

"That may not be necessary. I came to get you. The Captain wants us in the debriefing room."

STARING out through the windows at the iron-gray day, Noah's entire body tensed as Captain Bell continued.

"I warned you this could be the case, detectives. Deveau was a federal judge and the higher-ups in D.C. have taken interest. They know about the attempt on Ms. Leighton's life last week and they want to make sure that she lives to testify. They're putting her into the Federal Witness Protection Program until Draper's apprehended and goes to trial."

"This is *our* case." An angry heat flushed through Noah. He stood and paced the room, then threw out his hands. "WITSEC will move her to another part of the country. She'll have to live under a false identity. She won't want this—"

"What's more important is that WITSEC and the U.S. Marshals Service is the best way to keep her *alive*." Bell peered at Noah sternly. "You're going to convince her of that."

"It's just temporary, Noah," Tyson reasoned, swiveling in the conference room-style chair to face him. "Think about it. If we turn her over to the Marshals Service, we'll know that she's safe and we can put our full focus on the investigation."

Noah ground his teeth, aware that Garber and Durand, who had also been called into the room, were watching him. "This isn't what I promised her. Or her family."

"What's your problem, Detective Ford?" Bell's bushy, gray brows clamped down over his eyes. "You'll still get credit for your work. We're spread thin here and WITSEC has resources we don't. I've let you handle things your way until now, but that's over. This isn't my decision, anyway. I'm just the messenger."

Durand repeatedly clicked the top of a ballpoint pen he held. "The way I see it, we've got a lot on our plates already. Let the Marshals have her."

"I agree," Garber chimed in.

Noah focused on a line of Rotary Club commendation plaques on the wall, trying to bring himself under control. The matter apparently closed, Bell picked up his uniform cap from the table and began gathering papers spread over its top. Some part of Noah knew WITSEC made sense, but he saw it as another, larger betrayal to Mercer that he was making, even if it wasn't his choice. He felt a heaviness at the thought of sending her off into the unknown.

"I understand that you've developed a rapport with Ms. Leighton, so you and Detective Beaufain will be the ones to make the hand-off on Thursday," Bell said to Noah. "The marshals she's being assigned to are coming down from Columbia and will rendezvous with you at a halfway point. I've given the Marshals Service your contact information. They'll be in touch with you directly with the time and location."

Bell's attention turned to Garber and Durand. "While they're escorting the witness, you two will act as interim leads on the investigation should anything break here."

Bell departed the room. Garber and Durand rose from their chairs next.

"I guess that settles that." Durand gave Noah a victorious look as he followed his partner from the room.

Noah cursed under his breath, his face hot. Tyson got up

from his seat and walked to where Noah stood in front of the windows.

"I know you've become friends with Ms. Leighton," Tyson pointed out carefully. "You think that maybe it's coloring your judgment?"

Noah conceded to himself again that this might be the best thing for Mercer's safety. Still, the news he would have to break to her sat in his stomach like a stone.

"I'll talk to her tonight."

SEATED ON THE SOFA, Mercer looked up from her iPad, her stomach doing a little flip at the unexpected sound of Noah's voice coming from down the hall. He was speaking with Remy, who had gone to answer the knock on the rear door, which she had assumed was the change of guard for the overnight shift. But Detective Garber was the one who was supposed to be here tonight. Remy called out a good-night to her from the hallway and she heard the back door open and close again. Mercer put the iPad aside and stood, her heart beating harder as, a moment later, her eyes met Noah's from across the room. Looking at him now, she felt a hurt as well as a lingering yearning.

"What're you doing here?" she asked. "I thought it was Detective Garber's turn."

"I asked him to come a little later. I'll be here with you for the next hour or so."

Mercer glanced at her wristwatch. It was nearing eight p.m. As Noah moved closer, some of the anger she'd been holding on to evaporated. But there was a somberness about him—even more so than usual—that fanned a wariness inside her.

"I'm sorry about last night, Mercer."

Her chin lifted faintly. "Is that why you're here?"

He indicated the sofa. "Sit down."

She hesitated, then sat stiffly. Noah sat beside her. He was dressed in dark trousers and a white dress shirt, his tie hanging loosely around his neck. With the exception of his shield and the holstered gun at his hip, he looked more like a businessman who had come from a stressful meeting, not a cop who had been working a case. He released a heavy breath that sounded like dread.

"You're being transferred to the Federal Witness Protection Program."

Surprise and confusion made her skin prickle. "I don't understand. What does that mean?"

Leaning closer, he lightly touched her knee as if to brace her. "It means the U.S. Marshals Service will be taking over from here, at least as far as your protection is concerned."

She wavered in disbelief, trying to comprehend what she was hearing. On the verge of panic, she stood from the sofa, her arms wrapped around herself. Mercer took a few steps, then turned back to him.

"Are you doing this because of what happened between us?" she asked, an ache in her chest.

His eyes were pained. "I'm not *doing* this, Mercer. I don't have a choice. This isn't the Charleston PD's call. The Department of Justice is getting involved and my captain has given me my orders, which is to close down things here." He paused as if trying to figure out the right thing to say. "The Marshals Service has extensive resources. Now that we've had time to fully evaluate the situation, WITSEC just makes more sense. I don't like it, either, but I can understand it."

Mercer felt as though the floor had opened up underneath her. She didn't know a lot about the Federal Witness Protection Program other than what she had seen in television dramatizations. People were relocated, given new names, and forced to drop contact with everyone in their lives.

"No. That's not what I agreed to." She shook her head, vehement. "I-I won't do it! It's been bad enough being cooped up here in this house, but at least I was close to home. My mother lives just a few miles from here, Noah. That gives me some comfort. And what about Mark? This isn't what he agreed to, either."

Noah stood and closed the space between them. "I'll make sure that you get to see your family before you go. *I'm sorry*, Mercer, but this is out of my hands. You have to hang on to the fact that it's only temporary, until we can find Draper and put him on trial. After that, you'll be free to return home."

"You aren't listening. I'm *not* going."

His features were tense as he took her hands in his. "Yes, you *are*. I couldn't live with myself if anything happened to you. Participation in WITSEC is voluntary, but you have to do this. I...can't protect you anymore."

She shrugged out of his grasp. "This is insane! They're expecting me to go live in some strange town, completely alone and under a new name?"

"It's necessary to keep you *safe*."

"I'm *safe* right here, with you and Remy and the others," she argued, her throat thick.

He appeared defeated. "You'll be safer in WITSEC."

"And all this could go on for how long? Months? Years? What if Draper is never apprehended?"

"He will be," Noah said firmly.

"What if you're wrong?" Her heart squeezed. "I could be permanently separated from my family. I...might never see you again, either."

Noah swallowed. "I'll see you when they bring you back to testify. I'll be right there in the courtroom. You'll be out of this house, Mercer," he reasoned in a low voice, as if trying to find some silver lining for her, no matter how thin and tarnished it was. "You'll be able to move about freely again instead of being sequestered here. You can even get a job and work under your new identity, if that's how you choose to spend the time. The program offers a stipend for living expenses until you're established, but I'm pretty sure money isn't a concern for you."

"I *won't* be able to move about freely. I-I can't come back home."

"This isn't forever," he reminded gently. "It's just until there's a trial."

She felt sick. Her future looked vague and lonely. Closing her eyes, Mercer bowed her head, and she felt Noah touch her arm. She stiffened at first, still hurt and angry, but then realized all the fight had gone out of her. She leaned limply into him, her pride gone along with her courage.

It's not that I don't want you, Mercer. God, believe me, I do. But I can't let things go any further between us...

His words from last night echoed. She wanted to believe him, but didn't know what to think, who to trust, anymore. It was almost unfathomable that last night they had been laughing and shag-dancing together. That they had made out like two teenagers until Noah had stopped things.

"How long do I have?" she asked finally.

"Detective Beaufain and I will take you on Thursday to the marshals who will be handling your case. The time and location for the meet-up hasn't been disclosed yet."

He was talking about the day after tomorrow. Another shockwave passed through her. "Where are they sending me? Is that still undisclosed, too?"

"I don't know where you're going. I probably won't." There was a helplessness on his face. "I'll talk to your brother tomorrow morning, explain everything and make arrangements for you to see your family before you leave." Noah's voice hoarsened. "But you *have* to go, Mercer. After all you've been through the last thing I want to do is hand you off to more strangers, but I'm outranked here. Deveau was a federal judge and the U.S. Marshals Service is stepping in."

CHAPTER FIFTEEN

"YOU'RE NOT TALKING, man. This WITSEC thing is still eating at you, isn't it?"

Driving, Noah didn't look at Tyson, who sat beside him in the SUV's passenger seat. It was late afternoon and they were headed to Moncks Corner, a small town about thirty miles outside of Charleston, to follow up on a lead. A civilian there claimed to have passed Draper leaving a convenience store a day earlier and had alerted the local police.

"I've just got a lot on my mind," Noah said. He hadn't wanted to leave Mercer last night, but he had needed to get some sleep. When Tony Garber arrived for his shift, Noah had remained, ending up sleeping downstairs on the cot in the parlor.

"I offered to talk to the family instead of you," Tyson reminded, his eyes hidden behind dark sunglasses. "You've taken enough heat. Seems like it should've been my turn."

Noah had gone to see Mark St. Clair in person early that morning to break the news about Mercer being transferred to WITSEC.

"I made promises to them I couldn't keep," Noah said quietly. "I needed to be the one."

They rode in silence until Tyson used the radio in Noah's vehicle to converse with the Moncks Corner Police, who were in the process of setting up a roadblock in the area where Draper had supposedly been spotted. The civilian who believed he had seen him was elderly, and it had taken him a full day to report the alleged sighting since he hadn't realized who the man was until seeing a follow-up report on the news with Draper's photo. Noah hoped the civilian still had his mental faculties and wasn't mistaken. The arrestee who had claimed to have information on Draper had gotten what he wanted: a reduction in the charges against him. In exchange, he had connected Draper to another murder two years earlier, a local civil rights leader who had been supposedly shot in a robbery attempt, although it was now looking more like an assassination. That case was being reopened, but it did little to advance the current investigation.

Noah tightened his grip on the steering wheel. The sooner they caught Draper, the faster Mercer's nightmare would end. He stared through the windshield at the flat asphalt stretched out in front of him.

This isn't forever. I'll see you when they bring you back to testify. I'll be right there in the courtroom...

He had seen the upset in her eyes when she had pointed out that she might never see him again. The thought hurt him, too. He wondered if whatever flame that had kindled so quickly between them would be extinguished by the time the trial was over and she was no longer his witness. But he also knew that they came from vastly different worlds. The two of them...it just didn't make sense. Even more, Mercer might never forgive him for this newest hardship that had been heaved onto her.

"Did you catch any of that, Noah?" His exchange with the

local police finished, Tyson placed the speaker back on the radio's cradle. "You look like you're about a thousand miles away."

"I was listening." Despite his thoughts, Noah had been keeping an ear to the conversation, which had been mostly about the roadblock's logistics.

"It's true what they say—WITSEC's never lost a witness who follows the rules. That ought to give you some peace of mind," Tyson said. When he received no response, he added, "All right, I'm just going to lay it out there. You've got a thing for Mercer Leighton. And from what I can see, she's into you, too."

Noah shot him a hard look.

"How long have we been partners, Noah? I *know* you, man. You're all business, all the time. You're typically *Cool Hand Luke*, but not with this case. She's gotten to you."

"I've barely known her for two weeks." Noah's tone was dismissive.

"But something's there. It's like that for some people. You're just minding your own business and *wham*. I knew in the first fifteen minutes after meeting Lanny that she was going to be my wife." Tyson chuckled softly. "Of course, *she* didn't know it for another six months. Thought I was a damn fool at first. Took her six weeks just to agree to go out with me—"

"That's because she's smart."

"Go ahead and diss me. I don't care. You know I'm right."

"You're out of your mind," Noah grumbled, not wanting Tyson to know just how close he had hit to home. Changing the subject, he pointed out the intersection up ahead. "That's highway twelve. The convenience store should be on our left about three miles down."

MERCER WAS uncertain of how long she had been standing in

the unlit bedroom, just staring out into darkness, but the headlights of Noah's SUV as they swept over the backyard pulled her from her trance. He had kept his promise and returned tonight. Despite everything, a mix of emotions surged through her.

Going down the stairs, she reached the main floor in time to hear him closing and locking the door behind Remy, who had been here all day again.

Noah appeared from the hall. He had a small duffel bag and a suit bag slung over one shoulder.

"Have you eaten?" she asked, searching for something to say other than what was on her mind. She was determined to be braver this time, to not break down. "Remy and I had pizza. There's still some of it left in the fridge."

"Thanks, but I've already had something."

He went to place his things on the narrow cot in the adjacent parlor, his intent no doubt to sleep there again while his other former military friend, Tom, took the last overnight watch.

A long, emotional day lay ahead of her tomorrow, including saying goodbye to her family and then whatever the Marshals Service had in store for her once she was placed in their custody. Her thoughts were dull and disquieting. She looked around the house's bare rooms, recalling that just a few days ago she had complained about being held captive here, unaware of just how worse things could get.

"Lex Draper wasn't in Moncks Corner, was he?" she asked as Noah walked to her.

"How'd you know about that?"

"Remy said that you and Detective Beaufain went up there today, so I took a guess."

He sighed softly. "The convenience store camera footage is grainy and the man was wearing a baseball cap and sunglasses, but he does bear a resemblance."

His dress shirt already unbuttoned at the throat, sleeves rolled up, Noah pulled the already undone tie from his collar and tossed it over the couch's arm. "My gut tells me it isn't him, though. The guy was alone and we have reason to believe that Draper has a small group of men with him. Considering that Draper's face has been all over the news, I think he'd send someone else out to buy his cigarettes and beer. The local police are operating a roadside checkpoint and conducting door-to-door visits on households, but there's been nothing so far." Frustration and fatigue were evident on Noah's features.

"Did the man at the convenience store pay with a credit card?" Mercer inquired.

He shook his head. "He paid in cash. And since the man was actually in the store *yesterday*, the bills from the register were already deposited in the bank. Not to mention, it's notoriously difficult to isolate and lift prints off paper, especially bills since they've had so many hands on them."

Tiredly, he scrubbed a hand through his dark hair. "We're monitoring his credit cards and bank account, but so far there's been no activity that could help us to locate him. We've been working all the leads, talking to people who know him, but pretty much all of them are hostile to police. I even drove to the federal penitentiary in Estill to talk to Orion Scott, not that he gave up anything."

Sinking onto the couch, Mercer asked what she had been dreading. "How's Mark? I...know you saw him this morning."

"He's angry and upset. I'm pretty sure he wants to string me up, and I don't blame him."

Her voice fell nearly to a whisper. "It's not your fault that I was at that gallery, Noah."

"That doesn't make any of this easier." He sat down beside her, his shoulders slumped under his shirt. "Your brother's having the rest of your things packed. He'll bring them with him when we meet up tomorrow morning. Your mother will be with him. Your other brother is trying to make it in, but they're not sure yet if it'll be possible."

At the thought of Carter flying back in the midst of filming, leaving the rest of the cast and crew in the lurch just to see her, Mercer's heart hurt.

"This isn't what I wanted for you, Mercer. I thought I could keep you here," Noah said, his voice roughening. "I'd hoped that this didn't have to go as far as a formal witness protection program, that maybe we'd apprehend Draper quickly and his interest in you would subside if we could find other evidence against him that wouldn't make you the only threat."

He leaned forward on the sofa, head bowed slightly and forearms braced on his thighs, obviously still struggling with the decision that had been made for him. "But I was kidding myself. Keeping you here wasn't a sustainable plan for the long-term and now the Marshals Service is taking over. What they want, they generally get. It's just too much to fight."

An ache in her throat, Mercer was aware of the tension in Noah's frame. Finally, he blew out a breath and sat back.

"How're you doing?" he asked.

"Trying to hold on." Her composure was fragile and she paused to collect herself before speaking again. "But I'm afraid," she admitted softly. "Since losing Jonathan, I've been leaning on my family a lot. I don't know how I'll get through this all alone."

Sympathy filled his eyes. "I wish it were just the two of us tonight," he said quietly.

"You aren't superhuman, Noah. You can't stay up all night and lead an investigation by day. I'm glad Tom will be here with us so you can sleep." She did her best to smile. "Getting rid of me is the best thing for you."

"Don't say that," he rasped.

He placed his arm on the cushion behind her. Even if he had

hurt her pride when he had turned her down sexually, she needed Noah's presence right now. She wanted to be angry with him, but she needed to draw from his strength while she still could. They sat together in silence, neither of them speaking and instead listening to the old house's stillness and the occasional tinkle of a wind chime coming from a neighboring home.

Mercer had barely slept last night and she must have drifted off. She came awake only when Noah gently moved her away from him in response to the knock on the back door. She had fallen asleep with her head on his shoulder, she realized. As he went to let Tom inside, her anxiety rekindled like driftwood tossed onto a bonfire. Disoriented, she checked her wristwatch and saw that nearly an hour had passed.

Which meant that she was another hour closer to an uncertain fate. Her stomach churned.

By this time tomorrow, Mercer Leighton would cease to exist.

CHAPTER SIXTEEN

"PLEASE DON'T CRY, MOM," Mercer whispered as Olivia hugged her. Despite the early morning hour, her mother was dressed in a skirt and coordinating jacket, the gardenia-like scent of the perfume she had worn since Mercer's childhood evoking bittersweet memories. It concerned her that her mother felt thin through her clothing, reminding Mercer of how fragile life was.

"This isn't fair!" Olivia sniffled, still holding on to her daughter. "You were just trying to do the right thing, and now—"

"It can't be helped, okay? Everything will be fine, I promise." Mercer tried to sound upbeat. "I'll be back before you know it."

Olivia finally released her and Mercer looked at Anders, a tremor in her voice. "Take care of my mom?"

"It's my pleasure, dear." Wearing a sport coat and his trademark, bow-string tie, he stepped forward and kissed Mercer's cheek. "Don't you worry about us at all. We'll be right here when you come home. And you *will* come home, Mercer. Try to focus on that."

She was aware of Noah, grim-faced, standing with Detective Beaufain on the far side of the marina's office. The marina was located just outside Rarity Cove and was among the many commercial properties that the St. Clair family owned. Mercer had been ushered here under cover of darkness, her family arriving a short time later. The early hour meant that the harbor was largely uninhabited, save for the seagulls and terns fishing for breakfast. Through the picture window, Mercer could see several dozen pleasure crafts and other boats bobbing in their moorings alongside the dock. She looked out over the tranquil setting, a lump in her throat as she thought of her father and brothers teaching her to sail here. Mercer turned her gaze to Mark.

"It's a beautiful, young family that's buying the house," she said, referring to the home where she had lived with Jonathan in Atlanta. She tried not to think of the good years they'd had there, fearing it would bring her to tears. "He's a new surgeon at Emory University Hospital and she's a stay-at-home mom with a toddler and a baby. Their other home is already under contract, so I don't want there to be any delays."

"I have your power of attorney." Mark squeezed her shoulders softly in assurance. "I can handle the closing and anything else that comes up with Jonathan's estate. You don't have to worry about any of that."

She bit her lip and nodded. Mark had had his attorney draw up papers yesterday that would enable him to act on her behalf in her absence. He had brought the documents here and Mercer had signed them.

Samantha stepped closer, sadness in her eyes. "We'll miss you."

Detective Beaufain cleared his throat. "We have to go soon, Ms. Leighton," he reminded gently. "We have a schedule to keep."

"I need to see Carter and Quinn," Mercer pleaded to the detectives.

"They're not going to make it, honey." Mark broke the news.

"I just checked the arrival times at the Charleston airport. They're still an hour away, not including the drive here."

Her heart squeezed. Carter had tried his best to be here, but the overnight flight had had mechanical issues and had been delayed. His trip would be in vain if she left now. She turned hopeful eyes to Noah. But he appeared resigned, his stance unmoving.

"Detective Beaufain's right. We can't stay much longer." He glanced at his wristwatch. "I can give you all five more minutes. We'll go outside to transfer the rest of her luggage and make sure the area's still clear."

Hand poised on the butt of the holstered gun at his hip, attired in trousers, a white dress shirt and dark blue tie, he departed the office with Detective Beaufain. Mercer talked with her family a while longer before finding herself being hugged again by each of them in turn. Mark was the last to embrace her.

"Tell Carter I'm sorry." Her voice shook. "And...please tell the children that their Aunt Mercer loves them."

Mark's eyes held pain. "Do exactly what the Marshals Service tells you. We all love you and we'll be praying for you, every day. Just hang on. We'll see you again when this is finally over."

She fought back panic as Noah and Detective Beaufain reappeared. Squaring her shoulders and gathering what was left of her courage, she scanned the faces of her family once more. Then Mercer turned away, her vision blurring. If not for Noah's hand low on her back, guiding her as they left the office, she feared that she might collapse, overwhelmed with dread for what lay ahead. The sun had risen a short time ago and as they walked from the office, staying covertly under the building's eaves, she was aware of the sky that was just beginning to brighten with shades of pink and orange, the briny scent of seawater, and the sound of water slapping against the dock. She tried to memorize all of it by heart.

"You did good," Noah assured her as they stepped into the crushed-shell parking lot where Detective Beaufain's sedan sat waiting, its engine running. Mercer didn't respond, her throat too tight to speak. Noah opened the rear door of the vehicle for her. She climbed inside, aware of his concerned gaze on her, then he closed the door behind her.

It wasn't the metallic clang of prison bars, but it might as well have been.

A hollowness in the pit of her stomach, she fastened her seatbelt as the two men entered the vehicle, Detective Beaufain behind the steering wheel and Noah next to him on the passenger side. Their collective moods were somber. The lot's shells crunched under the car's tires as it pulled from the harbor and headed out.

THE RENDEZVOUS POINT was a non-descript diner located off the interstate, a few miles outside of the tiny town of St. Matthews, South Carolina. Noah sat in a vinyl-upholstered booth with Mercer, Tyson, and the two U.S. marshals. After making introductions and signing the transfer papers, they had ordered coffee, although Noah's sat mostly untouched in front of him. The conversation of other customers and the clink of cutlery against plates surrounded them. Mercer, however, stared absently out through the diner's windows.

Noah tensed as one of the marshals, a big, red-haired man named O'Hannon, spoke to her. "There'll also be papers that we'll need you to read and sign, Ms. Leighton. They indicate your understanding of the program and acceptance of our rules."

She looked at him. "Where am I going, Marshal?"

"For now, back to Columbia with us for a few days," the other marshal replied. A dour, prematurely balding male whose last name was Termin, he took another sip from a chipped, white mug before continuing. "You'll receive your new identity there as well as the supporting documents. You'll be staying at a hotel while being oriented to the program. After that, we'll be escorting you to Cedar Rapids."

Noah frowned. That was a long way from home.

"Iowa?" Mercer paled. "What am I supposed to do there?"

"Keep a low profile." O'Hannon signaled to the waitress to bring the check. "Obey the cardinal rule—stay out of contact with anyone from your former life—and you'll be fine. As your handlers, Marshal Termin and I will be checking in with you periodically. We'll bring you back to Charleston in the event there's a trial. But aside from that, you'll be on your own. An apartment and a stipend will be provided for the first several months, but WITSEC participants are expected to find employment and eventually take care of themselves." O'Hannon scratched at his cheek as he appeared to assess her. "You're a special case, of course, Ms. Leighton. Our understanding is that you have money of your own, some of which will be wired to a bank account set up in the name of your new identity so that you can access it."

Mercer merely looked out at the parking lot again through the diner's dust-covered blinds, her expression bleak. An ache inside him, Noah felt powerless to protect her. It surprised him that Termin had divulged where she was being sent. WITSEC information was highly classified and even police were typically kept in the dark regarding the location of witnesses.

Termin drained the last of his coffee. "We should get going."

"Excuse me." Tyson slid from the booth and stood. "I'll meet up with you by the cars so that we can transfer Ms. Leighton's things." As he headed off toward the restrooms, a white-aproned waitress laid the check on the table. Noah reached for his wallet, but O'Hannon picked up the check.

"We've got this, Detective Ford. You drove the farthest distance. It's the least we can do." Leaning to one side, O'Hannon produced a gold money clip that held several bills from his trouser pocket. His thick fingers concealed most of the clip, but a coldness ran down Noah's spine as he got a partial glimpse of it before it was stuffed away again.

It had some kind of design, maybe Celtic? It looked like a cross inside a circle...

The money clip had an engraving on its front. Was it the same design that Mercer had described on Draper's ring? At the prospect, Noah's heart began to race. He tried to process what he thought he had seen, at the same time considering the possibility that he was mistaken. Furtively, he scanned the diner, which contained a dozen or so people, including waitresses, a family with several young children, and a row of truck drivers who sat on stools at a long counter. Uncertainty tore at him. Was he wrong? These men had the proper U.S. Marshals Service identifications, including photo IDs. And O'Hannon and Termin *were* the names of the marshals who had been assigned to the case.

But if he *wasn't* wrong, this was no place for an exchange of gunfire.

"I meant to ask," Noah said with forced nonchalance. "How's Assistant Deputy Director McCann doing?" After several beats of silence, he added, "After his heart attack, I mean. Has he returned to duty?"

Termin squinted at him. "You know McCann?"

Noah's muscles went rigid. He had made up the name. He remained outwardly calm, however. "We served together. ANGLICO."

"Marines Special Ops," O'Hannon remarked knowingly.

"Good on you, Detective. I'm sure you won't be surprised to hear that McCann's already back behind the desk. He's one tough son of a bitch. We'll tell him you said hello."

Noah's mind searched for a way out of this that wouldn't leave Mercer and the others around them at risk. But there wasn't a chance in hell that he was letting them leave with her.

"Keep the change," O'Hannon said as the waitress came by to pick up the money that he had tossed onto the table.

"Have a nice day, officers." She smiled as she tucked the money into her apron pocket, apparently having noticed the badges and holstered guns the men wore. Once she had moved to another table, O'Hannon slid from the booth with Termin following. Noah stood, as well, although his insides were churning. Mercer emerged last. Appearing tired and drawn, she didn't look at him. He glanced to the restrooms, mentally urging Tyson to emerge. When he didn't, Noah followed behind the two armed men with Mercer between them as they exited the diner through smudged-glass double doors and stepped out into the gravel parking lot. At least it was devoid of others. The lot was shared with an insurance office and nail salon, and Noah hoped that no one would exit from them. As O'Hannon placed his hand on Mercer's back to guide her to their waiting sedan, Noah unsnapped the safety on his holster. Nerves crackling like live wires, he withdrew his Glock and moved into a shooting stance.

"That's far enough," he ordered in a loud voice, adrenaline making his skin pulse. "Turn around slowly with your hands up!"

The men as well as Mercer halted and turned. "Noah?" Mercer squeaked out, her eyes wide with confusion.

"What the hell are you doing, Detective?" O'Hannon's thick eyebrows clamped down over his eyes. "Have you lost your goddamn mind—"

"I said get your hands up and away from your weapons!" Noah advanced a step, his gun trained. "Now! I won't ask again!"

The men's expressions had turned to stone. A woman emerged from the nail salon. Her scream pierced the air.

"Get back inside!" Noah yelled at her. In the distraction, O'Hannon yanked Mercer in front of him, locking her against his chest with a beefy arm around her throat so that she was caught between him and Noah's gun. Noah tamped down panic as she struggled, dropping her purse and scratching and kicking at O'Hannon, who tightened his chokehold until she stopped fighting and wheezed for air. He began dragging her backward toward his car, which was parked near a line of eighteen-wheelers.

"Let her go!" The diner's door swung open behind Noah, and he heard Tyson's hard curse. In the chaos, Termin drew his gun and fired.

Noah fired back and dropped him.

He couldn't take his eyes off O'Hannon, but Noah knew in his gut that Tyson had been hit. Cold fear spread through him, but he kept his focus. O'Hannon had drawn his gun during the commotion, too, its tip now pressed under Mercer's jaw. She gasped against the hold on her throat, terror in her eyes.

"I said, let her go!" Noah advanced one step at a time, his gun still braced in both hands in front of him.

"She's coming with me! Unless you want to watch me blow her head off right here! Either way, you need to stand down! There're more of us up the road!"

Noah's heartbeat thrashed in his ears. If he let O'Hannon leave with Mercer, she was dead, anyway. He was using her as a human shield to make his escape or he would have already killed her. A trickle of perspiration rolled down Noah's back. He had to take the risk. Another six feet and O'Hannon would reach his car. Jaw clenched in determination, Noah advanced several more steps, steadied his aim and fired.

Relief nearly brought him to his knees as O'Hannon fell to

the gravel, leaving Mercer standing. Noah had shot him in the forehead. Appearing shell-shocked, Mercer swayed, then put her hands over her face. His ears ringing from his weapon's discharge, Noah turned and ran to Tyson, who had fallen in front of one of the diner's glass doors. Dropping down beside him, Noah released a shaky breath. Blood soaked the lower left quadrant of Tyson's shirt, but he appeared conscious. He groaned as Noah ripped the garment open to see the wound. His stomach dropped. Blood leaked heavily from a hole in Tyson's abdomen.

Screams had come from inside the diner when the shooting had started and people were now peering out through the windows. An African-American male in a white cook's uniform stood cautiously at the second glass door. When Noah held up his shield, the man opened the door and leaned out.

"I've got an ambulance on the way! Police, too! He gonna make it?" He stared down at Tyson.

"I need clean towels. Go get them. Now."

The man disappeared.

"How'd you...know they weren't marshals, Noah?" Tyson choked out.

"Don't try to talk. You're going to be okay, Ty." A lump in his throat, Noah glanced up at Mercer, who had moved unsteadily to where they were, her face ashen. The glass door reopened and the cook returned with a stack of white kitchen towels. Mercer took them and, kneeling beside Tyson, she gave them to Noah, who pressed them over the wound with his hands. Tyson moaned and writhed in pain.

"You were right about the leak, Noah," he managed hoarsely.

The screech of tires caught Noah's attention. Three vehicles were turning off the highway exit about a half-mile away and were traveling toward them at a high rate of speed.

There're more of us up the road...

Dread fluttered in Noah's chest. The others had heard the

shooting and were moving in. And there was still no wail of approaching squad cars.

"We've got company," Noah said tensely.

Tyson opened his eyes. "You've got to get her out of here, man."

Noah shook his head, aware of the blood already soaking through the towels. "I'm not leaving you."

"Take my keys and go!" Voice weak, Tyson grabbed at Noah's shirt, pulling him closer so that only he and Mercer could hear. "Take her to the cabin. It's not that far from here. Lay low until you can figure out who to trust."

Noah looked up at the cook, who still stood there, gawking.

"Drag him inside and lock the door," Noah told the man. "Keep pressure on the wound until the paramedics arrive and take over." He glanced up at the curious faces looking down at them through the diner's windows. "And get everyone in there into the kitchen."

The best way to protect these people would be if he and Mercer left. The men who were coming for them would give chase. But if they stayed, there would be another shootout and this time, Noah would most certainly be outnumbered.

"Oh, God," Mercer murmured, fidgeting in fear, her eyes on the approaching vehicles. They were now halfway down the access road. One of the men who had been seated at the counter emerged from the diner.

"What can I do?" he asked.

"Help him out," Noah said as the cook positioned himself behind Tyson. The sedan's keys lay on the concrete stoop where they had been dropped. With a last look at his partner, Noah snatched them up, sprang to his feet, and grabbed Mercer's hand, pulling her up, too. As they ran to the car, she tried to stop to pick up her purse, but Noah propelled her onward. "Leave it! There's no time!"

They jumped inside the sedan.

"Put on your seatbelt!" Noah quickly did the same, then started the engine and peeled out, the car's tires throwing up a gravel spray. They blazed past the three vehicles that were nearing the lot's entrance. Watching in the rear-view mirror, Noah saw the cars turn quickly around on the road and come after them. He floored the accelerator, the sedan's engine roaring. Several tractor-trailers were waiting to get on the interstate, creating a bottleneck that would slow them down. Noah headed east instead.

"Noah!" Terror ratcheted up Mercer's voice. "There're too many of them!"

"Hang on! I'm going to try to lose them." He gripped the steering wheel harder, his hands sticky with Tyson's blood. He had been up here a couple of times with Tyson recently, fishing and hiking. There was a patchwork of rural roads ahead and he might be able to shake them with enough turns if he could get some distance between them. As he drove, he used the radio connected to the dashboard to alert the local police of their location.

A short time later, they sped past a sign directing tourists to the Upper Santee Swamp System. Tires squealing, Noah took a sharp turn onto a two-lane road with heavy foliage on either side. A guardrail ran along the right side of the road and, just below them, murky, green-brown water could occasionally be seen between the trees and vines. For several minutes, it appeared that they might have lost them until the vehicles came shooting out from a side road. A Ford Mustang GT and a souped-up Camaro —both more powerful than Tyson's sedan—led the chase while the third vehicle was some type of large, off-road-capable SUV. Despite Noah pressing the accelerator to the floorboard, the two muscle cars were closing in.

Mercer screamed as the Mustang got close enough to bump

them from behind. Meanwhile, the Camaro had moved into the lane meant for travel in the opposite direction and was trying to get alongside them.

"Get your head down!" Noah yelled, flinching as gunfire shattered the car's rear window.

He had placed his gun and cell phone in the console between the sedan's front seats. Heart slamming against his ribs, Noah gripped the steering wheel with his left hand and picked up his Glock with the other, then twisted in the seat to return fire. He got off two shots, but the Mustang bumped them again, harder this time and causing the sedan to fishtail. Noah cursed, forced to put his weapon down so that he could get the car back under control.

"We have to stop, Noah!" Mercer cried, her hand on his arm. "We're going too fast!"

"We stop and we're dead!"

Using the side-view mirror, Noah watched the Camaro that was running nearly beside them now. His stomach flip-flopped as a gun barrel emerged from the open window on the passenger side. Noah reached for his gun again just as another gunshot rang out and his rear tire exploded. The sedan veered wildly before slamming into the guardrail. The velocity was too much.

The car sailed over the twisted metal and went airborne.

CHAPTER SEVENTEEN

DAZED, Noah hung upside down, secured into place by his seatbelt. The car had flipped, landing on its roof and skidding down a steep, rock-covered embankment before coming to rest in a grassy floodplain. After the din of crumpling metal and shattering glass, it was now eerily quiet except for a *plunking* sound that he realized was blood dripping onto the roof's interior below him. He turned his head to look at Mercer. Her long hair obscured her face as she hung upside down, too.

"Noah?" she whispered.

Closing his eyes briefly in relief, he swallowed and found his voice. "You okay?"

"I-I think so."

There wasn't much time. They had to free themselves before those men picked their way down the embankment after them. Noah braced his weight with his left hand on the roof's interior and strained against gravity to release his seatbelt before dropping down with a heavy, awkward thud. He tried to use the radio that now hung off the cracked dashboard, but it was dead.

His cell phone was missing, too, apparently having slid away somewhere inside the car when it had flipped.

"I can't get this off!" Panicked, Mercer struggled with her seatbelt.

"Hang on. I'll come around."

Opening his door, Noah pulled himself out, refusing to give in to lightheadedness. Although nothing seemed broken, he touched his left temple and his fingers came away wet with blood. Spotting his weapon inside the overturned, mangled car, he grabbed it and squinted up at the road. Surprise made his skin tingle. No one was trying to pick their way down the treacherous embankment after them. Instead, their pursuers had abandoned the cars and were climbing into the SUV. Noah recalled passing a side road a few thousand feet back that led down to a nearby fishing camp. He suspected they were headed to that road to take an easier route to reach them. Regardless, it bought them a little time. Noah jogged around the vehicle's smoking front and forced open the passenger-side door, which was wedged against a thick mound of sawgrass and sedges. Mercer now crouched on the upside-down roof's interior, having managed to free herself while Noah had been prying open the door. Her eyes were frightened as she looked up at him. Once she had climbed out with his help, Noah ran his hands over her arms and shoulders, needing to assure himself that she was uninjured.

"You're bleeding, Noah," she said worriedly.

Wiping at the blood trickling down his temple, his stomach tensed at the roar of an approaching vehicle. By the sound of it, the SUV was off-road and heading toward them. Noah had six rounds left in his gun's chamber. Not nearly enough to hold off these men.

Mercer's voice trembled. "They're coming!"

There wasn't time to search for his phone. "Are you able to run?"

Mercer stood white-faced and frozen, still looking off in the direction of the noise.

"*Mercer!*" Clasping her shoulders, Noah gave her a small shake to break her from her trance. "Can you run?"

She gave a tight nod and they sprinted together into a dense thicket of trees. The SUV wouldn't be able to follow. If they wanted to pursue them, they would have to do it on foot. Noah ran with Mercer deeper into the woods, sun dappling the leaves and creating shadows on the ground at their feet, their combined breaths coming hard.

"What're you doing?" Mercer whispered as Noah halted them a few minutes later. She leaned forward, panting, her hands on her thighs as she attempted to catch her breath.

"Trying to misdirect." His own chest heaving, Noah broke several thin branches on a young sapling in the opposite direction that he and Mercer were headed. Ripping off his tie, he tossed it onto the ground to make sure that their pursuers saw the broken branches. Blood dripped from Noah's temple. He couldn't see the men through the trees, but they were out there. Their voices carried in the not-too-far-off distance as they shouted directions to one another.

As Noah and Mercer continued on, the odor of stagnant water and decaying plants grew stronger, indicating that they were nearing the swamp. Standing water had begun to form small pools under the verdant foliage in between brown silt and moss-covered ground. Noah's dress shoes were muddy and slick, the stylish loafers Mercer wore equally so, and she had slipped more than once as the ground had grown wetter. Twigs were caught in her hair and her cheek was scratched, but she continued running beside him. She froze only momentarily as a snake slithered over the ground in front of them, but to her credit, she didn't make a sound.

Minutes later, the trees gave way to low-growing shrubs and

tall grasses. Noah wiped at the blood that had leaked into his left eye. The cut throbbed and perspiration made his shirt stick to his skin. He prayed that he was right about their location. Relief flooded through him as a sun-weathered, deteriorating shack on the swamp's edge finally became visible. Noah had recalled seeing it a month ago when he had been staying at Tyson's cabin but had taken off by himself on a long hike. The place had appeared abandoned then, as it did now. But it wasn't the shack that Noah was interested in.

It was the covered shelter off its dock where a canoe had been.

He estimated that Tyson's cabin was still four or five miles from here. Even if they were able to reach it on foot, their pursuers would track them every step of the way. But if they could get there by water, they had the best chance of leaving them behind.

"This is Detective Beaufain's place?" Mercer whispered. She followed Noah as he walked down the dock, which had rotted in places. Other sections of plank were missing altogether or were covered in slick, green algae.

"No, but I'm hoping it has something we need." He looked over his shoulder at her, his words low. "Careful. Step exactly where I do."

Upon reaching the covered portion of the dock and seeing the battered canoe still there, Noah released a pent-up breath. He thanked God that time moved like molasses in these parts and little changed. The canoe appeared to be water-worthy, so he pushed it across the rough wood planks until it slid into the swamp with a splash. Mercer fetched the two oars that leaned against the covered structure's railing. Noah steadied the canoe as she got in and sat at one end, facing forward. The canoe rocked as he climbed in behind her. Once he was seated, he took the oars from where she had left them on the dock's edge, handed her one and together they pushed off across the scummy water and began paddling.

Several minutes later, he squinted back to the dilapidated shack that had grown smaller with distance. Men were storming onto the dock. Six of them in all. Noah was too far away to make out their faces clearly, but one of them looked like Lex Draper.

Mercer glanced back, too. "Oh, God, Noah!"

They both paddled harder. The men fired at them, but they were too far out of range. Soon, both the men and the shack disappeared. Noah and Mercer continued dipping their oars in and out of the water on either side of the canoe until they were lost in the freshwater swamp that Noah knew to be comprised of more than sixteen hundred acres. After the bedlam of the last hour, it seemed strangely peaceful out here. When Lake Marion had been created in the 1940s by the damming of the Santee River, this area had been transformed into a deep water, flooded forest. A turtle's shell parted the floating algae as it swam in front of them, and the shadowy outlines of catfish were visible through the murky water below. His throat parched, Noah felt tension in his stomach. Even with his survival training, they were ill equipped to be out here. No water or food, no cell phones, both of them dressed in street clothes. He couldn't afford to get them lost out here. He had to find Tyson's cabin before nightfall. Noah stopped paddling to look at the compass on his sports wristwatch.

"Do you know where we are?" Mercer looked back at him, her expression worried.

"Not exactly." Determined, he used his oar to adjust their direction. The cut on his temple stung. But he wasn't the only one who had taken the brunt of the crash. Now that they were in less danger, at least for now, Noah noticed that Mercer was moving more gingerly when the oar was on her right side.

"Why don't you take a break?" he suggested. "We've got some distance. I can paddle by myself for a while."

She shook her head, then looked over her shoulder at him again. "You're still bleeding, Noah—"

"I'm okay. Put the oar down for a few minutes."

Placing her oar in the boat's hull, Mercer turned carefully around on the plank seat to face him. She swatted at gnats that swarmed around her, fatigue evident on her features. A bluish bruise had begun to form below her collarbone where the seatbelt had lashed tight to keep her in place. "What happened to the real marshals, Noah?"

"I don't know." Draper and his men had managed to somehow either kill or subdue the marshals who had been scheduled to meet them. Noah figured that the Celtic cross that had been on the man's money clip and on Draper's ring must be some kind of secret symbol worn by The Brotherhood's members, something that hadn't been known to police. He wondered who the two men posing as marshals were, since their images hadn't been among the ones of Draper's inner circle on the precinct's corkboard.

"How'd you figure out they were imposters?" Mercer asked.

As he told her what had given them away, her mouth slackened in horror. "God. If I'd left with them—"

"I wasn't going to let that happen." He paused, his throat tight with meaning. "I would've died first."

Their eyes held until she spoke. "You're worried about Detective Beaufain. He's more than a partner to you, isn't he? He's a friend."

Noah didn't respond as he thought of Tyson's wound. The abdomen was a dangerous place to take a bullet.

"Ty has a wife and twin daughters," he said finally. "The girls are just six years old."

Mercer's eyes were pained. Neither spoke much after that, too exhausted, thirsty, and shell-shocked to make further conversation. Noah veered them into a narrower channel shaded by black tupelos and cypresses, still heading south since the fishing cabin was located past the swamp's mouth near the upper end of Lake Marion. This area was isolated and it didn't surprise him that they hadn't seen anyone—not even kayakers—out here. Croaking frogs rested on gnarled tree roots and more than one snake glided through the water in front of them. Noah kept an eye out for the landmarks that he had noted either while hiking or fishing from Tyson's pontoon boat, but Draper and his men were never out of his thoughts. He wondered again how he and Tyson had been set up. Draper must also have a source inside the U.S. Marshals Service, Noah figured, since no one from his department—not even Captain Bell—had been privy to the time and location of the rendezvous point. The Marshals Service had contacted Noah directly with that information, including the names of the marshals assigned to meet them.

The men who had tried to take Mercer from the diner were dead. But Noah had no doubt that the ones who had pursued them by vehicle would soon have an engine-powered boat—maybe more than one—out here so they could look for them. If the men caught up to them, he and Mercer would be sitting ducks in the canoe.

They had to find the cabin soon.

DESPITE THE MILDNESS of the fall afternoon, Mercer suppressed a shiver as the canoe glided through dark water beneath a canopy of trees. This vast place was both beautiful and terrifying. Little sunlight reached this area of the swamp, and Mercer had glimpsed numerous species of birds as well as reptiles, including a large alligator as it dropped into the water from its resting place on a partially submerged tree trunk, possibly sizing up Noah or her as a potential meal. The creature had trailed them until it finally lost interest and changed course. Rubbing at the stiffness in her neck, she watched Noah as he paddled, his eyes on the bank, apparently searching for something that might tell him they were headed in the right direction. The top buttons of his dress shirt were undone, his shirtsleeves rolled up. The bleeding from his temple appeared to have slowed. Bloodstains marred his collar and shirtfront, some of it his and some of it Detective Beaufain's.

I wasn't going to let that happen. I would've died first.

She recalled Noah's words, all too aware that he might still lose his life trying to protect her. She had rested enough. Needing an outlet for her anxiety, Mercer reached for her oar again, but Noah's voice halted her.

"Look."

Her eyes fastened on an egret that stood on long legs under Spanish moss hanging from a tree at the water's edge. But she soon realized that Noah was looking past it at the ghostly, stone shapes jutting up from the ground among the undergrowth. "What is it?"

"A slave cemetery from the early eighteen-hundreds."

The sweat-dampened hair on her nape prickled.

Noah's muscles flexed in his forearms as he stroked the oar through the water. "There were cotton plantations not far from here. They were burned in Sherman's March to the Sea. Tyson showed me the cemetery when I was last out here. It means that we're headed in the right direction. I'm estimating that we're still about a mile from the cabin."

"The place must be isolated."

"That's the beauty of it. Tyson inherited it just a few months ago from his grandfather. I'm pretty sure no one on the force even knows about it except for me."

Taking up her oar and facing forward again in the canoe, Mercer began paddling, her spirit renewed. A short time later, they emerged from the narrow channel and its awning of trees, sunlight once again warm on her back and shoulders. As they moved out of the swamp and into the lake, she noticed that the water was becoming less encumbered with vegetation. They traveled another twenty or so minutes before Noah directed their path into a nearly hidden, tree-protected cove. A cabin made of mud-chinked cypress logs appeared in a small clearing in front of them. The rough-hewn cabin would have appeared primitive if not for the solar panels in its roof that collected light. A pontoon boat topped by a marine-blue sunshade floated in the water on the far side of a long, L-shaped dock.

"This property's been in the Beaufain family for generations," Noah said as they positioned the canoe adjacent to the dock. "Ty's grandfather built the cabin. They bonded over bass and catfish out here when Ty was a kid. His grandfather was a physician, but he also fancied himself an outdoorsman and wanted a place away from it all."

"It looks like he got it," Mercer mused as the canoe bumped against the dock's side. Still seated, Noah braced one hand on its wood planking so that he could keep the canoe steady while Mercer stepped onto the dock. After the time on the water, her legs felt rubbery, as if she were still afloat. Noah stepped carefully out behind her, then with some effort pulled the canoe up onto the dock.

"We're going to need to hide this," he said.

Together, they dragged the canoe to the pontoon boat and placed the smaller vessel inside it, then covered it with an opaque, plastic tarp. Mercer's body trembled with exertion. Noah looked nearly as tired as she felt. She turned to look again at the cabin. It sat on brick columns that were about five- or six-feet high, which raised it enough to protect against flooding, although the space between the cabin's foundation and the ground had been boarded up all around. Mercer followed Noah up the wood stairs and onto the cabin's porch where a whimsical, wooden plaque in the shape of a fish hung on the wall near the front door, its lettering spelling out *Beaufain's Folly.* There were also two rocking chairs with a fishing pail between them. A net attached to a pole, presumably for scooping fish from the water, leaned against the railing.

"I left Tyson's keys behind, but I know where he hides a spare. Stay here."

Mercer waited while Noah went back down the steps, jogged across a wide, dirt path that appeared to be a makeshift driveway, then disappeared around the cabin's side. He reappeared a minute or so later with a key. Coming back onto the porch, he inserted the key into the lock and pushed the door open. Hot, her clothes sticking to her skin, Mercer followed him inside. The interior was small but neat, with a rustic, wood-burning fireplace and a lived-in couch with an afghan thrown across its back. A bookcase on a far wall held an expansive collection of books while a utilitarian kitchen area completed the single room.

"There're a couple of bedrooms and a bathroom down the hall." Noah walked to a wall panel and flipped a switch. A trio of ceiling fans on poles that were mounted on the vaulted ceiling above them began to rotate, moving the sluggish air. "The solar panels store energy, at least enough for fans and lights. It's warm in here but it should cool off at night."

"There's a stove," Mercer noted.

"It's propane-fueled. So is the water heater. There's a freshwater spring on the property. It's non-potable, though."

Whether with hot or cold water, a shower sounded like heaven. Mercer followed Noah as he went to the kitchen and opened what appeared to be a pantry door. She glimpsed several cans of food and a few other non-perishables.

"God bless you, Ty," Noah murmured. "Looks like he had some groceries left from when he was out here last time." He took two bottled waters from an already opened, shrink-wrapped case that sat on the bottom shelf and handed one to Mercer. They both twisted the caps from their bottles and drank greedily. The water was tepid but in that moment, it tasted better to her than the finest bottle of wine in the St. Clair's climate-controlled wine cellar.

"I can't believe you were able to find this place." She wiped her lips with the back of her hand once she had finished her bottle.

Noah released a tense breath. "The one advantage we have is how big this area is. The swamp's well over a thousand acres and the lake itself is a hundred times that size, with over three hundred miles of shoreline. There're other cabins around here, but most are unoccupied until hunting season opens later this month. We need to make sure this one looks just as unoccupied." He indicated a kerosene lamp that hung on a hook on the wall. "The window blinds stay closed. We'll go down to low-flame lamplight after dark. This place has overhead lighting, but lamplight is weaker and less likely to be seen."

The initial relief that Mercer had felt upon their finding shelter faded. These men who were after them wouldn't give up easily. This place was too far off the grid for a telephone landline and maybe even cell coverage, not that either of them had phones. Tom, Remy, her family—anyone they could trust to help them were out of reach. Fear gnawed at her. "Is there anything we can do besides just hope they don't find us?"

"I'm going to set up some things outside to alert us if anyone comes onto the property." Seriousness darkened Noah's eyes. "As well as some things that'll hopefully stop any intruders or at least slow them down."

"What can I do to help?"

He placed his empty plastic bottle beside the sink. "Take the sign off the front door, for starters. We don't need the name

Beaufain being advertised out there. Then look around for dark blankets and towels we can layer on top of the blinds after dark. That'll make sure no light leaks out. Look for any guns, too, although I'm pretty sure none's here since Ty worries about break-ins and typically brings his weapons and ammo back with him. You can also take inventory in the kitchen so we'll know exactly how much supplies we have and how long we can last out here. We can boil water and supplement our food by fishing, but we need to lay low. If Ty survived, he'll send help to us."

Mercer felt an ache in her throat. "But...what if Detective Beaufain didn't survive?"

Noah swallowed heavily. "Then we'll need to wait it out here for as long as we can. Hopefully, until Draper and his men give up on finding us and leave the area."

Worry must have been evident on her features, because he touched her face. "I'm going to get you out of this," he promised in a low voice. They stared at one another in a charged silence until he took a step back.

"Go ahead and have something to eat." Noah tore a paper towel from a roll on the counter, then wet it in the sink once water began to trickle out from the faucet.

"What about you?"

Using the towel, he wiped carefully at the dried blood on his temple. "There're some protein and granola bars in the pantry. I'll take one with me. I need to get started out there."

"I can help outside."

"The fewer of us out there, the better. Stay inside."

She wanted to clean and bandage his cut, but he headed out. Mercer followed him to the door. As he stepped down from the porch, she went out to remove the wooden plaque and carried it back in, cradling it against her chest. It *was* warm in the cabin but they were lucky that the uncommon cool front from last week still lingered. The overhead fans were already helping and she suspected that Noah was right and the temperature would drop with nightfall. Slightly lifting the blind that covered the kitchen window, Mercer peeked out at the property's rear, where she could see Noah surveying the area, no doubt planning whatever he intended to do out there. She watched as he walked to a large oak tree and squinted up into its branches, one hand on his hip just above his holstered gun. Broad-shouldered, athletically muscled, his dark hair gleamed in the sunlight that filtered through the boughs. A weathered toolshed was located nearby and a tire swing hung from one of the oak's gnarled limbs. Mercer wondered if the swing was for Detective Beaufain's daughters—if he would even bring them out to such a remote location—or whether it had been there, unused and forgotten, for generations. Regardless, she said a silent prayer that those little girls hadn't lost their father.

Mercer thought of her own family. She wondered if they knew yet that she was missing, what the news might be reporting about the shooting at the diner, or whether the crashed car that she and Noah had abandoned had even been found. If it would *ever* be found. Mark, Carter, her mother—if they knew anything at all yet, they would be frantic with worry.

There was also one thing that Noah hadn't mentioned. If the police *had* figured out that they could be somewhere out here, they would be sending search parties of their own. But if there *was* a leak within law enforcement, someone so vile that he had been complicit in today's violence, there was a threat there, as well, and no one they could really trust.

CHAPTER EIGHTEEN

MERCER'S STOMACH quivered as she stared into the hip-deep, partially concealed pit that Noah had dug a few steps from the dock. He had strung netting over the hole, and sticks, their ends sharpened into points, rose up from its dirt floor. A shovel lay nearby on the ground. Carrying another armload of vegetation, Noah crouched beside the pit and spread it over the netting to conceal it the rest of the way.

"Anyone coming from the dock in the dark is going to get a surprise." Rising to stand beside her, he surveyed his work. Around them, the shadows had built and lengthened as daytime faded into dusk. "Neither of us needs to be out here much, since we're risking being seen. Still, you need to remember this area and avoid it."

"Like the plague," Mercer agreed, her throat dry. "But what if Detective Beaufain *does* send someone out to help us? Couldn't this hurt them?"

"Ty knows me too well. He'll know I've armed this place to the teeth and he'll make sure that anyone he sends out here knows to announce themselves before stepping onto the property." Dirt mingled with the dried blood that marred Noah's clothing, and he used his forearm to wipe perspiration from his forehead. "C'mon. Let me show you what else you need to know about."

As they walked around the clearing's perimeter, he indicated the fishing line that he had strung taut and low to the ground. He then pointed up into an oak tree's branches where a plastic trash bag dangled from a cord. "That's a bag of empty soda and beer cans that Ty was planning to take in for recycling. If anyone—or anything—trips the wire here, including coming across the driveway, we're going to know. I've got more of these noisemakers strung up in the trees on all sides of the property." He looked again at Mercer, his features serious. "Treat the wire like a fence. Don't go past it. I've set out some bear traps that were in the toolshed. They're old and rusted, but they'll get the job done." He showed her a beaten dirt trail that ran behind the shed into the woods. "If you do have to leave here without me, take that path and stay on it. It winds around through the trees and you'll end up on a road about a half-mile up. The path will hide you better than if you take the driveway out."

If you do have to leave here without me...

Noah meant that if something happened to him. Mercer prayed that she would never have to face that situation. She looked again at the wire that ran a couple of inches off the ground. "Did you learn how to do all this in the military?"

"I learned to avoid things like this. The Taliban and their sympathizers didn't have our weaponry, but they were masters at improvisation. Tripwires attached to handmade explosives were common. I lost a good friend in Kandahar that way."

Mercer touched his arm in comfort. His amber gaze seemed to assess her. "I like how you look. Without make-up, I mean."

She was aware of her bare face, her hair damp and falling around her shoulders. After completing the tasks that she had been assigned, Mercer had showered in the cabin's small bathroom. She had also inspected herself for ticks as Noah had instructed. She had been greatly relieved to find none, but when she glanced into the mirror over the sink, she had seen the scratch on her cheek and the bruising at her collarbone. The water in the shower had been warmer than she expected, and it had helped to ease some of the stiffness from her body. Afterward, she had changed into khaki shorts and a dark, scoop-neck T-shirt, women's clothing she had found in the back of a drawer when she had been looking for things that could be used to hang over the blinds. She was also currently without undergarments, since she had washed hers along with the clothes she'd had on earlier and hung them on a towel rack in the bathroom to dry. Self-consciously, she crossed her arms over her breasts and stared down briefly at the loafers that she had managed to mostly wipe free of mud. "I hope Detective Beaufain's wife won't mind about the clothes. Mine were pretty damp and muddy."

"I'm surprised you found any. Ty told me Lanny's only been out here once, right after he inherited it. He says it's too far out in the boonies for her and the girls."

Then the tire swing hanging from the oak's gnarled limb was as old as it looked, Mercer thought.

"There isn't much more I can do out here tonight." Noah briskly rubbed his palms together to brush away dirt. "It's about time I caught a shower and look for some clean clothes myself. I won't be in the shower long. I need you to keep an ear out for any noise while I'm in there."

Mercer nodded. "I found some toothbrushes still in their packaging in a drawer in the bathroom. There's toothpaste, too," she said as they walked back to the cabin's front once Noah had made sure that there was no one on the water nearby.

They went up the porch steps and entered. Noah looked around the cabin's darkened interior. "I see you've been busy."

Mercer had used the hammer and nails that Noah had brought in from the toolshed to tack up blankets and other bedding over the window blinds. "You had enough to do out there, so I went ahead and went to work. I nailed them just at the top, so we can pull the coverings back during the day to at least let some light in around the blinds' edges."

Noah took the kerosene lamp from its hook on the wall and placed it on a table. After retrieving a box of matches from the stone hearth's mantel, he removed the lamp's glass chimney, lit the wick and replaced the glass. Anemic, yellow light glowed.

"There's one other thing I want to show you." He bent to roll back a large, braided rag-rug covering the floor. To Mercer's surprise, a door with a hole for a handle was located there.

"It leads down to a crawl space. There's a removable board down there in back of the cabin so that things can be moved in and out. The space is used for storage, but if we need it, it's also an escape route." Noah replaced the rug. Straightening, he indicated the lamp. "Keep this one with you." He picked up the matchbox. "There's another one in back. I'll take it with me to shower."

"There're a couple of cans of ready-to-heat pasta. I was thinking I could make that for dinner? I'm hungry, but you must be starving."

He nodded. Mercer's heart constricted as she looked at him in the shadows.

"I...thought I'd be saying goodbye to you this morning," she stammered, her emotion rising. She couldn't stop thinking about the events of the day and how they had narrowly escaped with their lives.

"I guess fate had other plans for us. It's going to be okay, Mercer," Noah said quietly before turning and going down the hall.

HEAD BOWED, one palm braced against the shower wall's molded plastic, Noah squeezed his eyes closed as water rained down on him. The words of comfort he had offered Mercer belied his own inner turmoil.

He didn't know whether Tyson was alive or dead, whether any help would be arriving. If it didn't, Noah clung to the idea that if they could just remain out of sight long enough, Draper and his men might think they had escaped the area and would move on. At least for now, staying here was safer than being exposed and vulnerable outdoors where, if they were spotted, they would be outnumbered and outgunned.

If he did manage to get Mercer back home, what then? Protectiveness tightened Noah's jaw. As long as Draper was out there, she would still have a target on her back. Would she be handed over to WITSEC again? After this, how could he entrust her safety to anyone?

Noah thought of how she had looked outside in the waning daylight, the setting sun catching the gold highlights in her hair and making her skin appear luminous. He had noticed the flush that appeared on her cheekbones when he'd told her that he liked the way she looked. Noah couldn't imagine that a day had gone by that her husband hadn't told her how beautiful she was. He regretted that he hadn't made love to her—hadn't eased her loneliness—when he'd had the chance. That he had let protocol come between them.

The laceration on his temple stung under the spray, but it wasn't enough to distract him. Outside, Noah had thrown himself into the work that had to be done, but now, alone with his thoughts, he leaned his forehead against the shower wall, his breathing cramped. The gunfire and sprawled bodies outside the diner, Tyson's bloody wound, the shattering glass and crunching metal as the car flipped over the guardrail—it all came rushing back in on him.

It took him back to a helicopter crash and a prison built into a cavern in a mountainside.

He fought the images away. Angered by his weakness, Noah shut off his thoughts just as he shut off the showerhead. Standing in the flickering lamplight, he took a deep, calming breath, then used his hands to wipe water from his face. He reached for a towel that hung on the rack beside Mercer's lace-edged bra and panties.

Noah vowed that he wouldn't let her die out here.

After finishing up in the bathroom, he slipped on a pair of Tyson's jeans that he had found and brought in with him. Then he opened the door, planning to seek out a shirt in the bedroom's bureau. But he halted upon seeing Mercer. Her eyes flicked to the scars on his bare chest and abdomen before meeting his gaze again.

"I...just wanted to let you know that dinner's ready," she said, then went back down the hall.

MERCER ABSENTLY TWIRLED spaghetti noodles around the tines of her fork, discreetly watching Noah as he ate beside her. Since coming out of the shower, he had been quiet, even for him. She studied his even profile, his dark hair damp and tousled. The cut on his temple appeared angry, the skin bruised around it. Mercer had located a first-aid kit on a shelf behind the linens and, once he was done eating, she planned to try to convince him to let her at least apply some antibiotic ointment.

She could help the cut heal, if he allowed her, but there was little she could do about the wounds that he no doubt still carried inside.

Corinne had mentioned Noah's scars. Mercer had glimpsed five or six of them, each less than an inch in diameter and circular in shape. They were far different from Carter's scars, but their cause had been no less traumatic. She recalled the article that she had read about Noah's rescue and the torture that he and the other soldiers had endured.

"I'll take it for you," she offered when, having finished his food, Noah wiped his mouth with a paper napkin and started to rise from the couch to carry his plate into the kitchen.

"You don't have to do that."

"I know."

Taking his plate along with hers, working in the weak lamplight, she rinsed the dishes in the basin before leaving them there. Mercer went to retrieve the first-aid kit, then sank back down onto the couch beside Noah. She placed the kit next to his gun which lay on the rustic coffee table. He wore borrowed jeans and a white T-shirt, his feet bare. Hers were as well, although he had warned her to keep her shoes always close by.

"I suppose that's for me," he said as she opened the kit.

"I think it's a good idea, don't you?" Rummaging through the box, she extracted the antibiotic ointment and a small box of adhesive bandages. "I mean, after all that time in the swamp, what we both probably need is a tetanus shot, but this will have to do for now. I only wish you would've let me do it earlier."

"Daylight was burning. Besides, I didn't see the point until I could get a shower."

Mercer leaned closer and carefully dabbed some of the ointment against his injured temple which she assumed had been cut by the car window's flying glass. "You probably need stitches, Noah."

He frowned, but didn't resist her ministrations. As she worked, Mercer was acutely aware of his maleness and the strength that emanated from him. He smelled clean from his shower, like soap.

"There." She placed a small bandage over the cut. His dark, spiky lashes lifted and she found herself caught once again in his amber gaze. But she remembered how things had gone between them that night at the safe house, and she turned her attention to putting the supplies back into the first-aid kit.

"How're you feeling?" he asked. "Your collarbone's pretty bruised and you were favoring your right side earlier."

"I'm sore, but the shower and some aspirin that I found in the medicine cabinet helped a little. Considering things, we're both extremely fortunate. It's a miracle neither of us was seriously injured in the crash."

As she looked up, Mercer realized that Noah's eyes remained riveted on her face. Outside, the drone of insects and the repeated screech of some bird of prey could be heard, another reminder of just how isolated they were out here.

"You look so tired, Noah," she remarked softly, noting the faint lines of fatigue that fanned outward from the corners of his eyes. "Please don't tell me you're going to stay up all night and keep watch."

He shrugged. "Then I won't tell you."

"Well, I might not be able to handle a gun as well as you, but I'm perfectly capable of staying up and listening for noises. I'm probably too wired to sleep, anyway."

He shook his head. "No."

"I want to help," she persisted. "We can work in three-hour shifts, like Remy and Tom did the first day at the safe house. I'll stay up for the first three and then you can take over." When he still appeared resolute about doing it alone, her chin lifted faintly. "You can't do this by yourself, Noah. I don't want to be treated like some fragile piece of porcelain out here. I won't break."

"I'm not treating you like—"

"You trust me, don't you? *Both* our lives on the line here."

Finally, he released a breath of resignation. "Take the first shift. Three hours. If you think you hear *anything*, you wake me immediately."

Mercer gave a serious nod. "I'll go make coffee. At least we have a generous supply of that. The tin's almost full. It's just too bad that we don't have any milk to go with it."

As she rose from the couch, to her surprise, his fingers caught hers, stopping her. Her stomach fluttered as his brooding gaze held hers.

"Trust isn't easy for me," he rasped. "But I *do* trust you, Mercer."

His nearness gave her comfort. She ached with the need to climb onto his lap and lay her head against his strong shoulder, but she merely stood there. A moment later, Noah's fingers slipped from hers.

Aware of the dull beat of her heart, she went into the kitchen.

CHAPTER NINETEEN

THE STENCH of sweat and blood surrounded him.

Noah blinked, the light assaulting him as the blindfold he had worn for what seemed like days was snatched away. Throat like sandpaper, his heart hammering, he squinted at his captors—four this time, all bearded and raw-boned, wearing loose robes. Noah recognized the voice of the one who had beaten him on the first day nearly into unconsciousness.

"Your country says no deal." The man spoke to him in broken English, his eyes cold. "Unless they change their minds soon, it will not be good for you."

He turned to the others, his language shifting back to Pashto. Noah understood only some of it.

Show him. Let him see what we will do.

One of the men holding an AK rifle walked to a tarp in the room's corner. A video camera was set up there. As the man rolled back the heavy plastic, Noah's muscles went weak. He had heard Rodriguez's screams for hours. He now lay dead, naked in a puddle of blood, his flesh mutilated by long, weeping lacerations. Noah's bleeding wrists worked against the rough rope that bound his hands behind his back and kept him in place in a folding metal chair. Rage choking him, he vowed that if he ever got free, he would rip out every one of these bastards' lungs.

"Reeds soaked in water," the man who spoke English explained, his voice low in Noah's ear as he loomed over him. "They are like a sharp knife through meat, no?"

MERCER SET ASIDE the book she had taken from one of the cabin's shelves. For a brief moment, fear hardened her stomach until she realized that the male voice she was hearing wasn't coming from outside.

It was Noah.

Concerned, she picked up the lamp and walked uncertainly down the hall toward the bedroom he had taken. Her stomach tensed as she heard his voice rise and break with emotion. Reaching the room's doorway, she raised the lamp. She could see him lying on the bed, still dressed in what he'd had on earlier. Although he appeared to be asleep, he moved fretfully on top of the sheets, his dark head thrashing slowly back and forth on the pillow. He mumbled, some of the words unintelligible, some profane, but she clearly heard him say *Rodriguez.* Dread pooled inside her. Corinne had told her about the nightmares.

She had to wake him. Entering the room, Mercer sat the lamp on the bureau top before moving to the bed.

"Noah?" When he didn't awaken, she sat on the mattress edge. Looking down at him, she touched his shoulder, then gasped in surprise as he shot bolt upright and roughly grabbed her, shoving her back against the headboard and pinning her in place with his knee between her legs, his other hand at her throat. His eyes were wild, his face flushed. Mercer twisted underneath him.

"Noah!" she choked out.

It took him a moment to realize what he was doing. He quickly let her go and backed off.

"God," he whispered raggedly. "I'm sorry."

Chest still heaving, he moved to sit at the bed's edge. Elbows on his jeans-clad thighs, he dropped his head between his hands. Her heart squeezing, Mercer moved to sit beside him. She rubbed soothing circles on his back, wanting him to know that he wasn't alone and that he hadn't frightened her away. His T-shirt was damp with perspiration.

"Are you all right?" she asked. "You were talking in your sleep. You were upset."

"How long I have been out?"

"About two hours." Mercer hesitated. "Corinne...told me about your nightmares. She wasn't sure if you still had them."

Straightening, he scrubbed a hand over his features. "I didn't mean to hurt you, Mercer. I'm sorry," he apologized again.

"You didn't hurt me," she promised. "But you were talking about someone named Rodriguez."

The name didn't seem to come as a surprise. His breathing had begun to even out, and he dragged a hand through his hair before rising from the bed. He seemed restless, like an animal who had been forced into a cage. She could sense that Noah wanted to shut her out but she refused to shrink away. Mercer went to where he was and laid her hand against his chest to stop his pacing. She felt the hard beat of his heart under her palm.

"*Talk* to me, Noah." She implored him with her eyes. "Please let me help you, if I can."

He stood so close that she could feel the movement of his breathing. For several moments, they simply stared at one another in the shadows until his hand slowly lifted, his fingers skimming along her collarbone before sliding under her hair and gently cupping the back of her neck. She nearly stopped breathing, her skin tingling where he touched her.

The desperation she had seen in his eyes was now gone, his gaze shifting into one of male hunger. His hand buried more deeply in her hair and she leaned into him as he lowered his mouth to hers, sending a shudder of desire through her. His kiss burned with a soldering heat and Mercer clung to him, settling her body against his, her arms rising and wrapping around his neck. If *this* was how she could help him, if he wanted to use her to chase away his nightmares, she was willing. Out here alone, they had only one another. Mercer hoped that this time, he wouldn't pull away. Already, she could feel his male arousal, the sensation sending a spiraling, erotic thrill through her.

"Wait," she murmured. Her fingers trembled as she worked at the necklace's clasp at the back of her neck. The chain and its rings came away. Placing the jewelry on the nightstand, she briefly closed her eyes in bittersweet remembrance. Then she turned back to Noah.

His gaze was somber as the lamplight played over his features. "We don't have protection."

"I don't care." Mercer's throat tightened. "I...need this...I need you too much right now. Please don't tell me no."

In that moment, nothing outside the room mattered. The world around them seemed to stop. Noah crushed her to him, his mouth slanting over hers once more. His hands outlined the full circles of her breasts, then moved slowly down the length of her back before clutching the hem of her top. Mercer raised her arms to help him remove the garment, their kiss breaking so that he could pull it off over her head. Dropping it to the floor, his gaze raked boldly over her naked breasts. Mercer sighed as he fondled her, his fingers brushing back and forth over the marble-hard points of her nipples. She reveled in the feel of his big hands on her. His touch filled the aching void that had been a part of her for so long.

"Yes..." She whispered her encouragement before placing a kiss in the hollow of his throat. "Noah...yes."

His hands moved to the waist of her shorts, unbuttoning and unzipping them. Cool air met her heated skin as they joined her top on the floor. Without her panties that were still drying in the bathroom, she stood fully nude and unashamed in front of him. His dark lashes lowered as his eyes traveled over her again.

"You're the most beautiful thing I've ever seen," he murmured.

Impatient to see him, to feel him, too, Mercer tugged upward at the hem of his T-shirt. Taking her cue, he pulled it off over his head. She had glimpsed his powerful, broad torso earlier in the hallway, but she now stared at it freely—including its curious scars—instead of looking away. The sparse hair on his chest was as ink-black as the hair on his head, and a coarse, vertical line of it ran below his navel before disappearing into the waistband of his jeans. Determined to follow that trail, Mercer began to undo the top button at his waist but he stopped her, walking her backward to the bed and gently easing her down onto it. His gun had been tucked under the other pillow, apparently. Reaching over her for it, he picked it up and placed it on the nightstand beside her rings.

She lay there watching him, his face unreadable in the shadows as he removed his jeans and boxers. A tremor ran through her at the virile sight of him. Then he climbed onto the bed and braced himself over her. She moaned softly as his head lowered and he covered each of her breasts in turn with his mouth, his tongue caressing her sensitive nipples. Then his hand burned a trail down her abdomen before sliding between her thighs.

"God, Mercer..."

He stroked her slick, wet heat. She groaned with the sensual pleasure of it, her legs falling open more widely as his finger dipped into her. Noah watched her face as he moved it slowly in and out of her. Drunk with need, her hands explored the firm planes of his back as his hard body imprisoned hers. When his thumb began to expertly rub at her most sensitive spot, it was more than she could take. Mercer panted and cried out as her walls clenched in a shattering orgasm. She still rode the waves of it as his demanding lips took hers again. Heart beating wildly from her hard climax, she ran her fingers over the rough stubble on his jaw, over the strong cords at the back of his neck, before threading them through his thick hair. She clung to him like that until Noah trapped her hands above her head on the pillow, taking control again, his kiss deeper and more drugging this time. Mercer undulated underneath him, begging to be filled.

Burying his face against her throat, he breathed a hot kiss there before sheathing himself inside her in a single, hard stroke. Mercer cried out with the shock of it as her body stretched to accommodate him.

"Mercer, look at me." His command was a low whisper. Noah cupped the side of her face with a near reverence, his gaze holding hers until she stilled. Then he began to move inside her in deep, unhurried thrusts.

She lost herself in the dreamy haze of their lovemaking.

LYING against the pillows with Mercer's head on his chest, Noah watched the shadows dance on the wall in the flickering lamplight. Sated, their bodies wound together, her toes rubbed lazily up and down his shin as he traced a finger along the feminine curve of her hip.

It wasn't like him to be irresponsible. Still, he didn't regret what had happened between them. The taste of her, her sweet scent, the sounds she made when they had been in the deepest throes of sex—all of it was imprinted on his mind and heart.

He was aware of her fingers brushing lightly over the small, cylinder-like pockmarks on his chest. There were six in all.

"What caused these?" she inquired carefully.

Pensively, Noah curled strands of her long, silky hair around his index finger. If Corinne had told Mercer about the nightmares, he figured that she had mentioned the scars, as well, although his sister must have left out the grim details. As Mercer looked up at him, it was concern, not pity or morbid curiosity that he saw in her eyes. She wasn't the first woman who had asked about his scars after their being intimate. She would, however, be the first one of them in whom he had ever confided.

"I told you that the Taliban was good at improvisation." Even now the memory cut at him. "They were caused by a metal rod. They hooked it to a car battery and basically turned it into a cattle prod."

Her eyes filled with horror. "God. Were they trying to kill you?"

"More like they were just killing time. Torture was something they did to entertain themselves while they waited to see if our government would meet their demands." Noah's heartbeat grew sluggish as he thought of what had been done to him and the others. "They made us stand in water up to our ankles with our wrists chained to a steel bar overhead. The water intensified the shock. They took bets on which of us would be the last to pass out."

Much of the torture had been captured on video for sending to the United States. Noah knew that in a classified server somewhere there was footage of him.

Mercer slowly shook her head. "Was Rodriguez one of the men with you?"

"He was one of us who didn't make it back."

Noah wondered how long his nightmare might have gone on if Mercer hadn't awakened him. It had been especially vivid and, at times in it, Alonzo Rodriguez's body as it lay on the floor in front of him had morphed into Tyson's. What had happened at the diner had no doubt been a trigger, had thrown him back to that dark time.

"My brother Carter still has scars from the attack on him," Mercer mentioned quietly. She placed a soft kiss on Noah's shoulder. "I...saw the scars on your back, too."

They had faded with time, but the lash marks there were still somewhat visible. He didn't want to talk about it anymore.

"I need for you to know that if anything comes out of what happened between us, I want to be there for you," Noah said.

Looking up at him, she bit her lip. "You mean if I'm pregnant?"

"It's a possibility, Mercer. I'd stand by your decision, whatever it is. But if there *was* a child, I'd want to be there for him or her. I'd want to be the father I didn't have. Not that someone with the St. Clair family's resources needs someone like me—"

She sat up and turned to him. "If a baby resulted from what we did, Noah, I wouldn't expect anything from you that you didn't want to give. But I'd definitely be keeping it. The truth is... I've wanted a child for a while now." Tucking her honey-blond hair behind her ear, she hesitated before speaking again. "The treatments Jonathan had with his first bout of cancer made him sterile."

She didn't look at Noah. Instead, her fingers worried at the sheets that were tucked around the globes of her breasts. "He was in remission for two years before the cancer returned. The surgery and second round of treatments made him..."

She swallowed, not finishing her statement. She didn't have to. He understood.

"We were unable to have physical relations for more than a year before he died," she confessed quietly, a soft anguish on her features.

Noah's chest tightened. Mercer was a beautiful, vivacious young woman. He knew that she had loved her husband, but it had also cost her a lot. He ran a finger gently over the bruise that the seatbelt had left, unable to not touch her. "So, we put an end to your dry spell tonight."

"I mean, I *do* want a child but I don't want you to think that I was trying to—"

"Use me as a stud service?"

She actually laughed, and he was glad for it.

It was all that Noah could do to not make love to her again. Still, his heart felt heavy despite the soft curves that were snuggled against him. Things seemed calm now, but he worried that they were simply in the eye of the storm. His job was to keep her safe. He couldn't let himself think beyond that.

"My three hours are up." He kissed her temple as he held her in his arms. "Close your eyes and try to get some sleep."

CHAPTER TWENTY

"HOW IS SHE?" Mark asked, worried, as Samantha descended the curved staircase inside the Big House. He had been pacing in the home's wide foyer.

"Olivia took a sedative but I don't think it's doing much." Walking to where her husband stood, she slid her hand up his arm. "Anders is sitting with her now."

After learning what had happened, the family had set up camp here yesterday. Anders and Olivia had driven up from Charleston and spent the night, in fact, insisting that they all needed to be under one roof at a time like this. Olivia had convinced herself that the police would find Mercer overnight. When they didn't, she had grown increasingly despondent.

"Mom's had anxiety attacks before," Mark said. "Do you think that's what this is?"

There was a tightness around Samantha's eyes. "If it is, she has good reason."

"Yeah," Mark agreed hoarsely. They all did.

At the sound of Carter's voice in tense conversation, both Mark and Samantha peered into the front parlor. Standing in the morning sunlight in front of windows framed by ice-blue, silk drapes, Carter had his cellphone pressed to his ear, his posture rigid.

"He's on the phone with his manager in LA. The film's producer, the director—they're all giving him hell," Mark told Samantha in a low voice. "The halt in production is costing a fortune, but he's refusing to fly back until we know something."

What felt like talons closed around Mark's heart once more. It was hard to believe that just yesterday morning, he had stood by as Mercer left with the detectives, on their way to hand her over to the U.S. Marshals Service and its Federal Witness Protection Program. Where she was supposed to be safe. His stomach felt rock-hard. Now, no one knew where she was or whether she was even alive. The captain of the Charleston Police Department had called Mark personally with news of what had happened, and two of his detectives had visited the family last night, letting them know as much as they did at that time. The last sighting of her had been at a diner near St. Matthews where a shoot-out had occurred. Now two men who had been posing as U.S. Marshals were deceased and Detective Beaufain was in serious condition with a gunshot wound to the abdomen. The vehicle Mercer had fled the diner in with Noah Ford had been located early that morning, wrecked and abandoned in a floodplain near the Upper Santee Swamp.

According to witnesses at the diner, three vehicles had been in pursuit of their car. It went without saying that it was Lex Draper and his allies.

Sheriff's deputies and other law enforcement were combing the area for them, the police captain had assured Mark. Everything they could do was being done. But Mark figured that the men who wanted his sister dead were out there looking for her, too, unless they had found and killed her and Noah Ford already. He tried to tamp down his panic, his rising grief.

But he couldn't stop the gut-wrenching images of their bodies being somewhere out there in the swamp. He passed a hand over his eyes, wanting his little sister back so badly that his heart hurt.

"They're going to find her, Mark," Samantha said. "We have to keep believing that. We can't give up hope."

Mark took a breath. He had to stay strong for the rest of them. He briefly closed his eyes as Samantha hugged him.

"I love you," she whispered.

"Where's Quinn?" Carter asked. Off the phone, he stood in the doorway between the parlor and foyer. He appeared tired and stressed.

"She's with the children in the playroom, keeping them occupied. I'm going to go make a late breakfast for everyone." Samantha touched Carter's arm. "You look like you need some sleep, Carter. Why don't you take one of the guest rooms upstairs for a few hours?"

"No, thanks. I can't eat, either, but I could use some coffee, Sam, if you're making some."

"Of course." She divided a heartfelt look between Mark and Carter. "We're going to get her back. I refuse to believe otherwise."

The men watched as she headed to the kitchen. Mark knew that Carter and Quinn had arrived from their home on the north side of town well before daybreak. Like Olivia and Anders, they had wanted to be with family. Carter had carried a sleeping Lily into the house and put her in bed with Emily. He dragged a hand through his hair, faint lines of tension fanning out from his famous, midnight-blue eyes. "How's Mom doing?"

"Not good."

It was Carter's turn to pace. "I'm going to the police station. I want to talk to the captain and the detectives again."

"If there was anything new, I'm sure they would've told us.

And your being there is just going to add to the chaos. We don't need anything to distract the police from what they're doing."

Carter threw out his hands. "I can't just sit here and do nothing! If you don't want me at the police station, then let's go up there where they found the car and look for her ourselves." He drew in a tense breath. "They found blood in the car, Mark. She could be injured. And to top it off, they're calling for heavy rain up there overnight. They're talking about flooding. That's going to impact the search." His voice roughened with emotion. "I got here too late to say goodbye to her yesterday. What if that was my last chance to ever see her again?"

Mark braced his hand on his brother's shoulder. He felt the same fear and desperation. But there were dozens of law enforcement officers and a search and rescue team with dogs already up there. He wished again that he had stepped in and kept Mercer from cooperating with the police, somehow.

Noah Ford had promised to keep Mercer safe. Mark prayed that he remained true to his word.

He couldn't help it; he thought back to two bodies that had been disposed of in the government-protected salt marsh preserve not far from here. That had been more than seven years ago. His lungs squeezed as he wondered if karma might have reared its ugly head. Chances were that if Mercer and Noah Ford were dead, their remains might never be located, either. If Lex Draper and his men had killed them, they wouldn't want the bodies to be found. The thought of his sister being executed without mercy weakened his knees.

"I'm going up there," Carter said, emphatic. "Are you coming with me or—"

He stopped as Anders appeared on the upstairs landing. Worry churned inside Mark.

"We need to call an ambulance," Anders said. "Olivia's having chest pains."

IT HAD BEEN a night for dreaming. But while Noah had warred with his past in his own troubled subconscious, after she had fallen asleep, Mercer had dreamed of Jonathan.

He had been standing on the beach at sunset, dressed in slacks and a loose linen shirt, looking the way he did before illness had ravaged him. She had called out to him from a distance but he merely smiled at her, the breeze ruffling his salt-and-pepper hair. Then he lifted his hand in a goodbye wave before turning and walking off across the sand.

Mercer now lay alone in a strange bed. With a sigh, she sat up with the sheets tucked around her naked body. The lamp on the bureau had been snuffed out, leaving the room in grainy darkness. She ran a hand through her mussed hair, guessing that it was morning based on the chirping of birds outside. Rising from the bed, she took the top sheet with her and wrapped it around herself. She noticed that Noah's weapon was missing from the nightstand, although her wedding rings remained, their delicate, serpentine chain pooled around them. Thinking again of Jonathan, a lingering guilt washed over her, but she left the rings where they were for now.

Last night with Noah seemed like a dream itself, a hazy, erotic interlude that had been a respite from the mayhem that had taken over her world.

Leaving the bedroom, to her surprise she came face to face with Noah in the hall. There was a little natural light coming from the cabin's front, and she figured that he had pulled back the dark window coverings she had hung over the closed blinds. He was dressed, wearing the same T-shirt and jeans from last night, although he also had on a pair of boat shoes that no doubt belonged to Detective Beaufain.

"I...was just going to the bathroom," she explained, conscious of her nudity under the sheet and feeling suddenly awkward.

He held out a mug to her. "I was bringing this to you. I left the other lamp in the bathroom. There's a bottled water in there, too, in case you want to brush your teeth."

Mercer breathed in the pleasant aroma of coffee. Last night, she had used the old-fashioned, antique French press in the kitchen. It hadn't been as difficult as she'd expected. Apparently, Noah knew how to use it, too.

"Thanks." She accepted the mug. Her stomach fluttered as Noah cupped her face, his thumb stroking gently over her cheekbone. His hazel eyes held concern.

"You okay this morning?"

Mercer nodded, a sensual warmth spreading through her at the thought of their lovemaking. Lowering her gaze almost shyly from his, she took a sip of the rich brew. "I'll be out in a few minutes."

She turned and went into the bathroom. But as she closed the door behind her, the lamplight flickering over the beadboard paneling, she wondered if her dream hadn't been Jonathan's way of reaching out to her, assuring her once more that it was okay for her to move on.

AS MERCER ENTERED the cabin's front, Noah regarded her over the rim of his coffee mug. He stood in front of the stove.

"Protein or granola bars for breakfast—your choice," he commented.

She thought of the remaining food that included a half-dozen more bars, two cans of tuna, and a few cans of chili and soup. "It's food, though, right? At least we're not having to fish for our breakfast just yet."

Mercer had dressed again in the borrowed clothing from yesterday, although she now wore her underwear underneath them. Reaching for the glass coffee press, she refilled the mug that she had brought with her from the cabin's rear. She noticed that the kitchen was tidier than she had left it last night, the dishes she had rinsed and left in the sink after dinner now washed and put away. "You cleaned up."

He shrugged. "It's an ingrained habit. I've been told I'm kind of a neat freak."

"So, you *do* have a flaw." Mercer smiled softly at him. "I was beginning to wonder."

She left the coffee that she had just poured on the counter, intending to get a granola bar from the pantry, but Noah stepped forward at the same time and their bodies brushed against one another in the tight space. With the shadow of blue-black stubble on his jaw, his hazel eyes and tousled, dark hair, he appeared rakish, almost dangerous. Looking up at him, Mercer realized that they had both stilled, their bodies still touching, caught in one another's gravity. Noah's gaze was serious and intense as he towered over her. She laid her palms against his chest, a pleasant shiver running through her as she felt his strong arms encircle her.

Her lips parting, she raised her face to meet his kiss. It was slower and more unhurried than last night.

Maybe we're both crazy, she thought, her mind dulled by his mouth and his touch. Noah's hands slid leisurely down her sides before cupping and squeezing her bottom. Her stomach fluttered as he easily picked her up and sat her on the counter's edge. He molded his hands to her breasts, sending a hot current of want through her. They remained like that—kissing, exploring one another's bodies through their clothing—until Mercer's hands slid under Noah's T-shirt to meet the warm silk of his skin.

She gasped into his mouth as he picked her up again. Her

legs wrapped around his hips as, mouths still joined, he moved with her toward the couch.

They froze, however, at the tinny crash that came from outside.

The desire that had been simmering inside Mercer morphed quickly into fear. The cans that were in the tree.

Someone had tripped the wire.

Eyes locked on hers, Noah lowered her feet back to the floor.

"Don't go out there, Noah. Please," she whispered, her pulse racing.

But he was already reaching for his weapon that lay on the kitchen counter. Disabling the safety and racking the gun's slide, he moved carefully to a window. He lifted the blinds' edge just enough to peer out.

"What do you see?" Mercer's lowered voice sounded breathy with dread.

Noah went to another window and looked out from there, too. "Nothing. There're no boats or cars. I'm going to go have a look."

Panic squeezed her lungs. "What if it's them and they see you?"

"I don't think it's them. They'd be here as a group and they wouldn't be arriving on foot. But I still want to know who or what it is. Stay here." Opening the door an inch, Noah peered out again. Then, his gun held at the ready, he walked onto the porch and closed the door behind him with a soft snick.

Mercer forced herself to breathe as she waited, her ears straining for any noise. Just a few minutes ago, they had been about to make love again. But the reality of the danger they were in had now settled over her once more like a chilling mist. She sighed in relief when Noah returned and locked the door behind him.

"It's a freaking alligator," he grumbled. "It's only about six feet, so it's relatively young."

Mercer's tone held dismay. "What's it doing up here on land?"

"I didn't ask." Noah placed his weapon on the coffee table. "I'm just glad it didn't come across the pit or those bear traps. I'd just as soon not have a pissed-off gator on our hands. They can make a lot of noise when they're injured and putting it out of its misery wouldn't be possible."

A gunshot could give them away to the men who were looking for them, Mercer realized.

"An alligator." She shook her head in disbelief. "And I thought all we had to worry about out here were armed assassins."

Noah walked to her. Taking her hands in his, she felt a pang as he lifted one of them to his mouth and kissed her knuckles. But the scare seemed to have put a damper on what they had been about to do.

"We've been missing for twenty-four hours." Mercer voiced the thought that had been niggling at her. "If Detective Beaufain survived, wouldn't he have—"

"We don't know his condition," Noah interjected. "He was losing a lot of blood. Even if he survived, chances are he might not be conscious and able to communicate yet."

She nodded, doing her best to hold on to hope.

Noah released a tense breath. "But if no help is coming, we have enough food for a few more days out here if we're careful with it."

"And then what?"

"I don't know." His features were somber. "But the one thing I *am* certain of is that these men are still out there somewhere. They wouldn't have given up this soon. There's always the risk they could find us here, but we run into them out there and we won't stand a chance. Every day we can remain in hiding increases the chance they'll give up and go."

"What about law enforcement?" Mercer attempted to reason. "I understand that you think there's someone who's been feeding Draper information, but there have to be *good* guys out there looking for us, too."

Noah frowned. "There are. But they're probably focusing on the area where we left the car and are fanning out from there, figuring that we're on foot. Draper and his group know we left by boat and the general direction we were headed."

He didn't have to say more. Mercer felt a chill.

If anyone *did* find them, chances were much stronger that it would be the men who wanted them dead.

CHAPTER TWENTY-ONE

MARK HAD BEEN LEANING against the wall in the Charleston hospital's corridor, but he straightened as he recognized Detective Durand traveling past him. Mark had met him just the night before since he was one of the interim leads assigned to the investigation in Detective Beaufain and Detective Ford's absence.

"Detective Durand," Mark called out, halting him.

"Mr. St. Clair." There was surprise in the other man's voice as he waited for Mark to reach him. They shook hands. "What brings you here?"

"My mother, unfortunately." Mark felt a heaviness inside him. Once the small medical center in Rarity Cove had determined that Olivia hadn't had a heart attack, they'd sent her here by ambulance to the larger hospital for more thorough testing. "She had a pretty severe incident this morning. They're running some tests."

The detective appeared sympathetic. "God. I'm sorry."

"Thank you." Mark clasped the back of his neck. "Is there anything new in the search?"

"Unfortunately, I haven't received any new information." Durand shifted his stance to allow a nurse pushing an EKG cart to pass. "Detective Garber—you also met him last night—is taking part in the search and rescue mission with the Sumter and Calhoun County Sheriff's Offices. I'm sure he'll be in touch the second there's news." Appearing distracted, he looked down the hall before speaking again. "I apologize, but you'll have to excuse me, Mr. St. Clair. I'm actually here on business."

"Related to the investigation?"

"I'm here to speak to Detective Beaufain, hopefully. He's awake. From what I understand, he's extremely groggy but able to communicate somewhat. I plan to ask him if he knows anything that could aid us in finding Detective Ford and your sister."

"I won't keep you then, Detective. Please keep my family updated."

"I hope things turn out all right with your mother." Durand took a few steps on the shiny, tiled floor before turning back to Mark. "Your family's been through the wringer as of late. I guess I always thought that bad things didn't happen to people like you."

"People like me?"

Durand shrugged. "You know, being well-off, I mean. No disrespect intended. My wife and I spent our twelfth anniversary at your hotel, by the way. It's quite the place. It's a bit rich for a detective's blood, but she wanted to go all out."

He turned again and went down the hall. Mark stared after his departing figure before shifting his gaze to the increasingly gray, late afternoon that was visible through the hospital's plate-glass windows. Overhead, an intercom system paged a doctor to Oncology. Mark knew that he should get back to the waiting room to be with his family, but he felt on edge and needed to do something besides just sit.

Apparently, this was the hospital Detective Beaufain had

been helicoptered to after the shooting. It made sense, since it was one of the region's level one trauma centers. It also explained the number of police that Mark had noticed gathered in the hospital's lobby when they had arrived earlier. Briefly, he rubbed a hand over his burning eyes. Detective Beaufain had been shot at the diner before Mercer had vanished with Noah Ford. Chances of him knowing anything useful was a long-shot, but he had to hold on to something. He thought again about the strange comment that Detective Durand had made. At the least, it was tone-deaf considering his family's current plight.

"Mark."

He turned to see Carter approaching as others in the corridor —medical staff and visitors alike—stared openly at him. Carter had been in the ER waiting room with the others, but they had been sitting in back in a semi-private alcove. Mark took a tight breath and prepared himself.

"I came to find you." Carter seemed oblivious to the buzz of conversation that was focused on him. "You need to come back with me. The doctor's ready to talk to us about Mom."

STANDING in the lamplight in the kitchen, Noah removed one of the remaining bottled waters from the pantry. They would have to boil water soon for drinking. They would also need to refill some of the used plastic bottles and take them with them if they decided to set out. Taking a sip from the bottle, he lifted a corner of the window covering, opened the blinds a half-inch and peered out into the slate-colored dusk. He had been outside earlier, and the air had felt pressurized and heavy with impending rain.

Mercer came up behind him. She slipped her arms around

his waist, her body pressed to his. Her nearness seemed to calm some of the tension running through him.

Another day had nearly passed and no help had arrived.

"You're quiet, Noah," she said softly. "What're you thinking about?"

When he didn't respond, she slipped her fingers inside his. Noah allowed her to lead him to the couch where they sat together.

"According to Ty, there's a ranger station about five miles from here," he said. "With the cuts in federal spending it hasn't been manned for several months, but there's a chance there may still be a radio there that we could use to call out. I'm thinking that we should take a chance and hike to it. On Monday or Tuesday, depending on when our food runs out." Noah's throat tightened. "If Ty hasn't sent anyone by then, he won't be."

Mercer touched his knee, and he swallowed before continuing.

"We'll be less likely to be seen if we use the trees as cover instead of taking the road. If the station doesn't have what we need, we'll keeping heading south. The closest town is another three miles down."

Mercer appeared worried.

"Hey," Noah said softly. Hoping to lift her spirits, he bent his head closer to hers. "Remember back when you were complaining about not getting exercise? This'll be your chance."

Mercer released a soft breath before speaking. "I know we have to leave here at some point, but we're going to be okay," she said as if trying to convince herself. Her eyes searched his. "We *have* to be, don't we? We wouldn't have made it through everything that's happened..." Her voice faltered. "...for things to end badly."

Noah stared down at her fingers that were still tangled with his. Mercer's hands were finely boned, her fingers slender and elegant, and he once again felt a nearly overwhelming need to protect her. It reminded him of how he had felt when he had been a kid, trying to protect his mother and sister from the man who should have cared the most about them. Just like then, despite his outward bravery, he was worried, too. What he *hadn't* told Mercer earlier was that he had been thinking about the number of bullets left in his gun. Six. There had been six men on that dock yesterday. If they ran into them out there, he would have to make every one of those bullets count.

Noah looked at the cabin's door, which he had barred from the inside using two sets of eyelet screws, a hand drill, and two steel bars that he had found in the toolshed. The bars could be slipped off the door easily to allow them to exit, but they would keep out anyone who tried to enter, for a while. He had taken on the project earlier today. He had to stay busy or his thoughts came crowding back in on him.

He wrapped his arm around Mercer's shoulders and drew her to him. "We're going to be okay," he whispered into her hair.

She settled against him, her head on his shoulder. At least they had this. They had now. The first pings of rain hit the roof over their heads and thunder rumbled, ominous and low.

Storms around here could be wild, unpredictable things. Noah hoped that it was just the weather exacerbating his worry.

But he couldn't shake the feeling that something bad was coming.

CHAPTER TWENTY-TWO

"RELAX, BROTHER—"

"Don't call me your fucking brother!" The voice coming through Lex Draper's cell phone vibrated with rage. "I didn't have a choice in this!"

Lex smirked. Everyone had a choice.

"I'm done this time. You hear me?"

"You're done when I say you are." Disconnecting the phone, he bit down on a smile, maintaining his usual poker face before turning to the others. The men—five of them—sat around a table littered with beer cans and pizza boxes, taking a break after a long day of scouring the water and surrounding land. The house they were currently camped out in, a rundown split-level not far from the lake, belonged to a sympathizer to their cause.

"Well?" Mike Larkin—known as *Big Mike* since he stood at six-foot-five—narrowed his eyes inquisitively before spitting a brown stream of tobacco juice into an empty beer can.

"He came through again," Lex confirmed. "They're ours."

He moved his gaze to Lonny Cure, another of the men. "Get in touch with your contact at the county registrar's office. We need coordinates on a remote lake property. The owner's name is Beaufain."

"The county offices are closed by now," Lonny said.

Walking to the table, Lex picked up a slice of pizza from the greasy cardboard box. Making a face, he tossed it down again. "So? He'll find a way to get us what we need if he wants to get paid."

Scraping back his chair and reaching into his pocket for his cell phone, Lonny wandered out to make the call.

Lex looked around at his crew. When he was made the new leader of The Brotherhood—and he believed that he *would* be once the old man was six feet under—he vowed that everyone in this room would be rewarded for their loyalty.

Soon, his *loose ends* would be all tied up.

Taking out the witness would be merely business. But the cop who was with her was a different story. Killing *him* would be a pleasure. The pig had taken out two of theirs. Lex's stomach soured as he ruminated on the men who had died at that diner, both new recruits who had wanted to prove their devotion to him. Noah Ford would pay well for the blood he had spilled.

Thunder boomed like battlefield cannons overhead. Lex glanced out the window at the tattered rebel flag that flapped from a pole in the rain. It was barely visible in the iron-gray gloaming.

Eight inches were expected overnight, according to the weather reports. But Lex saw it as the perfect conditions for hunting. He absently caressed the butt of the Smith & Wesson .22-caliber firearm holstered at his side. He and his men had so far eluded the sheriff's deputies who were out there. That was because they were covering the land fanning out from the site of the car crash while Lex and his men had been south of them. He knew that the lawmen—like the government pussies they were—

would call off their search and take shelter indoors until the rain stopped.

By then, his work would be done.

Lex looked once again around the room. These men would share in his power. They would be the knights of his very own round table. He cleared his throat. All of them stopped their conversation and looked at him like eager bloodhounds waiting for their master to let them off leash.

"Get your rest now," Lex told them. "We're hunting tonight. And this time, it'll be by car."

CHAPTER TWENTY-THREE

THE RAIN HAD GROWN HEAVIER with nightfall. Seated on the couch, Noah listened as it beat a hard staccato on the cabin's roof. His fingers stroked through Mercer's hair as she slept, her head in his lap. Although he was currently the one keeping watch, she hadn't wanted to sleep in one of the beds alone so she had ended up here, curled onto her side, one cheek pressed into Noah's jeans-clad thigh.

Her wedding rings lay on the coffee table. They had made love again earlier that evening, right here on the couch, an impulsive thing that seemed almost as much about giving one another comfort as it did sating their shared desires. Noah recalled how his hands had settled at the swell of her hips as she straddled his lap and eased herself down onto him with a throaty gasp.

He would let that image carry him through these next few hours.

Noah remained as he was, simply watching her sleep until a sound—somewhere off in the distance—made its way to him through the rainfall. Cars. His skin prickled with foreboding.

They were coming down the long, dirt road that led to the cabin, their engines growing louder as they approached.

"Mercer, get up. Now!" Adrenaline catalyzing him, Noah swiftly moved her to a sitting position.

As he stood and snatched his weapon from the end table, she blinked at him in confusion, apparently still caught in a web of sleep. But a second later, her eyes widened and filled with fear as she heard the approaching cars, too. Noah slid on his shoes as Mercer stood and quickly did the same. There was a chance that Tyson had sent someone to help them, but the twisting in Noah's gut told him that wasn't the case. The bag of aluminum cans in the tree came down with a crash as the cars roared into the clearing. Their engines died and car doors—six of them—opened and slammed closed.

"Noah...oh, God." Mercer's breath rasped out of her.

His mind raced. He didn't have enough ammunition to wage a standoff. They *would* get inside here eventually. Their approach had been fast and deliberate, indicating that they had learned of their location, not just stumbled across it. A numbing sense of doom pressed down on him. Still, he touched Mercer's face. "Do everything I say, all right? We're going down to the crawl space."

The quiet outside the cabin—there was nothing now but the hard fall of rain—tightened his lungs. Moving to the crawl space's entrance, Noah peeled back the rug and lifted the hinged door. Mercer climbed down the ladder. As Noah began to follow, he flinched at shattering glass, his heart jumping. A crude incendiary device—a *Molotov cocktail*—had been thrown through the window, the bottle breaking as it hit the floor and bursting into flames that quickly spread outward and leapt onto the blanket that had been nailed to the top of the window frame.

Noah had been wrong about them coming inside. Their plan was to force them out or burn them alive.

Unable to take the lantern since its glow would be seen through the cracks between the crawl space's boards, Noah closed the door over his head as he descended, placing them in inky darkness. He had counted off the steps down here the day before and it served him now. Hunkered over, unable to stand to full height due to the low ceiling, he swept away cobwebs with his gun's barrel as he moved blindly to the space's rear, its dirt floor muddy from the rain that had leaked in. Mercer remained close behind him, her breathing fast and shallow and her fingers latched onto a belt loop on the back of his jeans. Once they reached the cabin's rear, Noah felt the boards until he located the loose one. He moved it an inch and peered out through the downpour. His stomach hardened. One of the men was back there, keeping watch. They most likely had the place surrounded. The man was armed and water dripped from his yellow poncho and baseball cap, his silhouette made visible by car headlights. They illuminated the trees and brush behind the cabin so that if anyone tried to leave using the dirt path, they would be seen. Two other cars to the right of the cabin's rear also faced out with their headlights pointed in different directions, creating another wide swath of light. Noah watched as the man headed to the toolshed with his gun at the ready and opened the door. Whether his intent was to look for anyone hiding inside or to determine if there was anything valuable to take, Noah didn't know. But either way, it was his opportunity.

"Stay here," he whispered to Mercer.

He couldn't see her features in the dark, but she grabbed his free hand and fervently shook her head. Still, Noah slipped his fingers from hers. With the fire above them, they couldn't stay here in the crawl space for long.

Now or never.

He moved the board away and climbed out. The cold rain was a shock on his skin as he moved quickly and soundlessly to the shed. Pressing himself against the structure's front beside the open door, water running from his hair into his face and his heart slamming against his ribs, Noah waited as lightning speared the sky.

A second later, the man walked out.

Noah swung the barrel of his gun as hard as he could, striking the man in the side of the head. He fell to the ground, unconscious. Noah hit him again, needing him to stay out. He dragged him back into the shed and out of sight, then wedged the door closed with a steel bar through its handle.

Confiscating the man's gun and tucking it into the back of his jeans, Noah looked to the cabin. The fire hadn't broken outside of the structure yet, but there was no doubt that it was being engulfed on the inside. He motioned to Mercer, who emerged from the crawl space and ran to him. Noah looked to the cars, wondering whether any of their keys had been left in the ignitions. But the option of going over there to find out was quickly taken away as voices could be heard through the downpour. Men were coming around the cabin's right side. One of them was giving orders to check the windows. It sounded as though there were three of them, which—based on the sounds of the slamming car doors—meant that two were unaccounted for.

Grabbing Mercer's hand, rain beating down on them, they took the path between the cabin's left side and the shed. But they didn't get far before Noah saw another of the bright yellow ponchos through the trees farther out, as well as the beam from a flashlight. Another of the men was searching the woods here. He and Mercer both dropped to the sodden earth. The scent of tall, wet grass around them, Noah searched desperately for some way out.

"Can you swim?" he whispered.

Her face went a shade paler, but she nodded. Noah kept his

voice hushed. "When he turns back to the woods again, we stay low and try to make it to those bushes up there."

That would give them a view of anyone who remained at the cabin's front. They waited, still lying on their stomachs until the man who was searching this side of the woods turned away from them with the flashlight. Noah and Mercer sprang up and made a run for the bushes' cover as lightning again lit the sky.

Kneeling with Mercer behind the foliage, thunder cracking like a gunshot above them, Noah squinted at the cabin's front. The glow from the cars' headlights made it possible to make out the sixth man. He stood behind the shelter of a large tree with his gun trained on the front porch, waiting for anyone who emerged. Flames were now visible through the shattered front window and black smoke billowed out.

Noah toed off his shoes and Mercer did the same.

"When I say go, we're going to slip into the water and swim under the dock," he instructed, keeping his voice low. "It's high enough, so there should be an air pocket underneath."

Her expression tense, Mercer gave a tight nod.

They would hide there until the men left or Noah saw a chance to climb onto the pontoon boat and get the canoe back into the water. The pontoon would be faster and Noah had the keys on him, but the start of its engine would draw attention and he didn't think there would be time to get far enough away before the hail of bullets began. Removing the confiscated weapon from the back waistband of his jeans, he handed it to Mercer, who tucked it into the back of her shorts. Noah did the same with his own gun, preparing to swim.

He peered through the rain at the man who stood guard at the cabin's front. Just like the one at the shed, he couldn't take him down with gunfire without giving their location away. He needed a diversion. Feeling around on the wet ground, he located a heavy, palm-sized stone.

Noah pointed to an area about ten feet from the dock. "We'll wade in there," he whispered. "The water's shallow at first but it drops off fast."

Mercer's eyes were large and frightened, but she wiped the rain from her face and again nodded her understanding.

His breath bottled inside his chest, Noah threw the stone. His aim was good. It hit an aluminum trashcan on the far side of the cabin's porch, creating a loud clang. It got the man's attention, who walked off in that direction with his gun drawn. Noah took off to the swollen water bank with Mercer close behind. They waded in until their feet no longer touched the lake bottom and then swam under the water's black surface. Noah came up for air when his hand met the dock's side. Heart pumping, he looked back as Mercer's head popped up above the rain-roughened water a few feet behind him. The dock was fixed, not a floating one that rose and dipped with the lake's depth, and he prayed that even with the rising water there would still be enough air underneath it.

A thunderous explosion rocked the night, causing Noah to look back to shore. His lungs squeezed. The fire had reached the cabin's propane line. Orange flames licked upward from the structure's shattered windows, lighting the area and reflecting off the lake. Noah could see Mercer as she treaded water beside him. Her blond hair was matted to her skull, her breath coming hard. He pointed downward, indicating where they would go next. Then, filling his lungs with air, he dove down into darkness, coming up seconds later under the dock. Mercer's head broke through the water's surface a few moments after his. Noah wiped at the water on his face as they both clung to one of the dock's algae-slicked support poles. There was still an air pocket between the water and the dock's underbelly, but not as large a one as Noah had hoped. His chest tingled, aware that if it continued raining at the current rate, the water would keep rising and they wouldn't be able to stay here.

The fire on shore created thin fingers of light between the wood planks above their heads.

"What if the alligator's still here?" Mercer whispered fearfully.

Noah had already considered that. Hopefully, it had moved on. He kept his voice low. "I haven't seen it around. Compared to what we're facing up there, I'll take the odds."

They clung to the pole in a charged silence for what seemed like forever. Noah's clothes—jeans and a button-front shirt borrowed from Tyson's dresser—were weighted by water, making him work harder to remain afloat. Mercer's shorts and top were lighter, but she still appeared at the point of fatigue. Her teeth chattered. Noah was cold, too. Although the South Carolina autumns were mild, the water under the dock was untouched by the sun and the hard downpour had dropped the temperature further. The deluge of rain drummed on the wood planking above them, accompanied by the roar and crackle of the fire as it continued to consume the cabin. The air around them smelled like wet ash and smoke. Noah hoped that someone was close enough to see the fire or have heard the explosion, that it had been reported to the authorities. But their arrival could still take more time than they had.

The rain showed no sign of relenting, putting their hiding place in jeopardy.

A pain-filled scream reached them over the fire's roar. It sounded as though it was coming from the woods behind the cabin. Noah's eyes met Mercer's as she bobbed beside him in the grainy darkness.

Someone had stumbled over a bear trap.

That left four men.

Noah's head bumped against the planking, confirmation that

the water was rising. He estimated that the distance to the far end of the L-shaped dock where the pontoon was located was about forty yards.

"Stay here," he told Mercer. "I'm going to swim to the pontoon and try to get the canoe out. We might be able to use it to get away."

Her hushed words held panic. "Don't leave me here, Noah! Please!"

"There's no point in us both taking the risk out there—"

"Why can't we stay under the dock and make our way to it together?"

"Because there's netting strung up farther down to keep out debris. When I reach it, I'll have to come out from under the dock and swim underwater the rest of the way to the pontoon. If I can get the canoe into the water, I'll come back for you. We can cling to its sides until we're far enough out, then figure out a way to get into it."

"You mean if they don't see you trying to get to it and kill you first! Don't do this!"

"I don't have a choice," Noah said hoarsely. "The water's rising. You can see that. Our air pocket's gotten thinner in the fifteen minutes we've been under here. We can't stay."

As thunder boomed again overhead, his eyes held hers for several strained seconds. Then, jaw set, he dove under the water.

CHAPTER TWENTY-FOUR

HIS LUNGS CRAMPING, Noah broke through the water's surface at the pontoon's stern. Holding on to the engine, he caught his breath. Although he couldn't see the cabin from here, the orange glow filling the sky indicated that it was now fully engulfed. At least it had provided enough light for him to see his way through the murky depths. Gray ash floated on the water around him and the air hung heavy with smoke.

Quietly, he pulled down the pontoon's ladder, climbed onto its narrow swim platform, and crawled into the body of the vessel. Padded bench seating and railings on the boat's sides provided partial cover, as did the sunshade and raised helm where the captain's chair was located midway to the bow. Staying on his knees, Noah could now see the flames that licked hungrily at what was left of the cabin. The sight made his blood run cold. Taking his gun from the back waistband of his jeans, he poured water from its barrel.

He squinted through the rain at the men, four of them, standing on shore with their backs to him, their voices caught within the fire's roar. Doing his best to stay out of sight, Noah pulled the tarp from the canoe. He would have to push it out, and he hoped that any scraping or splashing sounds it made would be drowned out by the fire's noise. His sodden clothes stuck to his clammy skin and water snaked from his hair, blurring his vision. Without standing, it was harder to push the canoe. Remaining on his knees, his muscles straining with the effort, it began moving slowly toward the stern.

The voices coming from shore became clearer. Peering cautiously over the railing, Noah tensed. Two of the men were now walking toward the dock. He dropped his head below the railing again. A few seconds later, anguished screams filled the night. Both men had fallen into the pit that Noah had dug and camouflaged. He felt no sympathy. With each pointed stick he had whittled, he had been thinking of Tyson and what this group had done to him, what they wanted to do to Mercer. As the men's cries and curses pierced the air, Noah heard the shouts of the remaining two as they realized what had happened.

The diversion was his best chance to get the canoe into the water. But it also meant that he would have to stand, at least partially, to turn it on its side to get it past the engine. One end of the canoe had reached the pontoon's stern. Noah's heart hammered as he raised up enough to use his body weight to turn the canoe. He had managed to work it halfway past the engine when another bolt of lightning split the sky, illuminating the pontoon. A second later, his heart clenched as a bullet hit the vessel's aluminum railing, creating a shower of sparks. Noah let go of the canoe and reached for his weapon. But before he could return fire, another shot echoed into the night. He fell backward into the pontoon, his upper left arm burning as if it and the cabin were one.

The air left his lungs as shockwaves traveled through him, trying to shut his body down. Footsteps thudded on the dock. Noah ground his teeth, attempting to clear his vision. Blood, bright red and glistening, bloomed high up on his shirtsleeve, below his shoulder. His gun. It had flown from his grasp. He searched desperately for it in the shadows.

One of the remaining men spoke. "Stay here and make sure no one leaves this dock."

Noah's heart squeezed as Lex Draper peered over the pontoon's railing, a scowl on his hard-featured face and rain dripping from the brim of his cowboy hat. The barrel of his gun was pointed at Noah's chest as he stepped on board.

"Where is she?" he demanded, his voice a low growl.

Noah spotted his Glock. It lay several feet away, just under the crumpled edge of the tarp that had concealed the canoe. Trying to push through the pain, he reached for it but Draper kicked it away, then picked it up and tossed it overboard. It went into the water with a heavy plunk. Noah cried out, black spots filling his vision as Draper viciously kicked his wound.

"I know she's around here somewhere, *pig*. You're going to tell me where."

HER WORLD TURNED OVER. Clinging to the dock's support pole, Mercer pressed her fingers over her mouth to contain the sob lodged inside her throat.

Noah. *Oh, God.*

Had he gone down in the gunfire? She could hear the low drone of men talking above her. But then a hard tremor passed through her at the voice that called out to her.

"Show yourself, sweetheart, or he's a dead man!"

Mercer's heart dropped into her stomach. She knew the monster shouting to her was Lex Draper.

"Come out now or I'm sending him to meet Jesus—"

"She's not out here! And you're going to kill me, anyway!"

Noah. Mercer swallowed hard. He was still alive. He sounded weak, but she knew that he had raised his voice because he wanted to make certain that she heard him.

You're going to kill me, anyway.

Her jaw clenched in terror. He was trying to tell her that he was a lost cause. To remind her that she had to stay under here until the men left or the last thin space of air was gone. The tears that had been welling in her eyes slipped down her face as her body shook uncontrollably in the cold water.

"Where is she, asshole? You got her stashed out there in the woods somewhere?"

Noah's moan of pain tore at her. Draper was hurting him.

"Come on out, baby doll! The longer you stay out of sight, the longer he pays for it!"

She heard Draper speak again.

"Go to the car and get my hunting knife. This cop's lying here like a fish, so we might as well gut him. He'll start talking soon enough."

Mercer tried to keep breathing but her lungs wouldn't obey. The footsteps that sounded above her indicated that the man Draper had given orders to was leaving. But he would be returning soon with a knife.

Do something!

The second gun. Mercer nearly gasped in realization. After swimming under the wood planking, she had taken it from the back waistband of her shorts and laid it on a narrow ledge created by the dock's construction. Her mind raced along with her runaway pulse. There had been two gunshots fired above her, but she had no way of knowing if either had come from Noah's weapon. Had his worked after being submerged? Would this one? She reached for the gun and drained the remaining water from its barrel. It felt heavy in her trembling fingers. Something brushed her leg as it squiggled past her in the water, but she had to ignore the revulsion that swept through her. Mercer squinted in the darkness at the menacing weapon, then disengaged what she guessed to be the safety as footsteps sounded again on the dock.

"Big Mike bled out." The approaching man's voice was thick with emotion. "That stick hit an artery. Lonny and Paul are hurt bad, too. You make sure that fucking cop feels this blade, Lex!"

If Mercer attempted to swim out to get closer, there was little doubt that she would be seen before she ever got a chance to aim the gun. But she could at least try to stop the man above her. Stop him from delivering his instrument of torture.

A silent prayer on her lips, Mercer let go of the support pole. Cycling her legs to stay afloat, she held the gun tightly in both hands and pointed the barrel upward. She waited, shivering hard from fear and cold, until the sound of footsteps indicated that the man was directly above her on the dock.

She pulled the trigger and fired.

The gun discharged with a deafening explosion, raining down wood fragments and the unexpected force of the kickback submerging her. Her insides sank as the gun slipped from her cold-numbed fingers. Mercer came up a second later, gasping and coughing, her head knocking against the wood planking above her in the ever-thinning air pocket. A high-pitched buzz filled her ears. But the man who had been above her had fallen into the water. She bit back a scream. Through a gap in the dock's siding, she could see him just a few feet away as he sank below the water's surface.

The buzz in her ears receded, replaced by thudding footsteps moving rapidly closer. Mercer looked up through the shattered wood. Her heart turned sideways as Lex Draper glared down at her. Quickly submerging herself again, she kicked away but still felt the water's current as a bullet whizzed past her. She dove downward and began swimming into the dark abyss under the dock, going low enough to touch the lake's floor. Her heartbeat thundered in her ears as Draper continued shooting down through the wood planks, trying to guess where she was. Seconds later, Mercer's heart suffered another hard jolt. She'd run into the netting that Noah had warned her about, the murky water making it hard to see. She turned and kicked away from it, but panic zinged through her as something held her back.

Her foot had gone through a hole in the slimy, ancient netting, anchoring her into place.

Oh, God.

Lungs begging for oxygen, Mercer fought frantically to work her foot free as bullets continued striking the lakebed around her. When finally, her foot slipped out, she tried to go back the way she had come, but the netting had unfurled around her. She must have partially torn it down in her struggle to free herself.

Please, God, help me!

Battling her way out of it, her need for air now so strong that her vision had begun narrowing into a tunnel, she accidentally came up on the outside of the dock instead of under it. Even as her instincts kicked in and she gulped precious air, grief clawed at her.

Her life and Noah's would end here.

Mercer dared to look over her shoulder. Terror speared through her. Draper stood in the driving rain on the dock above her, a victorious smile on his hateful face as he aimed the gun.

His chest exploded into flames.

What was happening? She blinked in stunned confusion as Draper howled and stumbled backward. It was as if fireworks were shooting out from his body, as if he were being electrified from the inside out. Screaming, he disappeared off the dock's other side. Treading water, still in disbelief, Mercer greedily inhaled the cool night air.

She turned again in the water. Noah stood inside the

pontoon. The flames from the cabin illuminated the glistening blood just below his left shoulder. His face was pale.

"Noah!"

Swimming to the pontoon's stern, Mercer used the ladder to climb up. She squeezed past the canoe that lay on its side, wedged between the larger boat's railing and its engine. Her heart froze. Noah now sat in the pontoon's hull, his back against one of the padded benches. What looked to be a brightly colored sidearm lay beside him. Mercer knew from her own boating experience that it was a single-use flare gun that he had discharged into Draper's chest. The seat of another of the padded benches was lifted upward. Various boating supplies were located in its compartment.

"Noah! God!" Mercer fell to her knees beside him, terrified by the blood soaking through his shirt. At her touch, he swallowed, his voice hoarse.

"We've...got to make sure Draper's dead."

"Of course, he's dead!" Mercer's throat tightened. Noah's skin was cold. Too cold. "You shot that flare into his chest! I shot the other man, too! He fell into the water!"

He tried to get up, but she wouldn't allow it.

"I need to see Draper," he persisted.

"I'll go look then, all right?" She peered at the spot where Draper had last stood. "His gun is on the dock. He's got to be in the water, too."

She didn't want to leave Noah. Still, she rose on wobbly legs and stepped from the pontoon onto the dock. The man she had shot was no longer visible in the water, and she imagined him on the lake's floor. Mercer forced herself to go farther. Wiping rain from her face, she avoided the bullet-shattered wood planks as she crept to the other side of the dock. Her heart squeezed in tightened beats. Draper floated just beneath the water on his back. Bubbles escaped his mouth as air left his lungs, and the gruesome cavern in his chest still glowed with green light. One hand pressed against her stomach, Mercer carefully picked up his gun. On shore, she saw two men hobbling toward one of the vehicles that was parked at the edge of the clearing behind the burning cabin. Both had bloody pant legs and one had his arm wrapped around the other's shoulders for support. They got into the car. The engine started, the car's tires spinning in the wet earth before gaining enough traction to speed off.

Mercer returned to Noah, who had managed to stand again inside the pontoon, one hand braced on the railing.

"Draper's dead," she confirmed, although her voice quivered. "And the last two men just left by car. They're both wounded. Noah, you need to sit back down."

"That leaves the one in the shed. We need to be sure he's still there." Noah closed his eyes briefly, as if to gain his equilibrium.

Mercer worriedly touched his uninjured arm. "I'll go look for you."

"I have to go with you this time. If he got out, it could be..."

They both stilled at the sound of an approaching engine. Mercer's wet skin prickled with apprehension. But it wasn't a car this time. The noise was coming from the water. Noah took Draper's gun from her as an airboat equipped with a spotlight lit the dock. But a moment later, he lowered the weapon as they heard recognizable voices calling to them.

Mercer nearly sagged with relief. "It's Remy and Tom!"

That meant that Detective Beaufain must still be alive. The approaching boat seemed to glide over the lake's roughened surface before coming to a stop beside the dock as the engine was cut.

"That Draper?" Remy asked, looking at the submerged but still glowing body in the water as he stepped from the boat onto the dock. Both he and Tom wore rain gear. Lightning lit the sky as rain continued to fall.

Noah nodded as they approached. "It's over."

Tom stepped onto the pontoon. Carrying a first-aid kit, he eyed the blood that soaked the entire upper portion of Noah's shirtsleeve. "You need to sit down before you fall down, Noah. Let's get you under that awning."

He helped Noah to the sunshade-protected captain's chair. Mercer followed.

"Hold this for me, Mercer." Tom handed her a flashlight. She took it and shone the light so that he could use the medical scissors he had taken from the kit to rip open Noah's shirtsleeve all the way up to his shoulder. Noah cursed softly with the action. Shoving her sodden hair back from her face, Mercer released a tense breath upon seeing the small round hole in his left biceps that oozed blood.

Remy remained on the dock. "How bad does it look, Tom?"

"Appears to be a flesh wound. It's bad enough, though." Tom continued to examine the wound. "Through and through to the biceps."

Mercer adjusted the light as he inspected the back of Noah's upper arm. Her stomach clenched as she looked at it, too. The bleeding was worse there.

"Entrance is clean but the exit left a bit of a mess. It doesn't appear to have hit an artery but it's too close to the brachial for my liking." Reaching for an item in the first-aid kit, Tom peered sternly at Noah over the bifocals he had put on under his rain hat. "You're bleeding pretty good. I'll patch you up here as best I can but we need to get you somewhere ASAP."

"There're two cars here," Mercer said.

Water dripped from the brim of Remy's hat. "The airboat will be quicker. The boat will let us take the most direct path, as the crow flies, back to the Southside Marina where we're parked. As soon as we're back in cell coverage, we'll call for an ambulance to meet us there."

He stared at what was left of the burning cabin. "Draper and his men do that?"

"Three are dead and two got away, but one might still be here." Noah frowned at Tom's ministrations. "I locked him in a shed out back, unconscious. He's unarmed but I don't know if he's still out cold or even still in there."

"On it." Removing his gun from its holster, Remy went down the dock, sidestepping the splintered holes Draper's bullets had made.

"Watch for the pit when you step onto land," Noah warned.

"You mean the one with a giant, dead guy in it?" Remy called over his shoulder. "Hard to miss."

"Don't go outside of the clearing!" Noah yelled to him.

Tom removed a roll of sterile gauze from the kit.

"Mercer, tear me off some strips of medical tape," he directed. She struggled with it in her wet hands, but managed the task.

"Ty's alive, then. He told you where to find us?" Noah winced as Tom pressed a large wad of gauze into the exit wound to occlude it. Mercer blanched inwardly but refused to look away, her concern for Noah too strong.

Tom wound more of the gauze around Noah's biceps. "Your partner is in serious but stable condition back in Charleston. He was helicoptered there for surgery. As soon as he regained consciousness and was able to clear his head enough to call, he tracked down Remy and told him where you were. He also warned us that you'd have this place booby-trapped."

Tom took a strip of tape that Mercer handed him and used it to secure the gauze in place. Blood was already seeping through it.

"We got the coordinates for the property, drove up here, borrowed that airboat from a pal, and headed out." Tom's expression was wry. "We figured you could use help. Although based on the body count around here, I'm not so sure."

"You okay?" Noah asked Mercer as Tom went back to the airboat, taking the first-aid kit with him.

"I should be asking you that," she replied softly. Her insides churned, however. Tiredly, she squeezed her eyes closed, opening them only when Tom returned with two blankets—the kind with waterproof backing to help keep someone dry. He slipped one around Noah's shoulders and the other around hers. Mercer hadn't realized how hard she had been shivering. Noah was, too. Outside the pontoon's sunshade-protected area, rain still fell in sheets. The fact that so far, no emergency personnel had arrived even with the blazing fire indicated just how far out they were.

"Bastard's still out, but he's breathing," Remy announced upon returning. "I've got him trussed up like a Thanksgiving turkey. That ought to hold him until we can get the authorities out here. Can't take him with us since the airboat only holds four. We could take the pontoon, but the airboat's faster and I'm more worried about you, Noah, than his sorry ass." Remy's rugged features appeared serious for once as he looked at Noah and Mercer. "Let's get you two out of here."

He assisted Noah in getting to his feet. "You okay to walk? You're not feeling lightheaded?"

"I'll make it."

Remy's voice roughened. "You know you're like a son to me, Noah."

"Me, too," Tom added. Mercer's heart pinched at their spoken affection.

"*Semper Fi*," Noah said somberly to both men.

"*Semper Fi*," they repeated.

CHAPTER TWENTY-FIVE

WEARING a hospital gown over his still-damp jeans, Noah lay in a curtained cubicle on a gurney inside the emergency room, his wound cleaned and dressed. He had received two units of blood to replace what he had lost and an IV line was currently delivering a strong round of antibiotics. His left arm had been placed in a sling to immobilize it, although he had declined pain medication other than a localized anesthetic. Tom was right; the shot had been clean, bypassing arteries and bone. The attending ER physician had marveled at just how lucky Noah was.

Remy stuck his head inside the cubicle. "The cafeteria's not serving breakfast for another half-hour, but they have coffee. Think they'll let you have a cup in here?"

"I'm good, but thanks. Where's Mercer?" It was early morning, based on the wall clock.

"She's with the sheriff's deputies."

Noah had spoken with them while he had been worked on, until the physician had strongly suggested they wait until she was done. They had left him and gone to speak with Mercer, apparently, although Noah figured they would return soon. He would also be debriefed by his own department. In fact, he would have to be cleared by an internal affairs board, standard procedure when there was an officer-involved shooting.

"It looks like the two men who left the lake property are dead," Remy said as he took a step inside the cubicle. "One of the deputies told me an accident was called in just a few miles from there. The car matches the description of the Mustang you gave them. Looks like the driver lost control at a high rate of speed, went off the road and crashed head-on into a tree. From what the deputy heard from the first responders, the driver had a pretty gruesome injury to his calf that probably wasn't a result of the crash. You said that one of your traps injured him. You think he might've passed out behind the wheel from blood loss?"

"Maybe," Noah said. "Are the local authorities at the cabin now?"

"More like what's left of it. They've also got the guy we left in the toolshed in custody. Two of the deputies are bringing him here for treatment. The fire marshal and coroner's office are up there, too, although they're going to have to bring in divers to recover the bodies from the lake. I figure some of your men are headed up there, as well."

"Mind if I borrow your phone for a while?"

Digging into his jeans pocket, Remy handed it over. "You should also know that Mercer called her family a little while ago. Her brothers are on their way up." He chuckled as he headed out. "Carter St. Clair showing up here ought to get this place buzzing."

Thinking of Mercer, Noah swallowed and stared at the inside of his arm where the IV needle had been inserted and taped into place. She had taken a life last night. He suspected how badly it was affecting her. She had appeared nervous and drawn when he had last seen her inside the ER before they had been separated. The hospital was small—only sixty beds—and wasn't equipped to handle major injuries, which was no doubt why Tyson had been helicoptered back to Charleston.

Noah punched Tyson's number into the phone. But it was Lanny who answered it, her voice low.

"Lanny, it's Noah."

"Noah, I didn't recognize the number. I'm so glad you're okay —I just heard."

He wondered if Lanny knew yet that the cabin had been destroyed. "How's Ty?"

"Sleeping. Do you want me to wake him?"

"No, but I'd appreciate it if he would call me at this number when he wakes up, if he's up to it. If not, I'll be by to see him, hopefully soon. How's he doing?"

Lanny's soft sigh held worry. "The doctors think he's mostly out of the woods now, but it's going to be a slow recovery. I spent the night here last night. I'm getting ready to go get the girls—a friend's staying with them—and take them to school. I'm trying to keep up as normal a front as possible."

"I'm here to help in any way that I can, you know that. Lanny...has Ty spoken to anyone from the department since the diner shooting?" Noah was still trying to figure out how Draper and his men had discovered their whereabouts. "I'm wondering if he told anyone on the force where we were."

"Well, he didn't tell anyone in front of me. He didn't even tell *me*, as a matter of fact. Police have been congregated here, as you'd expect, but the doctors wouldn't let anyone in to see Ty until yesterday afternoon. Even then, he was pretty out of it."

"Do you know who saw him?"

She recounted a number of detectives and higher-ups who had come by in her presence.

"Did anyone see him alone?"

"I don't think so. They were coming by in pairs or small groups, at least while I was here. But I went home to be with the girls after school. I came back around eight last night, so I don't know who might've been here while I was out."

They talked for a few more minutes, then Noah gave his best wishes for Tyson's recovery and disconnected. He had a few more calls to make. After he completed them, he leaned his head back against the gurney and closed his burning eyes. When he opened them again a short time later, Mercer was there. She stood quietly watching him.

"Sorry. I think I drifted off for a few minutes," Noah said.

"It's understandable. It's finally stopped raining, by the way." She came closer to him, her concerned gaze on his wrapped arm inside the sling. "How badly are you hurting?"

"I'm not looking forward to the anesthetic wearing off," he admitted.

"Didn't they give you something for pain?"

"I didn't want it. I have things I need to do."

"Noah, you need to rest," Mercer admonished. "I heard the doctor say that she wants to keep you overnight. They're moving you to a room as soon as one opens up."

Even under the harsh fluorescent lighting, her hair hanging limply around her shoulders and Tom's oversized raincoat over her wrinkled, damp clothing, Mercer still managed to somehow look appealing. But she also appeared fragile.

"Mercer...what happened out there, what you had to do, has to be weighing on you," Noah observed gently as she bit down on her lower lip. "Taking a life is never easy, even if—"

"I did it to protect *you*."

Still, he saw the shadows in her eyes. Noah felt an ache in his throat. "Did a doctor see you?"

"While you were being treated. They gave me a couple of injections. Antibiotics and a tetanus booster, I think. It was precautionary since I'd been in the water with some cuts."

Noah noticed that she now wore hospital-issued slippers on

her feet, just as he did. They had both arrived at the hospital barefoot.

"I called Mark," Mercer said. "He and Carter are on their way here."

"Remy told me."

"I'm sorry if I broke some kind of protocol, but I needed to let them know as soon as I could that I was okay. I didn't want to wait for someone from the police to contact them." She paused, her expression troubled. "My...mother was hospitalized in Charleston yesterday."

"I'm sorry. Is she all right?"

"They think she will be. Her sodium and magnesium levels were really low, which can be dangerous, but the tests ruled out any heart issues." Mercer absently smoothed the gurney's sheets, her voice fraying. "I think she just let herself get overwrought because of me. She'd been worried enough about my situation, but the last few days were just too much for her."

Noah's hand briefly covered hers on the gurney. He saw her swallow.

"You should know that the two men who drove off from the cabin are dead," he told her.

Mercer blanched slightly. "What happened?"

"They lost control of the car they were in. It left the road and hit a tree."

"And the man we left behind in the toolshed?"

"He's in custody. Deputies are bringing him here for treatment. The local authorities are up at the lake property now, processing the scene."

She seemed to take the information in. "So, what happens now?" she asked quietly.

"With Draper dead, there won't be a trial, of course. No one has any reason to come after you now. And even if they did, Draper's faction within The Brotherhood are all either dead or on their way to prison. The Charleston Police will want to formally interview you about what happened out there, but I'm certain you'll be cleared of any wrongdoing so you don't need to worry. You're free to leave with your family when they get here, if you want. It looks like you'll make that oyster roast at the St. Clair, after all—"

"What about *us*, Noah?" Mercer interjected in a hushed voice.

Just then, a uniformed deputy stepped inside the curtained-off area. He was among the ones that the ER physician had chased off earlier.

"Excuse me, Detective Ford. The doc says that she's finished with you for now. While you're waiting to be admitted, we'd like to go ahead and finish our conversation. I'm supposed to take you back there." He indicated a corridor through the open curtains. "We're in a conference room."

The deputy's timing left a lot to be desired. Unable to answer Mercer with the man standing there, Noah's eyes held hers for several heartbeats. Then, repressing a sigh, he sat up and dropped his legs over the gurney's side, but the deputy held up a hand to halt him.

"Whoa. They're bringing in a wheelchair."

"I don't need it," Noah argued.

"It's policy," a nurse in brightly colored scrubs announced as she arrived with the wheelchair. "Saddle up, Detective. I'll roll your IV stand along with us and make sure your line doesn't get tangled. You've still got a half-bag to go."

Noah carefully slid off the gurney and sat in the wheelchair. He flinched inwardly as the movement sent a flash of pain through his stiff biceps. As the deputy began to roll him out, Noah looked again at Mercer. There were things he wanted to say to her, but not with others around them and law enforcement officers waiting to debrief him down the hall.

"I'm glad your family is on the way," he rasped as he was rolled past.

MERCER SAT TENSELY on a vinyl-upholstered bench in the ER's waiting area, a foam cup of now-cold coffee on the low table in front of her that also held a collection of spiraled-out magazines. The antiseptic smell of hospitals had always unsettled her, but it was doubly so now. Her body felt wired, as if she were stuck in *fight or flight* mode. She could still feel the hard kick of the gun she had fired, could still see Lex Draper's body as it sank beneath the water's surface.

Staring blindly at an artificial ficus tree in the elevator bay, Mercer touched the space on her chest where her wedding rings typically lay. Regret mingled with her disquiet. In the rush to escape the cabin, she had left her rings behind. Could platinum melt? Had the inferno left anything intact? Unable to fill her lungs completely, she bowed her head and passed a hand over her eyes.

"Mercer!"

She looked up to see Carter entering through the hospital's automatic sliding doors. He was moving briskly toward her, past the medical staff and others who were staring at him. The strap of a leather tote bag hung over his shoulder. It no doubt held the clothes and shoes she had requested that he and Mark bring with them. Mercer stood as Carter reached her and she went into his arms.

"Mercer, thank God! Are you all right?"

She nodded. "Where's Mark?"

"He's parking the car." Carter's concerned gaze roamed over her. "Have the doctors checked you out?"

"They did. I'm fine."

He handed her the tote bag. "Quinn went to the bungalow. I hope what she picked out is okay."

Mercer pushed up the sleeves of the oversized raincoat she wore over her still slightly damp clothing. The ER had been chilly, and Tom had offered her the coat. "Considering my current state of dress, I'm sure whatever's in here is perfect."

"I thought I'd never see you again." At the emotion in his voice, Mercer touched Carter's arm. He frowned as he glanced around. "Are you all alone? Why isn't someone here with you?"

"It's over. Draper's dead. I'm no longer in danger. And I haven't been alone. Two of Detective Ford's friends were here with me until just a little while ago. They're the ones who helped us get here tonight. The authorities are likely to have more questions for me at some point, but for now I'm free to go."

"Where's Detective Ford?"

"He's being interviewed by local law enforcement." Remy and Tom had wanted to take Mercer to the cafeteria with them for breakfast, but she had politely declined, preferring to instead stay here to wait for Mark and Carter. Admittedly, she had also hoped to see Noah again before leaving the hospital.

She wondered what he would have said to her if they hadn't been interrupted.

What about us, Noah?

Mercer anxiously scraped a hand through her hair, regretting that she had asked the question. She reminded herself that Noah was wounded. He was also being interrogated about what had happened at the diner in St. Matthews and at the fishing cabin. The authorities needed to know the details leading up to the deaths of all those men. She understood that he had a lot of work ahead of him to close the investigation. For now, she would go with Carter and Mark. If Noah wanted to see her, talk to her, then he would.

"Merce?"

She realized that Carter had been speaking to her, but she hadn't been listening. "I'm sorry. What?"

"Are you sure you're all right?"

"I'm fine," she repeated, although just like the first time she'd said it, she wasn't completely certain that she meant it.

Medical personnel and hospital visitors had begun to gather nearby. Based on their excited demeanor, it was clear they hoped to meet Carter as well as take selfies with him since most of them held their cell phones. Still, they were waiting at a respectful distance and hadn't interrupted their reunion.

"Go be nice to your fans, all right? Mark just came in."

Carter glanced to the crowd. With a soft sigh of resignation, he affectionately clasped Mercer's shoulder before heading off. A moment later, she found herself in Mark's embrace.

"You're a sight for sore eyes," he said once he released her.

With a weak smile, Mercer tucked her hair self-consciously behind one ear, aware of her disheveled appearance. "More like a sight that would hurt your eyes."

"Never," Mark said. "Let's get you to a seat."

They stepped back to the bench where she had been waiting earlier. Mercer placed the tote bag that Carter had given her on the tiled floor and sat. Behind them, Carter talked with the crowd as he posed for cell phone cameras and signed autographs. Mark sat down beside her. "Can I get you coffee? Something to eat?"

She shook her head. "That's my coffee on the table, and thanks, but I don't think I'm capable of eating just yet."

His features hard, he looked around. Like Carter, he asked, "Where's Detective Ford?"

She placed a hand on Mark's knee for emphasis. "None of what happened is his fault, Mark. He kept me safe just like he promised he would. He saved my life more than once through all this." She felt a lump form in her throat. "If I'd been with anyone else, I don't think I'd be here talking to you right now."

"What happened out there?"

She couldn't help it. Her eyes misted. When Mercer had called her family, she hadn't given much detail, mostly telling them that she was safe, where they could find her and that Lex Draper was dead. Apparently aware of her duress, Mark put his arm around her and pulled her against him. "It's okay. We don't have to talk about any of this right now. I just want to get you back home. Anders called on the way up. They're going to release Mom sometime later today."

Mercer's heart lifted. "That's wonderful news."

"She knows you're safe now." Pausing, Mark swallowed as he looked at her. "I'd been trying to brace myself for the worst news about you, but I just couldn't do it. I can't imagine our family without you. You're its heart, you know."

Carter returned, his face serious upon seeing Mercer wiping at her eyes.

"Let's get her out of here," he said to Mark.

Standing, Mercer picked up the tote bag. "I just need to go change first..."

She stopped speaking, her stomach doing a small flip as Noah appeared from the corridor. He wore a clean shirt and sneakers with his jeans, his left arm in the sling. The cut on his temple had been re-bandaged, as well. He still appeared pale, however. She wondered where the shirt and shoes had come from. As he approached, Mercer worried that Mark and Carter would take him to task, but to her relief Mark stepped forward and shook Noah's unencumbered hand.

"Thank you for getting her back to us, Detective Ford," he said.

"I'm sorry to have put all of you through hell these last few days, Mercer included."

Carter shook Noah's hand next. "Thank you, Detective. I'm Mercer's brother—"

"I know who you are, Mr. St. Clair." Noah glanced at the crowd of medical personnel and others who were still gawking. "I'm pretty sure the entire world does."

Carter lowered his voice. "There're times like this that fame isn't all it's cracked up to be. And please, call me Carter."

"I think it's time you started calling me Mark, too," Mark added.

"May I have a word alone with Mercer?" Noah asked. "It'll only take a minute. I know you're anxious to get her back home."

Her heart beat harder. Mercer turned to her brothers. "Why don't you wait for me outside? I'll come out to the car after I've changed."

Mark and Carter headed toward the automatic, glass doors. Through them, Mercer was aware that sunlight had begun to break through the clouds that had brought last night's heavy rainfall. Before her brothers could exit, Carter was once again stopped by more fans. Apparently, word had spread about his being here.

"That must get old." Noah was looking at the commotion. But Mercer didn't want to waste what little time they had talking about Carter. She could tell by how Noah was dressed that he was ignoring the doctor who had wanted to admit him. Her voice held censure.

"Since you're not in a wheelchair and a hospital gown, I'm assuming that you're going against medical advice."

"I'm fine—"

"You're *not* fine." She frowned at him. "You signed yourself out, just like I was afraid of."

He sighed softly. "There're some things I have to take care of that can't wait. For one, I need to talk to the arrestee from the lake property—he's upstairs now. I'm just waiting for them to run an MRI on him. After that, I'm catching a ride with Remy and Tom back to Charleston."

Mercer fought the urge to argue. Without pain medication, she suspected that Noah was hurting. She noticed that he held his arm in the sling carefully. "Where'd you get the shoes and shirt?"

"A deputy offered them to me. We wear about the same size. He had his dry cleaning and his gym bag in the trunk of his cruiser and took mercy on me. I'll get them back to him."

Mercer indicated the tote bag she held. "I have fresh clothes, too. Mark and Carter brought them." Putting the bag down again, she shrugged out of the raincoat. "Can you give this back to Tom for me?"

Noah accepted the garment. They both took a step back so that two paramedics pushing a gurney with an elderly woman on it could roll past.

"It looks like The Brotherhood's taken another hit," Noah said. "I checked my messages at the precinct and had one from the federal prison in Estill. Orion Scott had a stroke last night. A bad one. The scans indicate he's brain-dead. They're preparing to take him off life support."

They stood there as more people passed by, doctors in white coats and scrubs-clad nurses.

"Is that why you wanted to talk to me?" Mercer asked thickly. "To let me know that the man responsible for starting all this is getting what he deserves?"

"I *wanted* to make sure you're all right." Noah laid the raincoat on a nearby chair and stepped closer, his voice low. "You've been through a lot, Mercer."

She felt a shimmer of electricity as he took her fingers in his and lightly squeezed them before letting go. It was a discreet gesture, one that wouldn't be overly noticeable to the others around them. Mercer glanced over her shoulder. Carter was still occupied with fans and Mark was in conversation with someone wearing a white lab coat.

"I'm sorry that the deputy walked in on us earlier," Noah said. "We *do* need to talk, but now isn't the time."

Mercer could only nod as her eyes searched his. Then she lowered her gaze. Uncertainty once again weighted her chest.

He took a step back. "Enjoy being with your family. I know how relieved they are."

"Have you called Corinne yet?" she asked.

"Yeah. Oh..." Noah dug into his jeans pocket. "With everything going on, I almost forgot."

A soft gasp escaped her as he withdrew the chain that held her wedding rings.

"I took them off the table at the cabin before we went into the crawl space." Noah pooled the delicate chain in her palm.

"Thank you," she murmured, her heart pinching. She was relieved to have the rings returned to her. But it also felt a little as though he were releasing her back to her world as it had been before he had come into it. Reminding herself that she wouldn't push for anything, she blinked and swallowed hard.

"Please take care, Noah," she urged softly. "You should be in a hospital bed right now. I know you think that you're invincible, but you're not."

As they stared at one another, Noah seemed to falter in the silence that engulfed them. Then, picking up the raincoat, he indicated the nearby restrooms. "Take care, too, Mercer. You should get changed. Your family's waiting. I'll be in touch."

She watched numbly as he turned and went down the corridor.

CHAPTER TWENTY-SIX

NOAH NODDED to the two armed deputies as he left the hospital room, albeit without any new information. The arrestee—the man he had knocked out at the toolshed—had been uncooperative, refusing to divulge anything, including how his group had discovered where he and Mercer were hiding. The man's responses to questioning, in fact, had been a repeated *fuck you, pig*. Despite his own wound, Noah might have had a more physical response to that if not for the medical staff hovering nearby.

He had, however, taken pleasure in letting the man know that he was going away for a long time. In addition to his role in Draper's plot, he was wanted on two warrants. The deputies who were stationed there to guard him would be taking him directly to booking as soon as the hospital released him.

"You look like something the cat dragged in—after he played with it," Remy commented when Noah stepped off the elevator and into the hospital's main lobby.

"You sure you don't want to take the doc's advice and stay here?" Eyeing Noah worriedly, Tom folded the raincoat that had been returned to him earlier over one arm. "A day of enforced rest would do you some good."

"I need to go." Noah had a filled prescription for painkillers in a paper bag from the hospital pharmacy. But just as he had explained to Mercer, there were things he needed to take care of before he allowed himself to sink into a fog.

Thinking of Mercer, Noah felt uncertainty tug at him.

There was no doubt that he had feelings for her, that he was even probably in love with her, but he had been reminded once again that morning that Mercer was indeed a St. Clair. Just a short time ago, Noah had stood in the waiting area with one of South Carolina's wealthiest families, one of them an A-list, Hollywood star. While being treated in the ER, Noah had even heard one of the physicians commenting that he had gone to medical school on a scholarship that the family provided in Harrison St. Clair's memory.

As Noah traveled with Remy and Tom through the lobby toward the parking lot, he heard someone call his name. He turned to see a tall, angular male with a badge and gun on his hip traveling toward him. Even from a distance, Noah recognized the badge as belonging to the U.S. Marshals Service.

"I'll meet you outside," Noah said to Tom and Remy. He tossed the pharmacy bag to Remy and the two men continued on without him, verbally sparring with one another as they went through the glass doors and outside.

"I figured it was you because of the sling," the marshal said when he reached Noah. "That and you have a cop's look about you. I received a report on what happened out at that cabin from the local authorities. How're you feeling, Detective Ford?"

"I'll live."

"I hear that." The man had thinning, ash-blond hair and appeared to be in his early forties. "I'm Jeff Emerson with the U.S. Marshals Service."

"Fool me once," Noah deadpanned.

"I can assure you that you've got the real deal this time." He reached into his back pocket to produce his shield, but Noah halted him. There was no longer a need for imposters.

"That's all right, Marshal. I'll take your word for it. How can I help you?"

"I just wanted to introduce myself and say hello, for now. I *will* have questions for you about what happened at the diner in St. Matthews in particular, but that can wait until you're feeling better. I'm here now to speak to the arrestee upstairs."

The clink of coins being put into a vending machine and the corresponding clunk of a soda can as it dropped down could be heard from a nearby alcove. "Good luck," Noah said. "I didn't get anything out of him. And from what I hear, he has a lawyer on the way. Not that it'll do him much good considering his record."

"Let's hope that's the case. You should know that we conducted a raid on The Brotherhood's compound yesterday."

"That'll make two within the last two weeks," Noah told him. "We conducted one ourselves in an unsuccessful attempt to find Lex Draper."

"At least you got your man last night."

Noah asked the question that was on his mind. "What about the marshals those men at the diner were impersonating? Did you find them?"

Emerson's features hardened. "They're both dead. We're still trying to piece things together. They were supposed to meet up in the field this past Thursday to travel to St. Matthews to rendezvous with you and Detective Beaufain. Both died in their homes from carbon monoxide poisoning in the early morning hours."

The news felt like a gut-punch to Noah. "Did they both live alone?"

"Yes, thank God. Or else we could be talking about entire

families right now." Emerson glanced to a man using a hand sanitizer stand that stood just inside the hospital doors before continuing. "Our theory is that once our men were incapacitated by the carbon monoxide, Draper and his group got into the homes —probably wearing gas masks—and stole the badges and IDs. They replaced the ID photos with those of the imposters. I've seen the doctored IDs. Someone did a professional job on them, right down to the authentication seal across the photos. You shouldn't worry that you missed some sign, Detective."

Noah told him what had eventually given the imposters away —the money clip that bore a similar design as the ring Draper had worn at the art gallery.

His stance wide, Emerson crossed his arms over his chest. "What we want to know is how the group knew the specifics—the where and when of the rendezvous point, who the assigned marshals were and their street addresses."

"I want to know the same thing. I'm still working the investigation from our end in Charleston. I would appreciate any sharing of intelligence."

Emerson nodded. "Of course."

"Draper was able to learn the identity of my eyewitness to a shooting that kicked all this off." Noah felt the need to be up front. "I thought then that there might be a leak within the Charleston Police Department."

"So, you think someone on your own force might've fed the group information?" Emerson lifted an eyebrow.

"I'm just saying that it's possible." Noah adjusted his sling, his upper arm throbbing. "It's just a theory at this point. I have no proof. But if I'm right, someone on our side wouldn't know where your men lived. That information would be classified to the U.S. Marshals Service."

"What're you saying, Detective?"

"I'm saying there might be a leak within your organization,

too. If Draper could get to someone on the Charleston PD, he could get to one of yours."

"I'll take it under advisement." Emerson pursed his lips together before speaking again. "You should know that within our ranks you're considered a hero for taking out those bastards at the diner. We lost two good men last week. It almost makes me regret that we agreed to get involved and bring Ms. Leighton into the program. We're backlogged and have a waiting list, but we jumped her ahead."

Noah looked at him. "You *agreed* to take her in?"

"Your captain requested it. My understanding is that some favors were called in to move her up." Emerson took a step back. "It was nice to meet you, Detective Ford. You did a hell of a job out there keeping your witness alive. Now if you'll excuse me, I'm hoping to have a chat with this asshole upstairs before the attorney shows up to shut things down. By the way, do you know what happens to a lawyer when you give him Viagra?"

"No," Noah said.

"He gets taller." With a wry smile, Emerson turned and walked to the elevator bay. Noah headed outside, his mind grappling with what he had been told. Captain Bell had clearly stated that the order to hand Mercer over to the Marshals Service had come from outside their department. Noah had just walked through the automated doors and outside when the cell phone he carried in his back pocket burst into a popular country music song. The phone was Remy's—Noah hadn't yet returned it. He reached for the device and peered at its screen. His heart felt a bit lighter as he saw the incoming number. Noah answered.

"Heard you burned down my cabin, Noah." Tyson sounded weak, but his tone was still familiarly acerbic.

Standing in the parking lot, Noah blew out a breath. "Yeah. About that..."

"You know I'm just messin' with you. It ain't on you. I know who I have to thank for that." Tyson's voice was rough and raspy, probably due to medical intubation.

"It's good to hear you, Ty."

"You, too. Know what else is good? This is over and we're both still breathing. So is Mercer Leighton."

As Tyson spoke, Noah stared across the parking lot at Remy and Tom, who were still in conversation and seated at a bench at a picnic table near a large magnolia tree. Tom's Jeep was parked nearby. Both men had slid on their sunglasses due to the now sunny sky.

"You back in Charleston?" Tyson asked.

"Not yet, but I'm headed that way."

"You come see me as soon as you can. All I've been getting is secondhand information. I want to get the details of what happened out there straight from you."

"Ty...Lanny told me that when the Cap came to see you yesterday, he was with Adkins and Bushnell," Noah recounted, referring to the police commissioner and the deputy chief of police.

"You know these *wounded cop* things." Tyson paused, his cough sounding painful. "They're a real dog and pony show. Higher-ups have to get in on the act."

"Did Bell see you alone at all?"

The airwaves went silent for several moments. "Now that you mention it, I think he did. Either that or I was dreaming. My memory is fuzzy. I was pretty stoned from all the pain meds, but I do recall him coming back by for a while."

Despite the sun on his shoulders, the hair on Noah's nape prickled.

"Why? What's this about, Noah?" Tyson asked.

"Did you tell him where Mercer and I were?"

"No, man. I didn't tell anyone but Remy when I called him."

Noah frowned. "Are you sure?"

"I wouldn't do that, considering things." Tyson hesitated, however. "At least I don't think I would've. But I *was* higher than a Georgia pine."

Noah paced a tense step, the phone to his ear. "Do you remember anything that you and Bell talked about? *Think*, Ty."

Thoughtful silence ensued again. Then, "It's real foggy, but it seems like we were talking about fishing."

CHAPTER TWENTY-SEVEN

"REMEMBER that time you took off in Dad's speedboat?" Mark directed an amused look at Mercer as they sat at the long, mahogany dining table inside the Big House with the rest of the family. Samantha had prepared dinner in honor of Mercer's safe return.

Mercer smiled despite the flush that she was pretty certain had crept onto her cheeks. Mark was preparing to tell one of his favorite stories about her, one of the few times in her youth that she hadn't walked the straight and narrow line her parents had set. "Do you really have to bring this up again?"

"Oh, he does." Carter smiled as Lily sat on his lap, nibbling on a yeast roll slathered in butter.

"And this wasn't just any speedboat," Carter recounted for the benefit of those who hadn't heard the tale before. "It was Dad's 1958 Riva Tritone. It was originally Grandpa Aiden's. That thing was a work of art—twin six-cylinder engines, 170 horsepower, and seafoam green leather seating. It looked like something you'd see Cary Grant boating around in."

"Mercer was fourteen." Mark passed the large platter of

handmade crab and shrimp ravioli in a rich cream sauce down the table. "We had three other watercrafts at our disposal, not to mention jet skis, and what does Mercer do? She loads Dad's vintage boat up with her girlfriends, sneaks it out of the marina, and takes off down the coast."

Laughter sounded around the room. Emily sat beside Mercer, and she played with a lock of her niece's blond hair.

"It had the best deck for sunbathing," Mercer argued. "And I'd had my boater education card since I was twelve." She shot a look at her brothers. "You both know that I know my way around a boat."

"Not that day, which makes the story even funnier," Mark replied.

Handing Lily off to Quinn, Carter picked up the tale again. "Anyway, Mark and I get this panicked call from Mercer. The boat wouldn't go. They had its engines running and straining, but they couldn't get it back to shore."

"We took another boat out and spent over an hour looking for them," Mark said.

"Obviously, you found them." Samantha smiled as she rearranged a stem in the table's centerpiece that was comprised of bush sage and asters from the Big House's fall garden. Ethan stood beside his mother, his head leaned on her shoulder. He had gotten bored with being seated and had been given permission to get up from the table.

"Merce and her friends spent the afternoon working on their tans," Carter said. "When they got ready to head back, no one remembered that they'd dropped anchor. It's a miracle they didn't burn the engines out."

Despite the ribbing she was receiving, Mercer warmly recalled how her brothers had tried to lecture her about the dangers of going nto open water, but neither of them had been able to keep a straight face, in disbelief that she'd made such a rookie mistake. It had also been the summer before Mark had left for college in Atlanta, the last summer that he and Carter had been close before the rift between them that had ended up lasting more than a decade.

"We got the boat back to the marina." Carter gave Mercer a wink. "She begged us not to tell Dad, since he had given all of us orders never to touch that boat. We didn't tell him what she'd done, but we made her work for our silence. She was our personal maid and errand girl for the rest of the summer."

Mark chuckled. "I've never had a car that clean since. I was having her wash it twice a week."

"You children were terrible, keeping secrets from us! That boat was your father's pride and joy." Despite her feigned dismay, Olivia was laughing, too. Mercer's heart lifted at the sound. Anders had driven Olivia here once she had been discharged from the hospital. Samantha had offered to move the dinner party to her and Anders's home in Charleston, but Olivia had insisted that Mercer needed to be here on the St. Clair property tonight. And while Olivia was supposed to be on bed rest, she had stubbornly refused the bed in the guestroom, not wanting to miss the family get-together. "I swear, Harrison pampered that silly boat more than he did me."

Laughing as he sat beside Olivia, Anders put his arm around the back of her chair.

"What happened to the boat?" Samantha asked. "I've never seen it."

Quinn shook her head, her fork poised over the porcini mushroom raviolis on her plate that had been prepared as a vegetarian option. "I haven't, either."

"It's on permanent loan to a museum in Charleston. It's part of a decade-by-decade *Yesteryear* exhibit. It belongs there. It really is a work of art." Mark wiped his mouth with a linen napkin, then replaced it in his lap. "They say Prince Rainier of Monaco had one just like it."

As the group went back to finishing their meal, the conversation turned to other topics. But everyone at the table continued to avoid asking Mercer questions about what had happened during the time she had been missing. No one wanted to break the festive mood and she was grateful for it. All she wanted to do right now was be in the presence of her family. She looked around the table, trying to imprint these moments forever in her mind.

Perhaps someday, they would replace the darker things that had been embedded there.

"COME SIT WITH ME, DARLING." Olivia patted the spot beside her on the camelback sofa in the home's rear parlor. The children played nearby while Mark and Carter stood in rapt discussion in front of the French doors that led into a sunroom. Samantha and Quinn were in the kitchen, cleaning up after dinner. Mercer had done her best to pitch in, but she'd been shooed out, her sisters-in-law reminding her that she was the guest of honor and forbidding her to help.

"How're you feeling, Mom?" Mercer asked, concerned that Olivia was pushing herself too hard.

"Much better, now that I have you back." She slipped her fingers briefly inside Mercer's. As always, Olivia's hands were perfectly manicured and she wore several rings, including the large sapphire that Anders had given her. Mercer thought of her own wedding rings. She had made the thoughtful decision not to put them back on. Instead, they were tucked inside her jewelry box back at the bungalow. After returning home and having lunch in the hotel dining room, Mark and Carter had dropped her off there so that she could shower and take a long nap. But Carter had ended up staying with her, watching television in the front room while she slept as if he feared she might disappear again.

"You should be in bed, you know," Mercer admonished her mother.

Olivia smiled. "And eat upstairs on a TV tray all alone? I wouldn't have missed this for the world—my family being together again after so much uncertainty."

"We could have come to Charleston."

Olivia shook her head, her silver bob swaying with the movement. "No. It feels right for all of us to be here in this house."

Mercer's gaze grew unfocused as bittersweet memories took over. It was little surprise to her that she was feeling emotional. Clearing her throat, she asked, "Where has Anders gotten off to?"

"He's outside on the porch, taking a call from Mary Lynn." Mary Lynn was Anders's daughter who lived in Falls Church, Virginia. "They're coming to visit over the children's fall break. It's going to time perfectly with the hotel's oyster roast." Olivia looked at her sons. "Carter's going back to Hawaii tomorrow to finish up filming, but he hopes to be back in time for it, too. Quinn and Lily are staying here this time. All that flying back and forth with a little one is difficult. I also think Quinn's starting to feel a need to nest with this pregnancy."

"She told me they're staying here." Mercer was reminded of the way that she and Noah had made love without protection, but she quickly pushed the thought away. Based on where she had been in her menstrual cycle, the chances were small that she was pregnant.

"Quinn offered to run me through some exercises and give me a massage tomorrow. I'm still a bit sore from the car crash,"

Mercer admitted. "I can always get a massage at the hotel spa, but it'd be nice to spend some time with Quinn and Lily."

"Then that's just what you should do." Olivia appeared contemplative before speaking again. "Mark says that you're not ready to talk about things. About what happened out there. In fact, he forbade me to mention it. He's always been so protective of you, especially after your father passed."

Mercer said nothing. Her mother didn't ever need to know what had transpired out there with Lex Draper and those men. It would only upset her all over again.

"Detective Ford seemed like a very nice man when I met him," Olivia said, referring to the night that Noah had been summoned to her and Anders's home on the Battery. "I do hope I get a chance to thank him for your safe return. He's quite handsome, isn't he? I mean, if you like tall, dark, and rather intense."

Mercer's hands fluttered in her lap. Olivia must have sensed her discomfort, because she touched the pearls at her throat and leaned back in apparent surprise. "What? I might be an old woman, but I still notice."

Anders appeared from the foyer. He held Olivia's jacket that matched her outfit folded over one arm. Even after just being discharged from the hospital, her mother was nothing if not put together.

"You ready to go, Olivia?" As Olivia stood and went to him, Anders held out the jacket for her to slip into. "I looked the other way tonight, but it's time for you to start obeying doctor's orders and get yourself to bed."

"Both of you *can* stay here tonight," Mark reminded.

"Thank you, darling," Olivia said to Mark as she guided her arms into the blazer. "But after that uncomfortable hospital bed, I want to spend tonight in my own."

Mercer hugged Anders and her mother goodbye. Olivia,

however, seemed reluctant to let her go. When she finally released her and stepped back, her clear-blue eyes shone with emotion. "I've prayed for you so much over these last few days. I'm so thankful we have you back."

As Mark and Carter walked Anders and Olivia out, Mercer remained behind. For a time, she watched Emily and Ethan arguing over an iPad as Lily played nearby with a doll, lost in her own imaginary world. Lily rubbed at her eyes, reminding Mercer that it was growing later, and she suspected the toddler wouldn't last another half-hour. Going down the hall, Mercer let herself out through the rear kitchen door, both Samantha and Quinn oblivious to her passage as they conversed while drying and putting away the last of the china and crystal.

Outside, there was a full moon. Arms wrapped around herself, Mercer wandered past the old carriage house and swimming pool to the children's swing set that was nestled under the gnarled boughs of an ancient live oak. Its garlands of moss swayed in the breeze that carried in from the ocean and held the scent of brine. The cheerful glow of the house behind her, Mercer sat in one of the swings, staring out toward the tumbled rocks on the shoreline and the dark plane of ocean made visible by the moonlight. The waves crashed with a rhythm that had been the soundtrack for much of her life. It seemed surreal that after living on the edge of mortal danger for so many days, she was now returned to the safety and peacefulness of her home, as if none of it had ever happened. She was free to go about her life again.

She couldn't help it. With a soft sigh of yearning, Mercer wondered what Noah was doing right now. Whether he was still working to finalize the investigation or was at home and recuperating as he should be.

She wondered when, if ever, she might hear from him.

THE FILMY GLOW from a streetlamp trickled in through the well-kept, suburban home's picture window. His muscles rigid, Noah waited in a shadowed corner of the living room as the front door opened. Captain Walter Bell walked from the foyer with heavy steps. It was late, but he still wore his navy-blue uniform with its shield and commendation bars. Not bothering to turn on the lights, he removed his gun belt, placed it on the coffee table along with his cap, and moved to a credenza upon which a collection of liquor bottles sat. Placing a death grip on a glass tumbler, he splashed whiskey into it, gulped it down, and repeated the act. Exhaling heavily, he then hung his head and braced his palms on the credenza's top.

Here, hidden away in his home, he looked like a guilty man.

As Noah clicked on the sofa lamp, Bell whirled and stumbled back a step, clearly startled.

"What the hell do you think you're doing, Detective? How'd you get in here?" Bell's face had paled with the shock. "I asked to see you at o-eight-hundred hours tomorrow morning and in my office, not here."

Noah had listened to the voice-mail message that Bell had left on his home answering machine. In it, he had expressed his relief that Noah and his witness had turned up safe and relatively unharmed. Bell had encouraged him to get some rest, then requested to see him the following morning for a full debriefing.

Bushy brows clamped down, Bell's eyes flicked to Noah's sling. "I understand you've had a rough few days, but this is breaking and entering. I don't care if you are one of my best—"

"How much did they pay you?" Noah's voice was deadly quiet.

Bell's jaw went slack.

Noah took a step closer, his hard gaze pinning the other

man's. "What does it feel like to be a traitor, Captain? I want to know."

Bell faltered before trying to adapt an air of indignant authority. "Did you get a head injury out there in the swamps, too? Because I don't know what you're—"

"Cut the bullshit," Noah snapped, an angry heat flushing through him. "I know you're the leak. You were the one supplying information to Draper all along. You turned your own men and a state's witness over for slaughter."

Bell made a move toward the coffee table where his weapon lay, but Noah stepped in his path and drew his gun. "Don't even think about it."

The bluster appeared to go out of him. Bell's eyes bugged with panic.

Holding the weapon in his unencumbered hand, Noah kept it trained on his superior. "What I want to know is why you did it. Start talking or I swear to God I'll shoot you where you stand."

Bell patted the air in front of him. "Okay. Okay! But you have to understand, it wasn't like that!"

Disgust, like bile, rose inside Noah. "Then, how was it?"

"I...need to sit down." Scrubbing his hands over his face, Bell sank slowly onto an upholstered wing chair beside the credenza. For several long moments, he didn't speak, instead rocking back and forth in silence, despair spreading over his weathered features. Then his voice thickened. "I...didn't mean for it to go this far. You have to believe me."

Noah waited tensely as Bell cupped a hand over his mouth. Slowly, he shook his head. "They found out from someone at the Fleur-De-Lis that there was a witness. They...came to me and offered money."

"Why you?" Noah's grip tightened involuntarily on his weapon. "Have you taken payouts before?"

The look on the older man's face was telling. "A long time

ago. Back when I was a beat cop, I took money from Orion Scott and Lex Draper knew about it. Draper had one of his men come to me." He took a tremulous breath. "He offered me a *lot* of money. He said all I had to do was give them her name. That I wouldn't be involved beyond that."

Noah glared at him.

"You have to understand! I *needed* the money." He leaned forward in the chair in a defeated posture. "Paula spent like a madwoman for years, trying to keep up with the Joneses. When she divorced me, she got half of everything, including my pension. I've put three kids through college. One through Harvard Law School." His voice roughened as he looked around the room's upscale furnishings. "All she left me is this house and that's only because it has a mortgage and a mile-high equity line against it. I'm paying a shitload in alimony. I still owe on loans and I'm barely able to cover the interest. I'm up to my neck in debt. The money they offered would get me out from under things." He jabbed his finger onto the shield pinned to his uniform shirt, resentment on his face. "I gave my life to this badge, and for what? Half a meager pension and some rat-infested, second-floor walkup when they foreclose on this place?"

His chin quivered. "All...he said I had to do was give them a name," he repeated in a choked whisper.

Mercer's name. Noah clenched his mouth tighter. "But this time, it didn't stop there, did it? They owned you."

Bell sighed heavily. "They knew she was gone from the St. Clair, that we'd hidden her somewhere. The man came to me again, wanting to know where she was." Looking up at Noah, Bell held out his palms beseechingly. "I tried to put a stop to it! Why do you think I didn't want to know where you were keeping her? Why I disregarded protocol and let you handle setting up her security your way? I-I thought if I didn't know, I couldn't tell them!"

Noah frowned. "Why the sudden concern for Mercer Leighton?"

"Not her. You. My men." Skin mottled, he used his shirtsleeve to wipe at the perspiration that had begun to bead on his forehead. "If Draper and his group ambushed that safe house, there'd be bloodshed."

Bell ran a shaking hand over his mouth. "But they started leaning harder on me. They threatened to rat me out to the department—"

"That's when you called in the Marshals. To get her off your hands?"

"That was my hope." Head bowed, Bell dragged a hand through his graying hair. "Turns out they have someone at the Marshals Service in their pocket, too. They found out about the transfer into WITSEC."

Noah's voice was cold with contempt. "So, they devised a plan with your help and the help of whoever their informant is within the Marshals Service."

Bell peered up at him. "As God is my witness, I swear that it wasn't supposed to go down like it did! They told me they were only going to detain the marshals until their men could meet up with you and Tyson for the hand-off. You'd have no reason to think they weren't the real marshals and the transfer would go peacefully. I-I didn't know they were going to kill anyone—"

"Other than an innocent woman." Noah seethed inwardly.

There was nothing Bell could say to that. His demeanor seemingly now resigned, his eyes reddened. "What are you going to do, Noah? You're going to arrest me like that?"

Noah understood that Bell meant in his current condition, with his arm in a sling. The wound throbbed steadily and his body nearly vibrated with exhaustion. He had barely been able to drive here. With every hour that passed, he could feel his strength ebbing away and he wondered if Bell could sense it. If he was considering trying to overpower him. It might have been foolish for Noah to come here alone, but this confrontation was profoundly personal to him. He had trusted and respected Bell for too long. The betrayal cut too deep. Noah kept his weapon trained on him.

"I'm going to keep you here until the uniforms arrive." With his words, Noah felt bitterness, as well as loss. "I'm not the only one who knows, Cap. Ty knows. I have two friends who also know. Even if you manage to get through me, it's too late. This can't be undone."

Despite everything, something broke loose inside Noah as Bell dropped his head into his hands, his big shoulders quaking with barely repressed sobs. But a minute later, he seemed to pull himself together. Noah swallowed thickly before moving to a phone console on an end table. Using the speakerphone function, he dialed 911, then trained his gun once again on Bell, who merely sat there with his shoulders slumped. When the dispatcher answered, Noah identified himself with his badge number, gave the house's street address, and requested that a squad car be sent. Once Noah disconnected, Bell stood to pour another large measure of whiskey into the glass he had used earlier, then gulped the liquor down.

"Will you let me go into the bedroom and change into civvies, at least? I'm an old man, Noah." Bell's eyes watered again as he made the request. "I...don't want to do the perp walk or go into lockup in uniform. I can't bear the shame of it."

Noah remained silent, trying to make some sense of the man he had thought he knew.

"Please, Noah," Bell pleaded, a tremor in his voice. Fatigue had settle into the pockets under his eyes. "I was your CO for over *ten years*. I was a good leader until I screwed up, wasn't I? Please? I'm begging you to let me keep some scrap of my dignity."

Noah felt the dull beat of his heart as they stared at one

another in a charged silence. Then he gave a faint nod. Bell turned and left the room. His slow footsteps echoed down the hall.

The world seemed to slow down as Noah stood in the deafening silence.

He closed his eyes as a gunshot rang out in the next room.

CHAPTER TWENTY-EIGHT

THE UNEXPECTED SIGHT of her nearly took his breath away.

Noah had answered the knock at his apartment door to find Mercer nervously biting her full bottom lip, her soft-blue eyes wide and her honey-blond hair framing her face.

"Hi," she said, although her gaze appeared uncertain. She wore a stylish denim jacket over a blouse and casual wrap skirt.

"Hi." Noah took a step back to allow her to enter.

"You're not wearing your sling. How's your arm?"

The wound was still bandaged underneath his blue dress shirt. As Noah closed the door, guilt flowed through him. Nearly three days had passed and he hadn't yet contacted her. There had been too many things going on. Things that he was still trying to process.

"It's still sore, but I got tired of only having the use of one arm," he told her. "The doc said it's okay to ditch the sling as long as I'm careful and I don't pick up anything over a few pounds. I have a follow-up appointment tomorrow morning."

Noah slid his hands into the pockets of his dark suit pants as

Mercer took in his small but tidy apartment with its spare furnishings.

"How'd you find my place?" he asked, knowing that his street address wasn't public information.

She fidgeted and scraped a hand through her hair. "I called Remy. He gave me his number and told me to contact him if I ever needed anything. I...needed to get in touch with you. You didn't return my voice-mail message. Noah, are you all right? Remy told me you were at your captain's house when he..."

As her words died away, the knot inside him grew larger. Bell's suicide had been in the news, as well as the allegations of bribery and collusion. Noah had just returned from the burial. Despite everything, it was something that he felt like he had to do. In light of the charges and the manner of death, the department had denied Bell a traditional police funeral with honors. There had been only a short graveside service with no more than a handful of police in attendance and none in uniform. Bell's family—his children as well as his ex-wife—had apparently wanted things handled as expediently as possible. The no-frills burial had taken place less than thirty-six hours following the autopsy's completion.

"I'm okay." Noah clasped the back of his neck. "And I'm sorry I didn't return your call. I mean it. I've been planning to."

Her eyes held doubt. She glanced to the sofa where his tie and suit coat had been neatly draped over its back. A paper funeral program lay on the coat's top. Mercer appeared contrite. "You just got back from the funeral. I didn't know. I'm sorry if I'm intruding—"

"It's all right. You're not."

"That must've been difficult for you. Attending the funeral, I mean. I imagine you have such mixed feelings."

Avoiding the topic, Noah took a step toward the kitchen. "Can I get you something to drink? Some water, at least?"

She shook her head, her hands fiddling restlessly with the clutch purse she held. "I'm not staying. I just wanted to check on you. I'm actually on my way to a meeting at the Charleston Area Convention Center."

"How're you holding up?" he asked. Other than the fading scratch on her cheek and bruise at her collarbone, Mercer appeared physically well. But Noah understood that looks could be deceiving. He also noticed that she wasn't wearing the chain that held her rings.

"I'm having a little trouble sleeping, is all." She played it down with a small shrug. "I've been having to keep the bathroom light on at night, but other than that, I'm okay. It seems strange, but everything is getting back to normal. What about you? Are you still working on the investigation?"

He nodded. "There're some last aspects of the case that need to be closed down."

"Have you learned anything new?"

"We got confirmation that Orion Scott gave Draper the bribe money," Noah told her. "After Scott's death, a family member reported a large amount missing from one of his bank accounts."

Mercer appeared anxious. "Do you know anything more about the marshals who were killed?"

"Both were laid to rest yesterday. My understanding is that the Marshals Service hasn't made an arrest yet, but they're zeroing in on the leak within their organization."

"How's Detective Beaufain?"

"They think he might be released from the hospital sometime next week. He'll be on paid leave for a while, and then he'll be riding a desk at the precinct for a couple of months."

They stared at one another in the late afternoon sunlight pouring in through the window, until Mercer broke the silence. She rubbed at her brow.

"I promised myself I wouldn't do this." Her soft mouth was

downturned. "That I wouldn't chase you, yet here I am. Before I throw what's left of my pride under the bus, I should be going. I just needed to see for myself that you're all right."

"Mercer," he whispered into the air, but she had already begun walking to the door, her narrow shoulders held rigidly. She hesitated before turning back to him. Her voice sounded frayed.

"You should know that I'm not pregnant."

His heart squeezed as guilt cut through him again. He couldn't let her go like this. It was wrong of him to shut her out without explanation. Noah fought past the paralyzing self-recrimination that had been gripping him.

"I...knew that Bell had a gun in the bedroom," he said roughly.

At the admission, shock appeared on Mercer's features. Noah's throat tightened. "All cops have backups. I let him go back to his bedroom alone. I knew what he was going to do. I gave him an out and I'm not sure I should've."

Dragging a hand through his hair, he tiredly closed his eyes. Mercer returned to him, her hand tentatively sliding up his arm. Her gaze was liquid with concern.

"Could you stay for a few minutes?" he asked. When she nodded, he led her to the sofa and they sat together. He released a slow breath.

"I'm sorry I haven't been in touch," he repeated in earnest. "Truly. It...hasn't been about you."

He looked at her with a searching gravity. "I *know* how I feel about you, Mercer. I've known it almost from the first moment I met you, although I did my best to fight it. I just need some time to get my head around some things."

By *things*, he meant Bell's betrayal and his own ethically questionable passivity the night he had gone to confront him. Although Noah hadn't entered out of respect for the crime scene, he had gone to the bedroom's doorway, had seen the bright splatter of crimson on the wall and Bell's sprawled body on the floor. By not stopping him from doing it, Noah felt complicit. He felt as though he had added yet another person to the body count that had begun with Lex Draper entering that art gallery. The gruesome sight of Bell's corpse joined a long list of the unspeakable things that he had witnessed in his life. As of late, it felt as if Noah was being pulled into an undertow. He had respected Bell, even looked up to him. He felt disillusioned by the career he had given his life to and what the man that he called his captain had done.

"Noah, you *are* a good person. Never doubt that." Mercer's voice soothed him. "But you have to understand that what your captain did—taking money from Draper in exchange for information—was *his* decision. He did that, not you. It set off a landslide he couldn't outrun."

Noah pensively ran a hand over his jaw, his voice low. "I should've done better. I should've forced him to face the consequences of his actions."

"If Walter Bell wanted to kill himself, he would've eventually. He would've found a way. And you couldn't have been completely certain of what he planned to do. I don't believe that." Mercer paused uneasily. "Regardless, pulling that trigger... that was his choice, too. Just like accepting the money in exchange for betraying his own men."

Noah swallowed, trying to keep his emotion in check.

"I'm glad you came by," he managed finally. "I should've been in touch. Don't think that I haven't been thinking about you. I just need some time to clear my head."

She appeared to understand, although there was pain in her eyes and her brow was creased with worry. "I don't want to leave you like this—"

"I'm okay," he assured her. "You should go to your meeting. I'm not the best company right now, anyway."

"I don't need for you to be good company." Still, honoring his wishes, she rose from the couch and picked up her purse that she had placed on a side table. "I'm a phone call away if you need me. But you need to talk to *someone*, Noah. If not me, would you consider seeing a therapist again? Just to talk some of this through? You told me that the one you saw after Afghanistan was helpful."

"It's a good idea. I'll think about it." He stood from the sofa, as well.

"We all go through rough spots." Mercer's voice was soft. "Losing Jonathan was my hurricane. But I think maybe the problem is that you've been through too many storms—bad ones—all on your own. You deserve to be happy, Noah, whether you believe that or not." She looked at him for several moments before adding, "If you're ever ready to talk about us, I'm here."

He walked her to the door. Their fingers mingled and then she pulled gently away. Noah felt the loss. As he watched from the breezeway, she went down the stairs. He recognized the black Audi sedan she climbed into as the one that had been parked in front of the bungalow the night they had packed up her things.

The car pulled onto the street and disappeared.

CHAPTER TWENTY-NINE

A COOLNESS HAD FALLEN over the beach in time for the oyster roast, which had taken place annually on the St. Clair property for as long as Mercer could recall. The crowd tonight was one of their largest, with hotel guests as well as invited locals enjoying the live music, cold beer, and seafood that ranged from oysters to Lowcountry boil. Paper lanterns were strung on wires between bamboo poles around the event's perimeter, illuminating the beach with a soft yellow glow. The ocean breeze blew Mercer's hair, and she shoved it back from her face as embers from the chef-manned trestle swirled upward into the star-filled night.

"It looks like you were right about pushing this back to fall." Mark appeared pleased as he came up beside her. Earlier, Mercer had noticed him seated at one of the long, paper-covered tables with Samantha, Emily, and Ethan as they ate. "The hotel's full, which is saying something for this time of year."

"There's so much competition in late summer. Schools are on fall break right now," Mercer replied. "People are looking for a getaway and not everyone wants to go to the mountains."

"Have you even taken time to eat?" Mark indicated the iPad that she held against her chest. It contained all of her notes that kept an event like this running smoothly. "You know what they say. All work and no play..."

"Considering who just made that comment—the original workaholic—I'm going to ignore it. And trust me, I've eaten. I've been picking at things all night. I'm stuffed to the gills."

Mark stared off toward a group of older folks. Olivia stood in their midst, holding court as her fingers toyed with the ever-present double strand of pearls at her throat. Anders was nearby along with his daughter, her husband, and their two young sons, the latter of whom were engaged with several other children, Ethan and Emily among them, in a game that required throwing beanbags into a hole at the far end of a slightly raised wood platform.

"This means a lot to her." Mark still peered at their mother. "This tradition. Dad started doing these oyster roasts back when he and mom were just newlyweds."

Mercer thought of Olivia's recent hospitalization. That had been over a week ago. "She doesn't look any worse for wear, does she?"

"You know Mom—she thrives on this stuff. She's always been the social butterfly of the family. Well, her and Carter." Mark grew more serious. "You did a great job bringing all this together, Mercer. Especially considering things."

She smiled her appreciation. Except for the food and the bar, which was the hotel's executive chef's territory, she had handled every detail of the event, from the decorations and planned activities to booking the band and marketing. Pensively, Mercer smoothed her hands over the leggings she wore under a shimmery tunic top, her feet bare in the cool sand. She didn't mind the work. She had been clinging desperately to it, in fact. Keeping busy meant that she was focused on the *now*.

"Look at this, won't you?" She pointed as Quinn, holding Lily's hand, came toward them across the sand. Lily wore a grass skirt, although she had on a light sweater over the rest of her *hula girl* outfit. A lei made of colorful plastic flowers hung around her neck.

"Lily, you look adorable!" Mercer exclaimed. "Did you get your outfit in Hawaii?"

Chewing on a small finger, Lily smiled and nodded.

"She insisted on wearing it." Quinn playfully rolled her eyes. "Even if this *is* South Carolina."

"I don't know. I think maybe we could use some pretty hula girls around here." Mark dropped down in front of his niece. "Want to show me how you dance?" He chuckled as Lily began to shake her hips and wave her arms, emulating the dancers she had seen in Hawaii. Mark bowed his head so that Lily could transfer the lei to his neck.

"Aloha," she lisped.

Mark ruffled her curly, auburn hair and gave the lei back to her before standing again. "Where's Carter?" he asked Quinn. Carter had wrapped up shooting on the film and returned to Rarity Cove a few days earlier.

"He's still back at the house. He said he'll join us later when the crowd starts to thin."

Mercer closed the cover on her iPad. "That'll disappoint Mom. She's been waiting for his arrival so she can show him off."

"She'll have to fight me to get to him," Quinn remarked jokingly. "We've gotten so used to being together that this last week without him seemed to go on forever."

Quinn looked down at Lily, who tugged at her mother's hand. "I'm only here now because of this little one. She couldn't wait any longer." Quinn laid her free hand on the rounded mound of her belly. "Not to mention, I'm starving as usual these days. Let's eat first, Lily, and then we'll have the artist paint a seashell on your face."

"There're some vegetarian choices on the buffet, too," Mark pointed out.

Quinn smiled at him. As she led Lily off toward the food, Samantha beckoned to Mark from the edge of the temporary dance floor that had been set up in front of the band. The musicians had taken a break from the lively beach music and were playing a slow, familiar tune. Samantha appeared beautiful, her long, dark hair lifting in the breeze.

"Go dance with your wife," Mercer said to Mark.

Briefly clasping her shoulder, he walked off. Mercer watched, wistful, as they went onto the dance floor hand in hand. They swayed together, Samantha's head on Mark's shoulder and his arms wrapped low around her back. Despite the pang inside her, Mercer was happy for them. They appeared still as in love with one another as ever. Carter and Quinn, as well.

"Ms. Leighton?"

Mercer turned. Kerry Bristol, a young African-American woman who Mark had just hired in a management training position at the hotel, stood in the sand. She was also working tonight's event, helping the cook and wait staff since the oyster roasts were typically *all-hands-on-deck* occasions.

"Hi, Kerry. And it's *Mercer*," she reminded with a smile.

Kerry nodded before pointing back to the boardwalk. "Someone is looking for you."

The shadow that had been across Mercer's heart for the last week lifted as she saw Noah among the couples and families who were making their way down the ramp onto the sand.

"Will you take this back to the hotel for me, please?" she asked and handed the iPad to Kerry.

Noah walked toward her. Mercer met him halfway, surprise as well as hope bubbling inside her. They had exchanged several texts, but she hadn't seen him since obeying his wishes and leaving him in his apartment to deal with his demons alone. Since then, her mind had been running circles, trying to figure out where they stood. Trying not to feel hurt that he had more or less shut her out. In the space of time since she had seen him, she had been summoned to the police precinct in downtown Charleston. But Detective Bobby Durand had interviewed her. The detective had told her that Noah had taken a few days off.

"So, I figured I'd crash the oyster roast." Reaching her, his gaze held uncertainty. He was dressed casually in jeans and a long-sleeved T-shirt that advertised a Charleston microbrewery. Like most everyone else, his feet were bare, his shoes no doubt left behind on the boardwalk above them. "Is that okay?"

"I wouldn't have it any other way." Mercer drank in the sight of him—his thick, raven hair that lifted in the ocean breeze, his fit, athletic frame, his sexily stubbled jaw and intelligent eyes the color of amber. He wore no shield tonight, nor was a weapon visible. "Have you eaten? We can fix you a plate and I'll introduce you around."

The live music nearly drowned out the ocean's roar. Noah looked off to the throngs of people crowded within the halo of paper lanterns. "I was thinking maybe we could go for a walk first?"

Mercer nodded her agreement and they walked southward away from the hotel, leaving the noise of the celebration behind. Here, waves crashed onto the shore. Making small talk, they walked past a compact fire with teenagers sitting around it. They had nearly reached the pier when Noah stopped, seashells and seaweed dotting the wet sand and cool, foamy surf ebbing and flowing at their feet. Here they were completely alone in a blanket of darkness save for the twinkling stars overhead.

"I should start by saying again that I'm sorry," Noah said.

Mercer tucked several long strands of windswept hair behind her ear as she waited for him to continue.

"I'm sorry for being so closed off these past few days." He stared onto the water. "They say that when someone has a traumatic event in their past like I do, it can make it hard for them to have a relationship. I...want you to know that I took your advice. I started seeing a therapist again. I think maybe my PTSD isn't as dormant as I thought."

Remaining silent, Mercer touched his arm.

"I also went to see my father this week. He lives in Tennessee. Corinne doesn't know, but I've known where he is for a while."

Her eyebrows drew together in concern. "How'd it go?"

He sighed in resignation. "I won't be seeing him again. But there were some things I needed to say. To get off my chest. I have closure now, at least."

Turning to her, he took her hands in his.

"I did a lot of thinking while I was on the road. And I also want you to know that you're right about something." Briefly bowing his head, he swallowed before looking at her. "I do deserve a chance to be happy. *You* make me happy, Mercer. If you're still willing, I'd like to see if we can find a way to try to make this work."

Mercer's heart sang out as she smiled softly up at him. As he drew her against him, her fingers threaded through the soft hair at his nape, her body pressed to his. He lowered his head and kissed her, his lips making her nearly dizzy with desire as she clung to him. Then, looking into her eyes, he buried his hands into her wind-whipped hair. His thumb stroked gently over her cheekbone.

"I haven't tried in a relationship in a long time," Noah rasped. "But I want this. I want *you*. I'm not the easiest person to live with at times. My job demands a lot from me. Sometimes I think maybe too much." He looked back to where they had been. Past the sand dunes with their swaying sea oats, the St. Clair stood majestically in the distance, lit from the ground up so that it glowed in the night. "And I'll admit to being a little intimidated by the St. Clair name."

"I don't believe that. You're not intimidated by anything, Noah." Mercer ran her hands over his hard chest, her mind reliving the velvet warmth of his kiss. "Besides, you shouldn't be."

As she looked up at him, her heart constricted. "All I know is that I want for us to try, too. After Jonathan, I...never thought that I could feel this way about someone again."

She raised her face to meet his kiss as his hands slid down her sides before settling at her waist.

"I respect who you are," he murmured, his head bent close to hers. "And I don't mean being a St. Clair. I mean being the *woman* you are. And that you had a past before me." His hands stroked over her hair. "I also think that I should get you back to the party before I end up laying you down on the sand and taking you right here on the beach."

The corners of her mouth lifted, and she touched his face. "Imagine Detective Ford getting arrested for lewd acts in public."

"That'd get things off to a good start with your family," he said wryly. His fingers reached for hers as they began walking back toward the hotel. "What if they don't approve of us?"

"I came out about my relationship with Jonathan at one of these oyster roasts years ago. If they could handle me with my middle-aged college professor, they probably won't blink twice at an alpha-male police detective." Although her tone was light, she was aware of a sweet ache inside her. She thought of the dream she had had at the cabin, the one where Jonathan had waved goodbye to her on the beach. Her throat tightened, but she squeezed Noah's fingers. "I know that all they want is for me to be happy."

Stopping, she buried her face against Noah's neck once more and clung to him. His arms closed around her. He was solid and strong.

"You okay?" His fingers gently lifted her face up to his.

She smiled. "I am now. I'm just so glad you're here."

He took her hand again. They left two sets of footprints in the wet sand as they walked back to the sounds of beach music and laughter.

EPILOGUE

SIX MONTHS LATER

"I'VE BEEN MEANING to ask if you've reached a decision."

At Carter's question, Noah took a pensive sip of his beer. They stood on the deck of Carter's gated beach house on the north side of town, the plane of gray-green ocean stretched out in front of them. It was a warm, sunny Saturday in May and he and Mercer had been invited over for an early dinner, although Noah suspected the real reason for it. He listened to the crash of waves as they swept ashore below. "It's a big decision. I've been a cop for over a decade."

Carter nodded thoughtfully. "But you've said yourself that a change might do you good."

The French doors that led inside the elegant home had been left open, and an infant's fragile cry could be heard. The meal over, Mercer and Quinn had taken Lily and the new baby—a girl named Daphne, just two months old—inside. Noah looked over at Carter, who appeared airbrushed perfect as usual in a polo shirt and cargo shorts. Over the past six months, Noah had gotten to know the entire St. Clair family.

Carter sat his beer on the deck's railing. "Just so you know,

Mercer isn't the reason we made the offer. We're offering it because you're the right person for the job."

The offer, if Noah accepted it, *would* be life-changing. The nonprofit fitness complex that was specially equipped for disabled military veterans in Charleston was seeking a new executive director. Noah had been told the position was his if he wanted it.

"There must be better fits for the job than me," he rationalized. "I don't have a background in nonprofits or administration. My degree is in criminal justice."

As seagulls squawked in the air above them, Carter placed a hand on Noah's shoulder as if to alleviate any doubts.

"We're going outside the box on this. *You* have the background we want," Carter assured him. "You're a decorated vet yourself. You understand these men like no one else. Your military background and life experience will benefit the center more than any guy in a suit with a master's degree. Our staff and board include financial experts and others who can give you whatever guidance you need." He looked at Noah over the top of his sunglasses. "You blew away the board in the interviews, Noah. They'd be interested in you even without my family's recommendation. The Charleston facility is our flagship center and we need a real leader for it. They believe that's you. If your hesitation is about the money—"

"You know it isn't." Although the center was nonprofit, the directorship still paid more than what the average detective made. He would be swapping out his pension for a 401K, but the hours and the environment would also be much more conducive to a better quality of life, something Noah had come to realize that he wanted more and more. Through the home's open doors, he could see Mercer as she paced with the baby in her arms, rocking her and trying to settle her down.

"Look. You know I'm not above guilt-tripping you." Carter

watched Mercer, too. "Being a cop is a dangerous occupation. I hope I'm not overstepping, but I'm pretty sure you have someone else to think of now."

Noah merely pressed his lips together. It was hard not to tell him more.

"Have you spoken to Mercer about this?" Carter asked.

"She's excited by the opportunity, but she says it's completely up to me." Noah had also talked to Corinne as well as Tyson, the latter of whom had given Noah his blessing even though it would mean an end to their partnership. Ty had called it a *golden opportunity*, in fact. He had made a full recovery following the shooting, and he and Lanny had used the insurance money from the cabin to buy a larger home in a better school district for their girls.

The thought of working with men who had been disabled in military service was something that very much appealed to Noah. The Charleston complex had also expanded to offer mental health and family counseling, as well as job placement services. If the center could give back those men's self-worth in some way, help them make the most of the lives they had—well, it felt like he would be paying it forward.

I deserve a chance to be happy.

Noah recalled what he had said to Mercer not all that long ago. And she *had* made him happier than he had ever been in his life. He knew that she was happy, too, but he also wanted to give her more. Carter was right. Police work wasn't only demanding; it could be dangerous and Mercer needed someone who she knew would be coming home to her every night. She had already been a widow once. He watched her as she placed a kiss on the baby's crown.

He wanted to give her that, too. The family he knew she desired.

Noah blew out a soft breath. As many reasons as his mind came up with for saying no, in his heart he wanted to say yes.

Maybe this was just all the pieces finally fitting into place.

"What the hell. I'm on board."

At Noah's announcement, Carter smiled broadly and the two men shook hands.

"You won't regret this, Noah," Carter said. "Hey, how about we ditch these beers and move to some celebratory champagne? Let's share the news. Quinn will have sparkling water because of the baby but Mercer can join us. And don't worry about driving. You two can stay here or we'll send for the hotel limo to take you back to the St. Clair."

Noah and Mercer hadn't officially moved in together, mostly because of logistics. Being a detective in Charleston required him to regularly be on-call at all hours of the day and night, and Mercer was working full-time at the St. Clair. But they often spent the night at one another's places. They had been taking it slow, partly to give Mercer time to adjust to being in a relationship again after Jonathan, but also because until recently, Noah had been in therapy. He had wanted to address any lingering trauma from his past and be able to drop the barriers that he had kept around himself for so long.

"Do you think maybe we can take a raincheck on that celebration?" Noah asked. "I sort of have something special planned for Mercer tonight."

Carter bobbed his head. "Sure. I'll let the board know of your decision."

A short time later, Noah opened the passenger door to his Ford Explorer and helped Mercer climb inside.

"I can't believe you're taking the job," she marveled once Noah entered on the driver's side. "I really didn't think you would."

He fastened his seatbelt and started the engine. In truth, once he had accepted the offer aloud, he had felt no regret, only excitement. "It wasn't a snap decision. I've been thinking about it a lot, and today just seemed like the day for big things."

"Won't leaving the force be hard?"

"I'll miss working with Ty, but I won't miss the violence and dealing with the worst of mankind. Besides, I think maybe it's time for me to shake things up a little."

"What made you finally decide to pull the trigger?" Mercer smiled. "No pun intended."

He turned to her as they waited for the property's electronic gate to open so they could exit. "You."

Her lips parted as he tenderly cupped the side of her face.

"And me," he said, then changed the subject as he sat back again and they pulled onto the road. "Do you mind if we take a detour before we head to Charleston? There's something I've been planning to show you."

"WHAT DO YOU THINK?"

"It's beautiful," Mercer said honestly as she took in the gracious, Lowcountry-style home that stood in front of them. "So, I'm finally getting to see your secret renovation project."

Leaning against the SUV's front, Noah stared up at the house, too. "It's close to a century old, but it has what you'd call *good bones*. I know it's pretty small by St. Clair standards, but I think it has a lot of charm."

The home's exterior appeared pristine, with a fresh coat of white paint and dormers that projected from a sloping, seam-metal roof, indicating a second floor. The main floor had generous windows and a deep, covered porch that appeared to be made from new wood. Mercer could imagine family and friends gathering at such a welcoming spot. The yard itself was a mixture of grass and sand common to homes not far off the water. But this house wasn't on the beach. Instead, a grassy marsh spread out behind the property. A chorus of bullfrogs croaked from the languid water.

Mercer shook her head in awe, the setting sun warm on her shoulders. "I don't know what this place looked like before, but you and Steve are going to make a killing flipping it."

"It's sold already, actually. Before our renovation work was even completed."

"I'm not surprised."

"It's only about a mile from the beach." Noah pointed eastward to some trees. "There's a bike and jogging trail that runs through there that leads to it. It might not seem like it from here, but there're neighbors nearby. The lots are large, so between that and the marsh, there's privacy. A lot of the homes around here are being renovated. It's an up and coming area that's about to go up in price. C'mon. I want to show you what we've done on the inside."

They went onto the porch together and Noah opened the beveled-glass door using a key. Entering, Mercer looked around the great room with its high, coffered ceiling and white-painted brick fireplace. Despite the home's age, the interior had been updated so that the living area opened into an airy, modern kitchen. A wide, wood staircase with a carved banister went up to the second floor.

"The hardwood flooring's original to the house. I did the refinishing myself," Noah said, pride in his voice. "It's made of cypress wood taken right from the land. We also had to knock some walls out to get a more open look." He placed his hand on a column. "These are load bearing, so they're here to stay."

Mercer nodded. "I like them."

"New pipes, new electrical wiring. The bathrooms are completely redone, too." He followed her into the kitchen that was replete with glass-fronted cabinets, a farmhouse-style sink, and stainless steel appliances. Mercer ran her finger along the handsome granite counters, her eyes drawn to a large window in the breakfast area that provided a stunning view of the marsh. She watched, transfixed, as a heron in flight came to a landing, making a splash in the midst of oat grasses and reeds.

"There're four bedrooms and two full baths," Noah said. "The master suite has a sitting area and its own fireplace."

Mercer stood at the window. The backyard had a gazebo and a private dock that extended into the marsh. "This place is plenty big, if you ask me. Does whoever bought it have children?"

"Not yet," Noah said, shoving his hands into the pockets of his trousers.

Mercer tilted her head at him. "Are you sure you want to take that directorship at the center? I'm thinking that you missed your real calling. You could have a full-time career in home renovation."

"Well, I did put a lot of extra work into this place. Actually, I'm the one who bought it."

Mercer stared at him in surprise. Moving to stand in front of her, his hands slid up her arms.

"It's for *us*, Mercer." He spoke to her in a gentle, hopeful tone. "At least, I hope that it is. I want us to live here in this house together. It was a real fixer-upper when Steve and I bought it. But the more work we did, I just kind of fell in love with the place. I kept imagining us here."

At his words, Mercer's pulse spun. "What're you saying? That we should move in together?"

"I'm saying that I want to *marry* you." He took her hands in his. "I want us to have a *family* together. We've been using birth control but I think maybe it's time."

Mercer's throat thickened with emotion. "Is that why you're leaving the Charleston Police Department? Because you think I wouldn't want to be married to a cop? I don't want you to change careers because of—"

"I want *this*. All of this," he assured her. "I want us to live a good, long life together. I want to be the kind of husband who comes home to you every night and isn't pulled out of bed at three in the morning to go to a crime scene. I think the job at the center will fulfill me in a way that police work hasn't. And I think it'll be good for me to get away from the darkness that's part of being a cop."

Nearly giddy with happiness, Mercer tried to get her bearings.

"I love you," Noah said tenderly.

"I...love you, too, Noah."

He lowered his head and brushed his lips over hers. It wasn't the first time they had expressed their love for one another. But while they had talked loosely of the possibility of marriage someday, until now it had been in the abstract.

"I've been banking my share of the money from renovation projects for years." Noah shrugged. "And you've seen my apartment. I haven't exactly been living above my means. I didn't pay for the house outright, but I was able to make a sizable down payment. I didn't want to do this with your money. That was important to me."

She felt wrapped in warmth as Noah slid his fingers through her hair. "You're only about ten minutes away from the St. Clair here. Since the center is on this side of Charleston, my commute won't be too bad. But if you don't like this place, just tell me and I'll—"

"It's perfect," she assured him, her throat tight.

His eyes searched hers. "Then say you'll marry me."

Mercer saw vulnerability on his face. She nodded eagerly. "Of course, I'll marry you, Noah. I love you more than anything."

"Don't say that just yet. I might have some competition."

Taking her hand, he smiled as he led her past the kitchen to a closed door.

"What's this?"

"Open it and find out."

Mercer looked at him, then turned the knob and pushed open a door that led onto a large, screened-in porch with a cushioned patio swing that faced the marsh. But it was the wicker basket that sat in the porch's center that caused her fingers to fly to her mouth. A puppy, a golden retriever, looked up at her from inside it. A large red bow adorned its neck.

"Oh, my goodness! He's gorgeous," Mercer exclaimed as she bent to pick up the puppy. It wriggled in her arms.

"*She*," Noah corrected.

"And she's ours?"

"All the St. Clairs have dogs. Even Olivia and Anders have that tiny designer dog. I figured that I better get us one, too, or we'd be left out of all the family dog park activities. I've got a friend whose dog just had a litter and they offered me one."

"You haven't left her here alone all this time, have you?" The puppy looked up at Mercer with adoring, chocolate-brown eyes, causing her heart to melt. "She's just a baby."

"Corinne brought her here a little while ago. I gave her a spare key and she texted me when she left."

Mercer nuzzled the puppy against her cheek. She had been seeing Corinne a lot lately. Mercer had introduced her to Mark and the hotel's executive chef, and she was now supplying fresh organic produce and flowers to the St. Clair. Corinne made the deliveries to the hotel herself, and she stopped by Mercer's office whenever she was there. Mercer had seen her earlier that week. Corinne had been keeping a lot under her hat.

"Corinne's had the puppy at her place for the last few days, although she's giving me hell about it because she says that now she's going to have to get Finn a dog." Noah rocked slightly on his heels. "What do you think of the bow?"

She nuzzled the puppy again. "I think it's about two sizes too large for this poor little..."

Her voice halted, her stomach fluttering as she saw the ring that had been secured in the center of the satin bow the puppy wore. The ring was simple in design, a white-gold band with a square-cut diamond. Noah peered at her uncertainly.

"Corrine helped me pick it out. Just like the house, if it's not what you want, we can—"

"It's exactly what I want." Mercer was nearly at a loss for words. "I...just can't believe all this."

"I know you're not a fan of surprises, but I hope this was a good one."

"It's the best. All of it is."

Stepping closer, Noah removed the bow from the puppy's neck and slid the ring from where it was secured. Mercer sat the puppy on the floor. It scampered off to a bowl of water that Corinne must have placed there. Mercer beamed up at Noah, her world full.

He had unlocked her heart and soul. He had brought her back from that lonely, desolate place that she had gone to after Jonathan's passing. She would never forget Jonathan. He would always be her first love, always be in her heart. But in Noah, she had managed to find love again. She blinked back tears of joy as he somberly slipped the ring onto her finger.

It fit perfectly. And as different as they were from one another, it seemed that *they* were the perfect fit, too.

Mercer thought back to that fateful afternoon at the art gallery. It had been the start of the nightmare that had brought Noah into her life. But he was the *good* that had come from such dark things. She vowed to always be his light. She wanted to have his children, wanted to make a family with him, grow old with him.

He was her second chance at having the life she dreamed of.

Noah placed a gentle kiss on her forehead. "So, what do you want to do now? We can go tell your family, if you want. I nearly spilled the beans to Carter earlier, truth be told."

"We will tell them. Eventually." Her heart ached with love and gratitude. "But right now, I'd just like to sit here for a little while and be with you."

Taking his hand, they walked to the swing that faced the marsh. The sun had dipped lower on the horizon, weaving streaks of mauve into the fading sky. Sitting together, Noah put his arm around her, pulling her closer as the puppy played with a chew toy at their feet. Looking out over the marsh, Mercer laid her head against Noah's shoulder, certain that it was the most beautiful sunset she had ever seen.

ACKNOWLEDGMENTS

Thank you for reading my Rarity Cove series. I hope you've enjoyed Mercer's story, IN DARK WATER. If you've read any of my earlier books prior to the Rarity Cove series, you know that I've always enjoyed writing law enforcement heroes, and Noah Ford was a welcome return to that for me.

There are several people I would like to thank for their assistance with this book. They include Katherine Knight, my friend and walking "buddy" who is also a fantastic beta reader and sounding board, authors Larissa Reinhart and Michelle Muto, as well as Sally "R," a special reader and friend from "across the pond." I'd also like to thank my husband, Robert, for his love and companionship for over three decades. Here's hoping for many more years together.

Most of all, I'd like to thank you, my readers. As always, you're the reason I write, and I'm so appreciative of your ongoing enthusiasm and support.

ABOUT THE AUTHOR

Leslie Tentler is also the author of BEFORE THE STORM, LOW TIDE, FALLEN, and the Chasing Evil Trilogy (MIDNIGHT CALLER, MIDNIGHT FEAR, and EDGE OF MIDNIGHT). She was a finalist for Best First Novel at ThrillerFest 2012 and is a two-time finalist for the Daphne du Maurier Award for Excellence in Mystery and Suspense. She is also the recipient of the prestigious Maggie Award of Excellence.

Leslie is a member of Romance Writers of America, International Thriller Writers and Novelists, Inc. A native of East Tennessee, she currently resides in Atlanta.

If you enjoyed reading Leslie's work, please consider leaving an online review, however short. Of course, simply telling others you enjoyed this book is also sincerely appreciated. Word of mouth is the best promotion.

Visit Leslie and sign up for her newsletter at www.LeslieTentler.com.